FANTASY ANNUAL 5

Books edited by Philip Harbottle & Sean Wallace

Fantasy Annual 1
Fantasy Annual 2
Fantasy Annual 3
Fantasy Annual 4
Fantasy Annual 5

Books edited by Philip Harbottle

Fantasy Quarterly
Fantasy Adventures 1
Fantasy Adventures 2
Fantasy Adventures 3

Books edited by Sean Wallace

Strange Pleasures

FANTASY ANNUAL 5

edited by

Philip Harbottle and Sean Wallace

COSMOS

FANTASY ANNUAL 5

Published by:

Cosmos Books, an imprint of **Wildside Press**
P.O. Box 45, Gillette, NJ 07933-0045
www.wildsidepress.com

For more information, contact **Wildside Press**.

ISBN: 1-58715-515-X

CONTENTS

LAZARUS

E.C. Tubb

It was something which never left him, a niggle in the mind like a nail scratching on slate. He tried to fight it. With scotch, heavy slugs followed with a beer chaser, a half-bottle at a time, scotch not beer. With the little pink pills which brought sleep, the purple ones which gave euphoria, the green which gave dreams, the black which gave nightmares.

The psychologist said, "The problem is simple, Mr. Oakley. You have an anxiety syndrome. Exactly what is it that is bothering you?"

"I don't know."

"Come now, can't you be a little more helpful?"

"If I knew what it was I wouldn't be here, because if I knew it wouldn't bother me."

"Selective amnesia, perhaps?" The psychologist hummed, swinging in his chair. "Let's tackle it another way. Go over your life. Tell me if there are any blank spots in your memory."

"My whole life?"

"Certainly. Look at it this way. If you had broken an arm you would remember it. If you'd killed a man, had an accident, been to jail. Well, this is the same. You don't have to remember every tiny detail of everything that happened since you were born. Just think of the parts you can't remember. A black-out, for example. A gap. A period which you know was unusual."

"Now?"

"You have an hour, Mr. Oakley. Most of it still remains."

Childhood was a mist, adolescence a blur. Sitting, eyes closed, he scanned the years. There had been that time on Mare Nubium when a fracture had shown in his air-pipe and he'd recognized the danger almost too late. He remembered the plain swinging around him, the dry retching of his lungs. The others had got to him in time and he'd regained consciousness back in the hut with blood on his mouth and a pulmotor whining at his side.

And then during a spree on Mars. The Syrtis Major complex had been completed and everyone had gone to town. There had been home-brew and some female technicians who had let their hair down in more senses than one. He had tried to participate but he'd never been much good with women. But that was nothing. He'd been stupid drunk before.

Too often for the good of his record. Back on Earth and how could a man used to space get a job? Dome-sealers had no place in an environment where air was all around. More drink, a fight, waking with bruises. A spell in jail which had dried him out. A job on a freighter patching a paper-thin hull and living in a suit, skin rubbed raw and sores all over. Back to Luna processing waste. Human waste.

"Five minutes, Mr. Oakley."

He opened his eyes, conscious of failure. No gaps. No periods in which something could have happened. No time when he could remember having been free of the thing which scratched at his mind.

"Your time is up, Mr. Oakley."

Outside it was Earthglow, a relief from the sun which struck hard and bright beyond the shields. He lingered on the upper deck watching the bugs as they crawled over the transparent dome. Two years ago men would have been busy up there with their sprays. Now machines built up the plastic eroded by the solar blast.

The sight depressed him and he went below. The levels ware busy as always, shops tempting tourists: with souvenirs of local rock tormented into rigid patterns, flasks of dust, the casts of the first footprints left so long ago by Armstrong and Aldrin. Other shops offering small packets of concentrates, candy, underwear, over-robes, magboots, junk.

Seats were set out about a fountain, a patch of green resembling grass, shrubs of plastic, flowers the same, a scatter of birds which had never flown and never would, an artificial dog which chased an artificial cat. The air stirred with a gentle breeze heavy with the tang of pine and roses.

He sat and watched the water.

Remember, the psychologist had said. Remember.

He'd forgotten nothing. There were no gaps, no blank spots. Three years ago up on the dome with the sun rising and his section still to finish. The hose was awkard to handle and the spray had to be just so or there would be visual aberrations. The suckers were weak and he'd stretched just that little bit too far. Slipping he'd had no choice. Fall and smash his bones or rip the dome and make a hold.

He'd fallen.

The water from the fountain turned green, then yellow, blue, red, orange then back to limpid clarity. Drugs, pus, cyanosis, blood, lymphatic fluids. The ache of splints and mending muscles. Russian sleep and intravenous feeding. A nasty time.

A come-down in more ways than one.

Rising he left the area with the fountain and fictiticious plants, wandering through corridors and passages which led around and down. The air changed a little, no longer scented with enticing odors, harsh and stale to nose and taste. In an alcove sat a figure, a transparent dome covering the skull through which the brain lay like a mess of gray spaghetti, pipes leading to a humming machine. In the pane before him was a slot and a printed card.

"Of your charity help to heal this unfortunate man."

Oakley felt something tweak in his mind.

He ran, leaving a part of himself behind, falling into the bar, the anodyne it contained. Scotch and a beer chaser. More scotch, more beer, enough to still the spider, to numb it for a while, to lull it while he sneaked up to crush it for once and all.

Find a blank spot, the psychologist had said.

Think.

The plastic of the dome running before his eyes, moving faster, faster, his gloved hands scrabbling for a hold. The rim which had caught him and thrown him clear to turn, slowly, slowly, pinwheeling as he fell to the rock beneath. On Earth he would have been pulped. On Luna he was simply broken.

Body and purse. Broken.

Of your charity help to heal this unfortunate man!

Insurance had helped, but not enough. His savings had gone. The money gathered by an entrepreneur who had watched him fall and who had passed the hat, handing in a quarter of what he collected. Medical fees came high. Ways had been devised to meet them. Parties who were guided through the wards, staring goggle-eyed at flesh displayed nakedly to view. A double amputee was sure of a donation. Operations drew a big crowd, their attendance money split between staff, some going to the patient.

Once it had been the arena.

Think!

Down to Venus with the sun growing all the time, a waiting furnace that would crisp ship and men. The cabin had been warm with more than physical heat. On the Venus run a man couldn't lose. Softness, waiting, arms extended to hold and caress, the voice a susurrating whisper in his ear. He had tried. It had been the last time. He had never been to Venus again.

The time when three men had broached him on the lower level. The time when he had slipped and fallen into the sludge and would have drowned but for luck. The sights and the smells of his new job. Farmers, they called them, the men who processed the waste. Scavengers too. There was always money in muck. Getting it was the hard part. But it was there.

All of it was there.

No blanks at all.

His entire life an open book.

Except that he couldn't remember what had happened to him when he was asleep. Nor during the times when he had been unconscious. And he couldn't clearly recall his childhood. Could anyone?

Back at the psychologist's the receptionist vaguely hostile.

"Your name?"

"You remember me. I was here a little while ago."

"Please! Your name? Your number?"

He looked down at the neat row of figures tattooed on his meter.

"They tell you everything, don't they?"

"Yes, Mr. Oakley."

"I bet they even tell you when I was born."

"Certainly, October 5th 2107."

"But you don't know that," he said. "Not really. You only know what the numbers tell you. I bet that it would be possible just to take a man and put a number on him. Any number. Then he would have to be what they say, wouldn't he? I mean, what he really is wouldn't matter. Only the number would count."

She wore a mask of metal foil, the eyes slanted, the mouth slit.

"I have never heard anything so filthy and disgusting in my life." A button sank beneath her finger. "Sir?"

"I never want to see, meet or talk with Mr. Oakley again."

She was a good receptionist and patients were a dime a dozen.

"Throw him out."

"Thank you, sir."

Back outside again, the bugs still swarming over the dome, the scratch in his mind worse than ever before. And the last hope gone. The word would pass, the ranks close, who wanted a heretic?

One place.

The queues were thick and the pedlars doing a brisk trade. Sweets, drinks, tantalizing hints of the pleasures within. The air held the stimulating odor of ether and idoform, a sharp, acrid, antiseptic smell. Inside a huddle of patients. A receptionist, no mask, just a set of features. The eyes were cold.

"I want," he said, and paused.

"Yes?"

"There's something in my head. I want you to cut it out."

A touch of animation, almost of interest. Masochism took strange forms, but this was unusual.

"Your head? Are you sure?"

"It keeps worrying me. I don't know what it is. Yes, I'm sure."

Tests, x-rays, doctors who fussed, whispers. A young man scowled.

"Head ops are bad pullers. Castration now, that brings in a crowd. And where do we cut? No tumor, no pressure, no implant. Trepanning is old hat. Sell him some aspirin and send him on his way."

"He has a right—"

"We're artists. To hell with his rights. A few feet of intestine, now, that would be something else. A head—phooie!"

"Ethics?"

"Sure. Sure. We mustn't forget ethics. No sign of organic trouble, right? So he's a nut case. So we send him on his way."

Outside again, always outside. Down to the lowest levels where the lights were bad and the air worse. Down to where the dead men lay.

"Mr. Oakley!" An old man, white haired, wet of mouth and liquid of eye. "What are you doing here? Is anything wrong?"

"My head. There's something in there. I don't know what it is."

"A thought? A dream?"

"A worry. Something I can't remember. If I knew what it was I wouldn't worry about it."

"Logic," said a woman. Others had come like ghosts from the shadows to stand, watching.

"Why did he come here?"

"Send him away."

"He doesn't belong."

"We don't want him."

"No one wants me," he cried. "No one will listen. But you know me, you called me by name."

"A name," said the woman, acidly. "The one we gave you. You should not have returned."

"A bad job," said the white haired man. "We should have taken more time." His hand rested like a feather on his shoulder. "Listen, son, I think I know what's bothering you. You had a bad time a while back and—"

"The fall from the dome?"

"No."

"That time in the crater?"

"No."

"On Mars then?"

"Not that either. Those things never happened. You only think they did. Those things and all the rest. We had to give you something."

"Complete erasure," said the woman. "You were dead too long. We managed to revive your body, but the brain was empty. It has to be filled. We picked a few things at random."

"Dead?" He looked from one to another. "Dead?"

"A freak. Organically unharmed. You fell into a vat of liquid helium. Once people thought that as long as cellular disintegration was halted the memories and ego would remain intact. That was a mistake. They do not."

"Dead," he said again. "I can't remember it."

"Of course not."

"Is that's what is bothering me? The fact that I died?"

"Hell, no," they chorused. "That isn't the thing that's bugging you. You can't remember it."

"Then?"

"You just hated to be re-born."

PRODUCTION MODEL

Philip E. High

The car stood on the grass verge at the edge of the runway gleaming in the warm afternoon sunshine. Produced by the Mecranan Company's top teams, it was designed to slot-in between the standard models of the same power and the luxury classes far above. It looked a good bet, it cost only a thousand more than the standard models, yet was seven thousand less than the luxury trade it sought to approach.

Stanford Wallace paid off the taxi and strolled over. A thin faced, dark haired man with pale but very astute gray eyes.

"Hello, Ray, starting production in the wilds now?"

Raymond Burke turned, a big untidy man in coveralls who seemed to exude cleaning rags from every pocket. He was, however something of a genius—so was Wallace. The two men had worked together on a project in Peru and become friends.

Burke waved his arm vaguely before shaking hands. "Wartime bomber station, we lease it from the local council as a testing ground."

"And this beauty on the verge is the one you want testing?"

"Beauty she may be but no one will drive the bastard."

"Mind if I start her up?" Without waiting for an answer he slid into the driving seat and started the engine. He listened for a moment shut down again. "Turbo-diesel, isn't it? An injection job by the sound of it. Congratulations, quite refined, no diesel-knock at tick-over at all."

"You're not trying to sell me the bloody thing," Burke complained. "I called you in to help me figure out what's wrong with it."

"Fair enough, but I'm only a car buff not a specialist."

"True—but you have a talent for an obscure approach. You showed that in Peru with that metallurgic problem."

Wallace frowned at the car. "And what's wrong here?"

"The trouble is, my friend, that no one wants to drive the bloody thing."

Burke paused before hurrying on to explain. "It's nearly had two accidents in the street and four more on the private road at the back of the complex. Actual distance covered, each time, eighty to a hundred meters."

"Then it packed up?"

"No, the individual drivers packed up. Sudden stomach upsets, dizziness, you name it. There were all sorts of excuses."

"Did none of the drivers offer a reasonable explanation?"

"Only one, a chap named Ryan but I don't know if the word reasonable applies. He said, and I quote, '*I wouldn't get into that bastard crate again for a top win on the State Lottery. It's from the Dark Side—bloody well jinxed!*'"

"You believe him?"

"Of course not, but there must be some sort of psychological problem somewhere."

Wallace looked the vehicle over carefully. It was exceedingly well equipped—over and above normal safety factors. Satellite navigation, climate control, parking sensors, engine management—it seemed on the verge of being almost able to drive itself. All it needed was steering and braking.

"Let's get in." Wallace slid into the driving seat and waited for the other to join him.

"What I'm going to do," he said, "is creep the entire length of the runway at minimum speed. I seem to think better in the old terms, around three miles an hour, a walking pace."

"Before we start," said Burke, "I forgot to tell you we're probably being watched. Hidden cameras all the way, quite a few directors worried about industrial espionage—with reason now that we're chasing the big boys."

In the viewing room at the plant, one of the directors, Harrison, had reduced his cigar to a shapeless lump.

"They intend to get moving this week, I hope—ah! At last they're actually . . . No! Hell, they've stopped again. Come and look at this, Jensen, three damn lengths and they've stopped again. Now they're getting out, going to the side of the road, they're looking at something in the grass—what the hell is going on?"

Burke was wondering that himself. A brief distance then Wallace had stopped the car, cut the engine and got out.

"You had better come with me."

At the verge he pointed. "It's that."

Burke scowled at him. "It's a little bush about knee-high, what about it?"

"It's a little red bush with bright green berries, like an inverted holly bush. The point being that it wasn't here when we climbed into the car."

Burke's scowl vanished and his face lost a little of its color. "Are you absolutely sure?"

"I have no doubt whatever, I have a photographic memory. These verges were clear as far as I could see."

"You think it has something to do with the car?"

"I don't know if has anything to do with anything, but it does seem relevant that as soon as we start moving something odd occurs."

Back in the passenger seat Burke said. "I'm getting a very uncomfortable feeling about all this."

Wallace started the engine. "My description is stronger than that and I have a perfect word to describe it—that word is apprehension."

Burke looked at him and nodded. "Yes, put like that, I have the wind up, too. I have no idea why."

He pulled a notebook from an inner pocket and produced a pen. "I'll make notes about this and I'm beginning to understand their feelings. Most of them made eighty meters, we've covered only thirty five and look at us already. Anything else you noticed beside that bloody plant?"

Wallace nodded slowly. "Maybe its me, perhaps its purely emotional, but the sun or, more aptly, the sunlight doesn't look right."

"I noticed that, too—thought it was just my eyes playing up. It's got a sort of metallic tinge as if it was being reflected by a gigantic copper disc."

Wallace started the engine again. "You think I've been going slowly? Watch this! As far as this car is concerned, snails are going to break the sound barrier."

In the observation room, Harrison had thrown away the wreckage of his chewed cigar but his face was flushed and his fists were clenched.

"Don't tell me they're actually moving again! Dear God, if they go any slower they'll be in reverse—now what!?"

He leaned forward and swore obscenely. "Now the bloody picture is breaking up, that's all we need."

Almost before he had finished speaking the picture dissolved into a mass of wavy black and white lines.

In the car Burke said: "I feel bilious and my eyes have gone funny. My notes are all over the pad."

Wallace got rid of some verbal obscenities before answering. Then he said: "Eighty bloody meters. I would have made a run for it like those other drivers. The entire vehicle feels distorted, rubbery and the camber of the road is all wrong."

"Camber! This is a runway, an airstrip, there *is* no camber."

"I think you should lift your eyes from that note book and look ahead."

Burke did so and felt that some unknown power had tightened every muscle in his body. The flesh of his face and scalp had become rigid and locked.

Dead ahead, the outlines and shadows of trees filled the horizon. They were already bumping along a dirt road towards them.

He thought: we must have run off the runway somehow—in eighty meters! They were literally crawling; the explanation was just as insane as immediate events and, yes, he felt so bloody *sick* to add to all this.

"Have you any explanation?"

Wallace shook his head. "Sorry, I'm having job enough to maintain my concentration. I have to keep reminding myself that I'm driving this damn thing."

"Sorry I got you into this. If you want to turn back—"

Wallace cut him short. "I accepted the job, my responsibility. On a purely practical level, however, look behind you."

Burke did so and felt trapped. The dirt road upon which they had been crawling no longer existed behind them. There was no gap between the trunks of the acacia-like trees through which the car could have passed

It was only a few seconds before both men realized why. The view ahead was constantly changing, a kaleidoscope of swirling shadows and shifting landscapes. Scenes that pulled at the eyes and made the urge to vomit even more difficult to suppress.

The sensation lasted only a few seconds and then seemed to stabilize abruptly. There was change but not a change that either man could welcome. They were in a landscape so utterly alien to them both it was terrifying. It was not only the surroundings, but the feelings that came with it which increased the terror. Both men felt that they were under observation, that the very sky itself had come down even closer to see them. They felt threatened, overwhelmed and trapped by the very terrain which surrounded them.

One thing only was familiar—they were on a road. A wide, solid road with lining curbs, side drains, and a just perceptible camber. It was a dull red in color and it ran through a desert of red dust that was only slightly brighter than the road.

Huge, jagged slivers of reddish rock, of varying shapes and heights, rose from the sand like the remains of an ancient city long fallen to ruin.

Somehow it reminded Burke of a cemetery and he shivered inwardly.

The sky above was also red and, to both men hostile. An enormous scarlet sun was just visible through a covering of thick cloud. Both began to wonder to wonder uneasily if they had ended up in Hell . . .

Desperately trying to reject the idea, Wallace continued to drive forward at a steady crawl. It was, in this case, a very short journey.

Directly ahead, two huge slivers of rock rose on either side of the road like two vast trees.

A bare six meters from them, something walked from behind the right hand one, gained the center of road and raised its arm, hand extended

Wallace stopped. There was no mistaking the meaning of the signal.

The thing that stood in their way wore a skin-tight black covering up to the neck. It was also tall and incredibly thin.

Burke, trying to take in what he saw, was unable to use the adjective humanoid. It might have two legs and two arms but there the comparisons stopped. In the first place, the thing was yellow, bright yellow, brighter than a canary.

As it started to come forward, Burke had to resist a tendency to cringe back in his seat. It looked—although obviously it wasn't—like a polished yellow skull, a skull with a thin lipless mouth. There was no nose, just two long black slits and apparently no ears.

The tiny, livid, bright red eyes were sunk so deeply into the sockets that the impressions of a skull were heightened. A black wavy line crossed the forehead but Wallace thought it artificial and probably a mark of rank. What looked like short-clipped yellow feather covered the upper scalp.

The thing pointed a short black tube at them. "You will lower your defensive screen or face the consequences."

The black tube pointed briefly away from them and then something happened. There was no report and no flash but one of the huge slivers of rock turned abruptly silver. Then it collapsed into a huge heap of glowing white ash.

"A demonstration only. You will observe that I have instruments of destruction. You appreciate that you are intruders?"

"Yes."

"What are you doing here?"

"The simplest explanation is that we lost our way."

"Are you hostiles?"

"Most definitely not."

"How is it that you speak *Golthru*?"

"How is it that *you* speak English?"

The two intelligences stared one another, both realizing that they had come to an impasse.

"Make no movement," said the alien. "I will send for a Science/Five."

The two men never discovered if this race had matter-transmission or some secret means of transport, but he arrived almost immediately. He was almost the same as his companion save that he had three wavy green lines drawn across his forehead and sported a blue feathery moustache.

He wasted no time asking questions but screwed a round object, like a thick monocle, into his right eye-socket and began to study the vehicle closely.

"We never lowered our defensive screen," said Burke in a low voice uneasily.

"I put down my bloody side window—that's all I could think of," said Wallace. "Any way, it seemed to work, he never questioned it." The alien walked round the car three times, studying it closely.

Finally he stopped by Wallace and the open window.

"I perceive you are not hostiles. I also perceive you are not responsible for your presence here. Sadly, however, your appearance here has created a situation of immense danger for both our life-forms."

He paused and pointed both at the car and the two men. "Somehow you have accumulated a mass of surplus energy, a mass so enormous that it is far beyond our science to disperse. As you proceed, that energy will accumulate even more until is becomes critical. When this occurs, a fiery nucleus of immense heat will begin in the center of your vehicle and spread outwards. It will consume you, much of the surrounding area and finally detonate—an explosion large enough to erase a continent."

Both men stared at him with the curious feeling that their eyes were fixed in their heads. Burke knew his mouth hung open idiotically but he was unable to close it. After all they had been through, they had become a bomb, a nuclear warhead capable of destroying a planet!

It was some time before Wallace gained control of his vocal cords but when he spoke his voice sounded cracked and unfamiliar—inwardly he was shivering with cold.

"Is there anything we can do?" he asked

"For yourselves, sadly, nothing. It is possible, of course, that should you continue your journey through time/space you may shed this load as easily as you have acquired it, but I cannot raise false hopes."

"And you, yourselves?"

"If you decide to remain, we must share the end with you. On the other hand, you may move on, perhaps traveling well clear of the cities—but we cannot order you to do so."

Wallace, feeling numb, started the engine and heard his own voice say: "We will move, of course."

"Our thanks, but go slowly, speed will increase the energy."

They moved, neither man spoke, each lost in his own thoughts. Although terrified, both were conscious of a numb resignation. There was nothing they could do about it, no escape, nowhere to run. It would be pointless to fling open the doors and make a break for it. They were part of it, a mass of accumulated energy, walking bombs in their own right.

Dully Wallace realized that both sides of the highway were packed with yellow faces. Crowds stretching as far back as far as he could see and all, without exception, with their arms raised high above their heads. Despite his terror he found that part of his mind was working clearly and detachedly. What was it all for—some form of alien supplication? Were they being sacrificed? Perhaps a bomb had been placed in the car in readiness.

Wallace looked resignedly at the mass of yellow skull-like faces and found himself suddenly riveted to one. One yellow skull in a sea of yellow skulls yet there was contact. Abruptly his consciousness seemed to up-end and his conceptions, despite his fear, changed beyond recognition.

He sensed that she was female and he was seeing this world through her eyes, with her knowledge, and it was not the same world at all.

It was only red through *his* eyes but not hers, through hers there were glorious ranges of colors which his own could never reach.

The dust of the desert was not dust but a common life form as ordinary and acceptable to her as grass was to him.

This was not a desert, this was a public park; her people had picnics here. As for the slivers of rock, they were not rocks at all, they were merely a different form of organic life, growing things as familiar to her as oak and elm were to him.

The thing which had stopped them was not, as Wallace had supposed, a policeman. This civilization had no conception of a police force. This man, a volunteer, was a protector of the people. Sometimes wild creatures got into the park and he was there to make it safe.

When he saw an alien machine containing alien life he had done his duty. He had barred their way, issued a warning and called for higher authority,

Wallace realized he had only begun to understand. The raised arms were not a supplication but a salute both to himself and Burke. They had decided to go on, thus possibly sparing thousands of lives.

On the other hand they were not here for tribute alone—they were here to *contain*. The thousands round the car never lessened and all of them carried objects that he had assumed were natural things like handbags and umbrellas. They were none of these things and he could only describe them to himself as counter/fires.

When an eye-searing glow appeared in the center of the car, all those instruments would be switched on. The mass attempt would not stop it, would not slow it. The crowds out there would be incinerated in their hundreds of thousands but in the extreme the magnitude of the detonation would be reduce by one third. These people were prepared to die that others might live

He found himself forced to simplify the picture for his own benefit. They were like villagers on an active volcano defying a wall of lava. People with only a pathetic defense; perhaps an old fire pump, a hose, buckets of water. Knowing they could not stop the advance of fire but, perhaps, slowing enough to spare the next village.

He turned to Burke. "Put your hands high above your head like them. If we live long enough I'll tell you why later—they deserve it."

It was some time before an explanation was given, both men were becoming acutely aware of the increasing energy, their clothing crackled at the slightest movement and the interior of the vehicle seemed to glow.

Wallace had become resigned; fear was still there but in the background. His thoughts were mainly concerned with his recent experience and he found it sad that he had such a short time to live. He had learned so much and his horizons had been widened beyond belief. It had changed him and, inwardly he knew he was not the same man.

Burke also had changed but mainly due to the immensity of events. He was no longer afraid, perhaps the immediate terror had numbed or burnt out his nervous system but death no longer seemed to have meaning. There was sadness for all he had to leave behind, all the unfinished work, but it was remote like the memory of a long lost friend.

Far ahead, beyond the edges of the desert, dark outlines began to mass themselves on the horizon. The city, he thought. I hope to God we don't blow when we're half way through it. Visually these creatures are not exactly appealing but they've been fair with us.

He closed his mind to the subject and focused his attention on the trivial. He was surprised to find it shocked him beyond belief.

One kilometer! All this, all they had seen, all that had occurred, and the instrument in the car said they had only traveled one kilometer! Relatively speaking, more than three quarters of the runway still lay ahead.

He was still turning the matter over in his mind when there was a 'click.' There was no other description, both men were aware of it but neither heard it with their ears. It was something that they both felt, something which occurred inside their heads yet still, could only be described as a click.

Almost instantly they were plunged into darkness, it was as if someone had turned out the sun.

Both were aware, however, that this was something more than a switch into darkness, this was a new dispensation altogether.

Their circumstances had not changed, if anything it seemed increased. Their clothing still crackled with every movement and, in the darkness, their hands and faces were glowing.

Outside it was not an impenetrable stygian darkness, it was a warm almost velvet darkness.

As their eyes became accustomed to it, they saw it contained darker shadows, which might or might not denote solids.

"I think we're in a forest," said Burke, "those darker things could be trees. I'd say put your headlights on but I don't think it would be safe."

Wallace nodded, he'd thought about that himself but in their situation it was taking a chance.

He leaned forward, frowning. "Is it my eyes, or is everything linked together with a tracery of tiny white lines?"

Burke nodded vigorously. "My eyes as well—." He did not finish the sentence but began another. "Close! To your right, eye level."

Wallace turned his head. There was a small white spot, slightly large than the head of a pin and it was moving. It was moving in equal distances with brief stops in between. Around it was a strange, yet curiously familiar tracery of fine white lines.

"It's a bloody spider," he said in a shocked voice, "it's a spider building its web."

Burke had no time to make a comment, something glowing, about the size of a human hand dropped from above and clung moistly to the window beside him. It clung there for perhaps fifteen seconds then fell away only to rise uncertainly then soar erratically away.

Burke shook his head. "I know it sounds quite mad but I think it was drunk."

"Any idea what it was?"

"None whatever, but I am still certain it was stoned out of its mind." He grinned uneasily. "I seem to have developed faculties." Wallace nodded, he knew exactly what is friend meant.

He had no time to dwell on it, things started coming in from all angles, clung briefly to the car and fell way—some did not rise again. They were immediately replaced by others. One, a huge glowing moth-like thing clung to the screen with suction pads. It was so large it almost completely obscured their forward vision.

It was not there for long; that, too, fell away only to be replaced by other things.

It was Wallace who noticed the change first. "We're not crackling any more, our faces and hands have stopped glowing." His voice held a dawning hope.

Burke was silent for a few seconds, then he said; "Got an idea, probably crazy but it might fit."

He swallowed audibly then continued. "Seems pretty obvious we're on a queer world, one that hasn't been thought of before. Note all linking threads, little flashes, a shining web with spider. Could there be a world with electronic life forms? Suppose there is and we come blundering in with an overload of energy, perhaps the very sustenance of an electronic form of life. There is so much here in fact that the first creatures to take advantage of it, get an overdose."

Wallace turned and stared at him. "Your blob, the thing you said was drunk?"

"Precisely."

Wallace laughed to himself softly and, he admitted to himself a little hysterically. "Rightly or wrongly, I think those things have saved our lives. They've devoured, sucked up or bled off all that energy. I don't think we're a moving bomb anymore."

Burke nodded. "If things were normal I could almost cry with relief but we're still at the back end of time/space if that's the true explanation."

"Yes—I, too, seem to have developed faculties—but there is one hope. That click."

"It meant something to you?"

"Not psychically, if you can call it that but practically. It sounded familiar, an everyday sort of sound, like points being switched or signals being changed. As if something said; 'they're on the wrong track, got to switch them over to the correct one quickly."

"You think someone or something is looking out for us?"

Wallace shrugged helplessly. "Don't misunderstand me, terror has not reduced me to a state of religious fervor. On the other hand I've rejected the theory that the universe created itself out of nothing. Somehow, somewhere, particularly in the light of all we have experienced, there must be something which thinks and, most certainly, intelligences far greater than ours."

They moved on and Burke, musing over Wallace's words, thought: we have crossed the immensities of time and space yet, according to that little instrument in front of Wallace we've only traveled one kilometer and twenty two meters.

They moved on, Wallace still keeping the vehicle to a snail's pace. Their eyes had become used to the velvet darkness and it seemed they were in a forest not of trees but what appeared to them as the shapes of pipes or girders. All seemed to be linked by the web-like gossamer everywhere. Periodically sections of it lit vividly and bluely with almost gun-like reports. There were numerous and continuous sharp flashes near and at a distance.

Burke wondered if it was always dark and if such a place had seasons or storms. In the midst of his musings there was a distinct click. Wallace was aware of it also. "Now what?"

There was no immediate change but the shadows in front of them began to fill with mist. An attempt to use the headlights was no help whatever, merely reflecting the light back.

Wallace stopped and cut the engine. "No point in going on through this lot, we could go straight into a tree or over a cliff edge."

They waited, the mist thickened but gradually lightened as if somewhere, dawn was breaking. Slowly the light increased and the mist cleared. The velvet darkness and all pertaining to it had gone and in its place was almost normal countryside. They were on a high hill and the grassy meadowland fell greenly away in a succession of hills to a distant sparkling sea. A few trees were visible, a small lake and a few birds, but that was all.

Burke shivered. "It's not real," he said. "I know that doesn't make sense but that's how I feel. The insane scenes through which we have just passed had the stamp of reality; frightened as I was, I believed in them. This I don't, this is a picture put there as a background. It's a setting for something else if you know what I mean?"

Wallace did because something was happening, not out there but inside him. He had begun to experience things and new emotions which had never touched him before. He did not ask if Burke was feeling the same—he knew he was.

He tried desperately to rationalize his feelings and failed in the middle of it. There was fear—no, sheer choking terror—yet there was a light inside him, an exultation and, yes, no doubt about it, a reverence. He thought of burning bushes, heavenly choirs, and the wings of angels. If a towering figure, robed in shining light, had appeared in front of the car he would not have been surprised. He knew, however, that none of these things had relevance. These things were happening in his and Burke's minds. They were being assailed, brought into line for purposes as yet unknown.

Then, abruptly, it was gone, washed out of his mind like a sponge wiping marks from a blackboard.

Wallace started the engine and they moved forward again. The sun grew warmer and brighter as they moved. The green grass gave way to tarmac.

They looked at each other without speaking; they were back on the runway—if they had ever truly left it.

"What the hell will we say when we get back?" asked Burke. "Ten to one Harrison has left his office and come to meet us."

Wallace grinned twistedly. "Give me a minute or so, I'm working on a convincing story for his benefit."

24

"Which is?"

"Part car computer, part sonic, acting directly on the nervous system and effecting the stomach, hence the reaction of the drivers. We can clear the matter up in half an hour, no problem. Oh and yes, you saw a piece of silver paper in the grass as we pulled away. You thought it might be the lens of a timed micro camera so we pulled up to make sure. I'm convinced Harrison will both buy and applaud that one."

Burke was silent for a few seconds, then he said: "Do you know what really happened, the main cause?"

"In outline only. I can't prove it, of course, but I'm fairly sure the theory is O.K. I can put it right, it only needs some adjustment to the car computer and a fragment of metal in the engine bay replaced by plastic."

"The computer is the answer?"

"Not exactly, all the factors by themselves are completely harmless. Put together, however, the functioning of the computer, the engine vibration setting up a miniature electrical field in the engine compartment coupled with normal sonics—"

He did not finish the sentence but began again. "Whatever it was, sonic or high frequency electrical reaction or the two combined, it directly affected anyone using the car. At first it was only the nervous system—hence the tendency to vomit and the alarm felt by the drivers."

"So the car was responsible?" Burke looked worried.

"Not entirely, the conditions set up—call it a high frequency condition, if it helps—directly effected the brain. I don't know why and I admit that much of this theory is supposition. Anyway, I think it stimulated part of the brain giving it abnormal faculties and it became attuned to conditions beyond our conceptions, to worlds perhaps beyond the normal time and space continuum as we understand it . . ."

Wallace paused and laughed weakly. "Sorry if I simplify this, it's for my own benefit as much as yours. I've got a general outline but making sense of it in words is not that easy. Take a radio, you turn a dial or push a button for the station you want. When you've done so you're precisely tuned in to that particular station. We had no choice, the artificially stimulated parts of our minds did that for us. Once tuned in and locked on, we became more and more involved with that section of time/space to which we had become attuned."

Wallace paused again and made a helpless gesture with his hands. "Take a drama on television which is really gripping for you. It involves you almost completely, you almost forget the chair in which you are sitting and precisely where you are. Push this idea to the Nth degree and you will begin to see what happened to us. Physically we may not have moved but mentally we were so involved we were *there*. So much so, in fact that our thought/images had substance to an alien lifeform. Again, the contact had such reality that if the dangers we faced had occurred, any one of them could have killed us."

Burke wiped his forehead quickly. "This is all theory but you're not only making sense, you're also making me sweat. But how did the car get there?"

"It was in our minds, wasn't it? Perhaps it was still on the runway but since it was in our minds it had reality in this presumed illusion."

Burke paused and looked ahead. The sun was out, shining warmly on the runway and, at the far in he could see three of the directors' limousines waiting for their return.

He scribbled on his note pad and handed it to Wallace. "Directions to the Ferry Inn. The big boys are bound to keep you talking, expect you around seven."

At the corner table Burke ordered a meal and said: "Drink?"

"Thanks, no, I don't feel like one tonight."

"Very wise." Burke held up a large empty bottle. "Brandy, I drank the bloody lot while I was waiting, could have been water! We've changed, y'know."

"Don't remind me, old friend, a few hours ago we were normal people. We thought we knew this world exactly with every danger recognized and neatly labeled. When we were held by traffic at Romford's Corner—" He shook his head and changed the subject.

"Mind if I summarize?" asked Burke. "We set out as normal people, now we've got faculties that we don't care to think about. In point of fact we've come back as bloody aliens."

Wallace looked at him tiredly. "Sadly you've overlooked one point. We have also come back to what is now, to us, an alien planet."

THE TAPESTRY

Sydney J. Bounds

Brand was on the run.

On swift sandaled feet he darted first down one alley, then another, penetrating ever deeper into the native quarter of old Vegapolis. Far behind, forgotten, lay the glitter and brashness of the spaceport.

There, in sour-smelling lanes, shadows appeared to exist without benefit of light. Narrow alleys, filthy with refuse, crowded one on another, twisting in a maze of arches and passageways and ancient hovels behind whose walls lurked the vices of three solar systems.

There came the soft patter of feet behind him, a susurrus of voices.

Brand stumbled in his flight, half-drunk, the sword gripped in his right hand, trailing blood over the cobbles. It had been an exhilarating fight while it lasted, but even the outlaw known as the Tiger could not stand forever against massive odds. So he ran, a mob of Vegan at his heels.

The evening had started innocently enough. He had come to Vega seeking forgetfulness after the unfortunate affair of the golden-haired Luyka. It had seemed right to drown his sorrow; and poteen juice had led him to a harlot whose name he never learnt, then to a quarrel with her admirer. Brand had run him through and, instantly, a score of the admirer's associates fell upon him.

Brand's blade whirled in new action and. two more Vegans fell before others joined the fight. It was only then he had calculated the odds against him were too great, and fled.

Drums beat through the Vegan night, filling the dank air with an insistent throbbing, setting the ground a-quiver. *Vroom . . . vroom . . . vroom.* And the voice of the drums was a hunting call.

Brand ran with his lean body thrust forward and nostrils dilated, cursing the perpetual cloud that cloaked all light from the sky. Darkness aided his pursuers, for they knew these twisting passages better than he.

He hared on, seeking sanctuary.

The way he took led him through a street so narrow his shoulders dislodged dust from the walls on either side. He passed the open door of a shop, glimpsed bric-a-brac designed for bazaar-sale to space-happy tourists. Then a high wall barred his escape; he had entered a blind alley.

He turned. Vegans crowded the distant end of that narrow passage, howling in triumph because they had finally trapped him. Brand did not hesitate; he doubled back, into the shop, slammed the door in the face of the mob and shot the bolts. He leaned against it, swallowing air through his open mouth, looking about him.

There were silks in plenty, heavy to the touch; rugs of ornate design; bronze pots glinting in a dim light; ceramics and finely wrought metalwork. The aromatic smell of incense hung on the air.

A hammering started on the door at his back, shouts of frustration echoed. Brand bounded forward, checked in mid-stride as pattering feet sounded along a passage leading from some backroom to the shop. He waited, poised and tense, sword extended before him.

A Vegan appeared carrying a lighted bowl in his hands. He was old, his skin crinkly as faded parchment, clad in a dirty toga.

Brand moved, lunging to bring the point of his blade against the old man's throat. "Show me a back door—and hurry if you value your hide!"

The Vegan looked at him in silence. There was no fear in him, only a timeless calm. Brand leaned on his sword till the point broke the parchment skin and blood seeped.

"Violence will gain you nothing," the old man said gently. "There is but one door to my dwelling, that through which yon have so recently entered."

Brand cursed, turned the shopkeeper about and pushed him back along the passage. "I'll see for myself," he rasped.

But the Vegan spoke the truth. Behind the shop was a small room of thick stone walls, the only opening a narrow slit set high up. A rhythmic thudding at his back informed him that those outside were ramming the door, and it would not hold them long.

He was trapped. Fumbling in the pouch at his waist, he cast heavy coins upon the table. "See? I have gold—it is yours if you hide me well."

The Vegan smiled. "Keep your gold, Earthman—I have no use for it. But I can hide you."

Brand glimpsed a sudden flash of cunning in the old man's eyes and tightened his grip on his sword-hilt. "No tricks," he warned, "or I'll split you as I would a swamp rat."

"I can hide you, Earthman, in a place none can reach—if you have the courage to take the way."

Brand laughed, eyes lighting recklessly. "My courage has never been questioned. Am I not called the Tiger, hunted by the police of three solar systems? Show me this way you speak of and you will not regret it."

The old man stooped and drew back a rug to expose a trapdoor. He lifted this. Steps led down through darkness to a cellar. "Follow me."

Brand descended stone steps worn with age and presently stood on bare earth. The cellar was entirely empty except for a faded tapestry hung about one curved wall.

"There is no place to hide here," he snarled. "Fool, must I spill your guts in the dirt?"

The Vegan watched him calmly. He raised his lamp high and the flame wavered, throwing light and moving shadow across the wall.

"O Tiger," he said softly, "look into the tapestry before you say there is no sanctuary here. Look well, and tell me what you see."

Brand stared. The tapestry covered the entire wall and held a rare beauty. The warp was of the finest, the weft a muted rainbow of color, faded now, with no two threads of identical hue. It was a close-meshed web, shimmering in the lamplight in way that suggested movement, subtle beyond words.

"This is no ordinary work, old man."

"True." The Vegan sighed wistfully. "It is an ancient work, so ancient that mortals cannot comprehend. It is said it was left by the Gods . . . but tell me, 'what do you see there?'"

Brand strained his eyes to read the elusive picture woven into the tapestry, and found it difficult to focus. The result of too much poteen juice, he wondered, or some quality inherent in the design?

"I see," he began, "walls that contain passages, walls without end and passages that intersect haphazardly. A Labyrinth! And more . . . "

His voice trailed off, his spine tingled, for there were no words to contain the alien thing roaming those passages. It was not of Earth, or Vega, he was certain. He doubted if such a being had spawned within the Federation of known worlds.

"I see . . . a monster!"

The old man chuckled slyly. "A monster, yes. And one worthy of your blade!"

Brand raised his sword. "Old man," he growled, "do not mock me."

'Look again, Earthman—you have not seen all the tapestry holds."

Brand flexed irritably, aware of distant sounds, the battering against the upstairs door. Soon the mob would be on him; yet the pattern of colored threads held him entranced.

"I see a girl . . . and what a girl . . . beautiful . . . "

"A princess," the old man murmured.

Yes, she would be a princess; it was in her bearing. She carried a regal pride, and sadness too. Her hair shone like burnished copper and the shape of her roused desire in him.

"Is she real?" he wondered aloud. "Can she truly exist where a man can lay hold of her?"

The Vegan chuckled and rubbed withered hands. "Aye, she is real enough. She exists—somewhere. The land of the tapestry is no figment of an artist's imagination; rather, regard it as you would a mirror revealing a reflection of the truth. I am the keeper of the tapestry, and even I know not in what strange realm of space or time the reality exists."

Cunning inserted itself into his voice. "Yet I have the means to send you there, Tiger."

Brand removed his gaze from the tapestry, the labyrinth, the monster and the princess. He straightened his lean frame, muscles bulging, lank black hair tossed back in a wild mane.

'Then you shall send me to her, old man!"

The keeper of the tapestry inserted a skeletal hand beneath his toga, brought out a vial of amber liquid.

"Drink this," he said, "and you will enter the world of the tapestry and join your princess. It is no potion designed to harm you, but an ancient sorcery. The vibration-rate of your body cells and aught you touch will change to allow you to pass through the web of space-time—to her. Drink, and she shall be yours!"

Still Brand felt suspicious. Then a splintering sound came from above, the sound of rushing feet. Armed Vegans surged down the cellar steps.

He swing round, sword ready, baring his teeth wolfishly. There were too many and he was trapped. He laughed in their faces as they came for him, snatched the vial from the old man man's hands and jerked free the stopper with his teeth. He drank . . .

The liquid tasted bitter. Fire spread though his body and his head spun as the cellar faded from view.

Now the world of the tapestry loomed large. It sprang up about him. The walls of the labyrinth soared over his head. He stumbled, and his legs trembled under his own weight. He felt vicious hands jab into his back, thrust with surprising strength. As he fell forward a voice croaked: "One more victim for—"

Brand sprawled on hard-packed earth, sword gripped in his hand. The silence, the stillness of the air, was oppressive. He scrambled quickly to his feet and looked about him. On each side, some five meters apart, massive stone walls reached away before and behind him. The light was not strong, tinged with crimson, and it cane from a source he could not immediately identify; its range was short, a few meters only.

There was no sign of the cellar, the keeper of the tapestry or those who sought his death. Thoughtfully, he reached out and tapped the wall: solid. Without doubt, he was in the labyrinth . . .

He stood a moment, considering this. His memory of the interlocking passages was not clear; and what he could recall availed him nothing, for the illumination of this strange place isolated him in disconcerting fashion.

Somewhere the princess waited. The princess, and a monster.

Brand barked a laugh and started forward, swinging his sword vigorously. He roared a war-song as he advanced; his head was clear and his body tingled with anticipation. He would kill the monster and claim the princess and she would love him . . . naturally. He was not called the Tiger for nothing.

He stopped abruptly, impressed by a bizarre phenomenon. As he moved, so the source of light moved with him. His flesh crawled. It was as if the crimson glow were part of him. He walked back a pace, and the light moved with him.

It solved one problem—how he was to find his way through the labyrinth—but he didn't like it. The whole thing was unnatural, giving the impression that the ground unrolled before him as he needed it, then fell away to nothing behind.

He paused, looked both ways. Beyond the reddish glow was dark blankness, impenetrable; and now a tremor of fear racked his lean frame, fear of the unknown.

He went on, taking a left turn, and left again, counting. The walls of the labyrinth were three times as wide as the passages between them and he felt stifled, imagining the maze to be mere slits in the rock buried deep under . . . under what? For the first time, he looked up.

The walls rose past the range of light, vanished. How high did they go? And what might he see from the top?

To think was to act. Brand sheathed his sword and, impatiently, began to climb. The rock was old, grooved with age and ho found foot and hand holds. He went up the vertical face like a spider on a web—to discover yet another disconcerting facet of this strange place.

The light did not follow him. It remained at ground level and, soon, he was climbing through darkness. Yet the wall continued to rise and still he climbed, moving more slowly now, feeling for holds and testing each in turn before placing his weight on a new one. Below, the crimson glow shrank to a dot, faded away completely.

His muscles ached and he despaired of ever reaching the summit. He rested a moment, clinging to the vertical face of the rock wall, peering up. He saw nothing but blackness.

Even the tiger must give up sometime. The wall had beaten him; if there was a limit to it—and that he began to doubt—he knew he would never reach it. Slowly he descended.

Once more at ground level, enclosed by his crimson halo, he set about exploring the labyrinth. It was only when he found the first pile of bones that it occurred to him to wonder how he might return to his own space and time.

The bones were human and in disorder, giving the appearance of having been ravaged. Some were snapped across, others crushed as by some tremendous force. Further on Brand found more bones scattered in his path; he did not investigate closely.

Till then, he had given no thought to his return. It was enough that he should find the princess; now, however, he began to worry. Was there a way out from the maze? Or was he doomed to wander these endless corridors forever?

He called, again and again, urgently: "Princess . . . princess!"

A distant bellow answered, a noise half-animal, half-alien. Brand halted in his tracks, scalp prickling. The bellow came again and there was fury in it, hunger, and a challenge.

Brand pulled his sword free and held it ready. Somewhere beyond the ring of light, the monster hunted him. A bestial odor pervaded the air, like nothing he had smelt before—it made him want to retch.

He waited, poised, for the monster to appear, listening to the sonorous echoes of its challenge roll through the passageways.

The minutes dragged. Now and again, the frightful bellowing would seem close at hand and his grip tightened on his sword, then it would fade into the distance. Brand guessed the monster knew no more of these labyrinth ways than he.

A figure appeared at the rim of the circle of light. Instantly his blade flashed, lunging. He barely checked his stroke in time as a feminine voice murmured: "Quiet! Every sound betrays you—Mintor hunts by sound alone."

Brand let his sword rest at his side and looked the princess boldly up and down. Her beauty stirred him, made him reckless.

"Let him hunt then. I am called the Tiger and, for your love, will kill this monster. Forget your fears, princess—truly I have come to deliver you."

She made a smile for him, a smile that quickened his pulse, but still sadness shadowed her face.

"You speak well, bold Tiger, but others have spoken such phrases and their bones litter this place. Unless you wish a similar fate, be silent. Take my hand and follow—at least I know the path better than Mintor."

Brand took her hand, soft and warm, and together they traveled the passages between the stone walls. She danced on light-shod feet, copper hair draping bare shoulders, filmy veils fluttering about her. Mintor's strident challenges faded to a whisper.

Suddenly tired of flight, Brand pulled her to a halt.

"Enough," he said abruptly. "This running before an enemy affronts my dignity! First, tell me your name. Then how you came to be in this place. Finally who—or what—is Mintor."

"I am called Haidee—"

"Princess Haidee." Brand pressed her hand to his lips. "So young and—"

She laughed, and her laughter held a bitterness he did not understand. "I am ten thousand years young!"

Brand released her hand. Ten *thousand* years? It was impossible, of curse; his mind dizzied trying to imagine it. Her lips so ripe for kisses, her supple figure . . . and yet her eyes were haunted by a strange truth. Eyes that held a wisdom greater than any lifetime could command, a fire that had once blazed; now sad, burdened by unnatural youth.

"I am here because my father punished a sorcerer, an evil man who placed this spell on me," Haidee said quietly. "For ten thousand years I have wandered this labyrinth, alone with Mintor, creation of the same magician. So many men have been lured here, food for the monster. So many have died for me."

Brand listened, her tale chilling the passion she roused in him. Her voice was a lost echo, her face calm as carved marble.

"A tapestry was fashioned to mirror this place, a keeper appointed. Through generations it has been handed on, passing from world to world—and all who look on it are lost. Why did you come here? Because of me . . . now do you understand? I am the bait to feed Mintor. I, daughter of a royal household . . . bait!"

Brand lifted his blade in a big hand, showed his teeth in a rapacious laugh. "Tell me what I must do to break this spell, princess. Tell me, and I'll bring you peace."

"There is only one way—kill Mintor. But he is strong and cunning. Many have tried and failed."

"The Tiger will not fail! Have no fear, Princess Haidee, this time the keeper of the tapestry has brought death to his charge. My sword shall put an end to Mintor."

He threw back his head and shouted: "Hear me, Mintor! I am the Tiger and am here to kill you. Come if you dare."

Far off, the monster bellowed.

Haidee spoke again, swiftly. "Now he comes. Mintor comes in answer to your challenge and once more I pray deliverance. Now I kiss you, for a warrior should always carry the taste of his lady's lips into battle. Truly, I shall love the one who brings me peace."

She stepped close, reaching out her arms, raising her hand. "Close your eyes," she murmured, "that we may put ten thousand years behind us. I am eighteen again and I love you."

Brand crushed her in his arms, eyes tight shut, kissed her long and hard. The heat of her body came to him through filmy veils; her breasts and thighs molded to his muscles. Her lips were fire and passion such as he had never known before. Her hands locked behind him and her embrace contained an eternity of experience.

"And now—kill Mintor for me!"

The alien stench grew stronger. The ground trembled and the monster's challenge sounded close at hand. Brand stepped free, sword lifted.

"Take your position at an intersection," Haidee advised. "At all costs, you must avoid being trapped when he charges. Evade him, and strike as he passes."

Brand moved to a T-junction in the maze and waited. Haidee hung back, gazing fiercely at him. And Mintor came . . .

There was a rush of air along the narrow corridor, billowing dust and an alien fetor, a terrifying roar. The stone walls vibrated, Brand glimpsed sharp curving horns, bone-white, and a glistening snout. Obscene hands struck blindly at him as he dodged, hands that struck his steel aside as though it were no more than a leaf.

Then Mintor was past, beyond the rim of crimson light and swallowed in darkness. Brand turned sharply, readied himself for a second charge. Braced, he held his sword horizontal and at full length before him. He was sweating slightly.

Back thundered his enemy, bellowing frustrated rage. Brands barely had a second in which to wield his sword; the time between Mintor's appearance in the ring of light and his attack. A massive horn deflected his thrust.

This time the deflected steel sliced the snout a glancing blow and Mintor howled. Good . . . he *could* be hurt!

Now a massive bull-shoulder almost crushed him against the wall, driving the breath from his body. Blind Mintor turned again, out-reaching hands groping for him.

With some cunning, Brand climbed the wall, sword between his teeth; hauling himself beyond the reach of Mintor's horns, climbing to vertical rock.

Mintor commenced another charge—and halted, uncertainly, below him. The monster raised its head and bellowed, buffeting the walls in its rage. And suddenly, looking down, Brand knew what kind of beast it was he fought—the mythical minotaur of Gnossus. In appearance half-man, half-bull; the creature was neither; it was *alien,* from another space and another time and the resemblance to a man-bull was entirely artificial.

The shoulders were broad and the body heavy, half as high again as a man, and nearly filling the labyrinth corridor. Coarse hair covered a hump-back and the withered eye-sockets set in the snout were also overgrown with hair. Short forearms ended in muscular hands. The horns were curved and sharply pointed. It stood on two powerful limbs, naked and obscenely manlike, scaly hide scarred from encounters with previous challengers.

Brand could form no guess as to how this alien thing had become part of Crete's ancient history—unless the tapestry had been known on Earth—and did not care. One thought only lay in his mind; he must kill before it killed him.

Dropping from his perch, he slashed at the huge head. Mintor snorted, tossing his horns to gore the attacker he could not see. Brand clung with one arm wrapped around Mintor's shoulders and sought to stab again.

He was tossed away, and Mintor lowered his head and charged. Brand rolled sideways, slashed at. sinewy limbs. He dived between the minotaur's legs and scrambled upright behind it.

Haidee called: "Now bold Tiger—strike him dead!"

Brand lunged, aiming for the immense bull-neck, but Mintor turned in time to ward off the blow. Flailing hands forced Brand back and, as the horns lowered and thrust for the kill, he dropped his sword and grasped the horns with both hands.

Mintor bellowed and shook his head vigorously, but Brand vaulted nimbly onto his back.

Stumbling, dragging the Earthman with him, Mintor lurched forward, smashed into one wall, rebounded to another. Brand changed position, squatting astride the broad shoulders; he levered on the horns, dragging the head back.

Locked together they fell. Still Brand clung on, exerting every ounce of strength in an effort to break the monster's neck. Dust rose as they struggled, covering them. The air grew foul as Mintor's breath labored.

Haidee's voice came again: "You have him, Tiger! Now . . . now!"

Mintor weakened as Brand twisted his head on his shoulders. Sweat covered the Earthman, mingled with blood and dust; his muscles ached as the stain grew.

Then he let go, bounded the short distance to his sword and scooped it up. He ran in as Mintor still struggled to rise. The steel flashed, crimson in the weird light. He hacked and stabbed at that monstrous body till his blade was wet and bloody.

Mintor made a last effort to grasp his opponent, failed. The strength was leaving him.

Brand paused a moment to set himself, both hands tight on the hilt of his sword. He lifted and swung . . . and severed the bull-head from its body in one mighty stroke.

Mintor's hands groped at air. It seemed that a scream came from his mouth even as blood fountained from the stump of neck. Then the immense body convulsed on the ground, legs kicking.

Brand backed off, gulping air into his lungs. Weary and bruised, he yet felt exultant; one more foe had fallen to his blade. He turned, smiling, to seek his princess.

And that which had been the princess Haidee grimaced mirthlessly back at him. The spell broken, the years rolled over her, remorselessly grinding her beauty under the wheels of time. Gone the lustrous copper hair, the suppleness of youth. Age changed and wrinkled her to a hideous crone.

Brand stared, appalled, as sagging flesh rotted and wasted away before his eyes. The flesh liquefied and bones turned to dust. A graveyard smell forced him back . . .

He closed his eyes against the horror and, when he opened them again, saw the cellar and the tapestry. Those who would have killed him had fled; and, on the floor, lay the keeper of the tapestry, head severed from his body.

Brand stood motionless, his sword a useless weight in his hand. After a time, he lifted his gaze to the tapestry—and that too, had changed.

No longer faded, its colors blazed out a new story. He saw Haidee—a happy laughing Haidee—surrounded by people who came running to her, through every corridor of the labyrinth. A white-haired man of royal bearing took her in his arms and kissed her forehead. A king had been given back his daughter.

As Brand looked, the people of the maze turned their faces to him in silent gratitude. The king raised his hand and the people fell to their knees. Only Haidee remained standing; a young and lovely princess, her eyes shining with a love she could never give . . .

The vision faded. The tapestry too rotted and fell from the wall till there were only moldering threads, musty as withered grapes on a vine.

Brand wiped his sword and sheathed it. He climbed the cellar steps and went out into the Vegan night. He wandered the cobbled alleys till he found the light of a tavern, to seek his reward in the arms of the first harlot he met; for all women would wear the face of Haidee this night.

BLACK OUTLOOK

John Russell Fearn

It was dark when I set off over the hill—dark and windy, with a thin, driving rain. I glanced back once towards the spot from which I had come, satisfying myself that it was unlikely anybody would come in that direction, and on such a night. Come to think of it, the conditions could hardly have been worse, or else it was that I felt them more being so accustomed to warmth and sunlight. But there it was. I had a job to do, and that as quickly and efficiently as possible. For that purpose I had been chosen.

I covered perhaps three miles against blinding rain and gale-force wind before I saw ahead of me the gleaming lights of a drive-in cafe. In another ten minutes I had reached it. I found my way through a convoy of parked lorries and then practically fell inside the place, slamming the door against a deluge of rain. An ancient-type bell tinkled noisily over my head.

Faces turned and eyes looked at me—swarthy, weather-beaten faces most of them. Everywhere there seemed to be men in leather jackets—drinking, smoking, eating, talking. They looked at me in cold disregard and then turned back to their tables.

I went across to the counter and slid onto one of the tall stools. The proprietor looked at me dispassionately, a complete void on his face. I was there, yet as far as he was concerned, I was not.

"Can't you read?" he demanded, as I asked for a cup of coffee, and he nodded his shiny bald head towards a notice pinned on the wall. "If you can't, I'll read it for you. It says 'Colored People Barred!' And that means *you!* Get out! Get off my premises!"

"But I . . . Surely just a cup of coffee?"

"You heard me! *Out!*"

I studied him for a moment. Back of the counter a mirror reflected my features. Coal-black, black as the columns of Hades. Yet in my eyes there must have been a faint surprise.

"Does my color matter?" I asked at length.

"You know damned well it does! Now get out—before I throw you out!"

I hesitated. In feeling for the money in my pocket with which to pay for the coffee I had also encountered something else—the hard outlines of a lethal weapon.

"Are you going, or not?" demanded the angry voice; and around me at the tables the men were getting up. All of them tough, burly individuals. Though they had not touched me as yet, the air crawled with the menace of their intentions.

"I'll go," I said quietly—and I went. I was not really thirsty, but I was certainly surprised. Vastly surprised.

Out into the wind and rain again. Cold, inhospitable, friendless: how could anybody live in such inclemency? It was five miles to the town itself—a south country town drenched in the rain of winter, yet with the lights of homes gleaming behind curtains of varicolored hues. I tramped on. I thought of what might lie behind those curtains. Happy homes, maybe. Or angry homes. Friendless homes. Families enjoying the peace of security. Children. Company. Laughter

I chose one of the houses at random and knocked on the door. A little girl opened it. The hall light showed she was white-skinned and neatly dressed. Yet her bright young face filled with a shocked surprise when she saw me. She took a step back.

"Mummy!" she shouted urgently, into a side room. "Mummy, there's a black man at the door . . . !"

All the time she was backing away until she came up against a young woman who was presumably her mother. Although her face was pleasant her voice was harsh.

"Well, what do you want?" she snapped at me, coming to the door.

"All I wanted, madam, was to have a word with you. To ask you if . . . "

"I'm sorry, but I can't help you. In any case I don't encourage tramps even when they're white ones, and I have certainly no time for negroes.

Good night!"

The door slammed in my face. I was left staring at it, the rain streaming down its green paint as it caught the reflection from the street lamp opposite.

My thoughts were strange ones—baffled ones. I had never expected anything like this. I felt like going home—back to warmth and security—but because I had a job to do I went on. I knocked on the doors of four more homes at random, and each time I got a rebuff. One old lady even seemed scared to death. On the sixth occasion, however, I was more fortunate. A middle-aged man came to the door.

"Well?" he asked—not with intolerance but with a touch of genuine interest.

"Forgive my bothering you, sir, but you have a notice over your front door—'Board Residence'. Would that apply to me?"

"I can't see why it shouldn't. Come in."

He held the door wide and I passed into a bright hall, then into what I assumed was the lounge. The place was comfortable, even though there was a rather ancient coal fire burning. The middle-aged man followed me in, sucking his pipe.

"So you want board residence?" he asked, motioning to a chair.

"Not really." I sat down. "Most of all I want to talk to somebody."

He looked vaguely surprised for a moment, then he shrugged.

"All right, fellow, talk. I've been told I'm a good listener. First, let me tell my wife what I'm doing."

He went out. I studied the room. Comfortable, yes, but capable of enormous improvement. In one sweep I could very easily . . . My host came back and stood near the fire, drawing at his pipe.

"Now?" he invited, and his eyes were curious but by no means critical.

"I'm a stranger here," I said. "I arrived tonight. So far I have been treated like an animal, if not worse. Can you tell me why?"

"Surely you can guess? Racial intolerance. You're black, my friend, and this is America, in the year 1959!" He paused, pipe balanced, and stared at me. "God, you *are* black! What are you? West African?"

"No," I answered, and did not elaborate. "I have a mission to fulfill. I want to contact various important people—heads of State, civic heads, all those in whom rulership is vested. Also the chiefs of the medical profession."

"You don't want much, do you?"

"How do I set about doing it?"

My friend—for I felt he *was* my friend—extended a cigarette case towards me. I shook my head quickly.

"I wouldn't know what to do with those," I said.

"That's a pity. The offer of a cigarette signifies peace. It's an old custom."

"I see . . . Could you answer my question, please?"

"I would if I could, black man, but I can't. The prejudice against the blacks is colossal, and you'd never break it down. As for meeting important people, I don't think even a white man could do that—an ordinary, everyday white man, that is—without tremendous influence behind him. I'm afraid you don't stand any chance whatever."

I said: "Is it possible for such prejudice to exist in an ordered, progressive society? In a community of men and women that considers itself enlightened and progressive?"

"Yes. It's more than a possibility: it's a fact." He put his pipe back in his mouth and looked at me. "You speak surprisingly good English."

"I have spent nearly five years learning it. It seemed the wise thing to do since it is spoken by the major nations. I can speak any other language at will."

"You are of good education, and yet you don't seem conversant with the color bar. You wonder why you are unwelcome, and yet you come unheralded out of the night and seek audience with the great ones! And you come to a prosaic boarding house to make a start! In heavens' name, man, who are you? *What* are you?"

"A seeker after facts," I told him. "I want only to see how the people of this country—any country—live. And I want to do it without them knowing I'm coming." I got to my feet. "This is utterly different from what I had expected. I had expected surprise, perhaps, but certainly not hatred. All because of my skin. I came to confer great benefits and nobody will listen to me—except you."

Silence. I noticed a clock on the mantelpiece, one that seemed to work by spring. So incredibly archaic.

"Suppose," I said suddenly, "I were to find others with skin like my own. Would *they* help me?"

"Possibly. As you know, there are some very clever colored people, but as a force they are in a minority. The whites would never be influenced by them. In fact, if they felt like it, some whites could—and probably would—exterminate them from the earth."

I stared at him. "Then how am I to confer benefits? How am I to give the precious information I am carrying? How am I to *begin*?"

"Begin what, black man?"

"Begin . . . " I stopped. There was no point telling him. If this vast prejudice was so inflexible, what was the use?

"I am a simple man," my friend said. "I try to understand everybody because I think it is the only way to gain peace when I die. I believe any man—or woman—is really perfect no matter what the skin . . . be it black, yellow, or red. But most other people of white stock don't think the same as I do."

"Then how do you achieve unity and peace?" I demanded.

"We don't. The world has always been on the verge of an explosion. Not against the blacks, particularly, but against each other. And the discovery of nuclear power has made things worse. H-bombs, cobalt bombs. Outer space. I suppose the fools will carry their infernal machines out there too."

"Not for long," I said quietly. "There's a very good reason why they won't be allowed to."

"You mean the hand of Providence? Well, perhaps . . . " He stopped, sucking at his pipe. It had gone out. He said, "I don't know who you are or where you have come from, but if you want board residence you can have it."

I hesitated; then he added, "Mind you, I don't guarantee how the others in the house will react. If there's trouble because you're a black man you'll understand why it is."

"I am not going to stay, my friend," I told him. "I prefer to go, and to remember you as one man who had the courtesy to try and understand me. I shall go—never to return. Some day perhaps it will become plain how much has been thrown away. Never in all the careful analyses we made did we foresee this."

"Analyses? *What* analyses? Can't you stop talking in riddles?"

He said something further but I did not catch it. I was already on my way, out of the house, into the wind and rain, back to the spot whence I had come.

It is peaceful where I am writing now. There is no sound except the faint hum of the engine utilizing the illimitable power of the magnetic lines of force. There is no quietness comparable to that of infinite space. So, I write my report for transmission by ultra-beam:

"Report to his Serene Excellency,

"Always conscious of the immense trust your Excellency has placed in me, I must nevertheless in this case report the failure of my mission. I have traveled across interstellar space from our happy world of Dexa filled with the conviction that my ambassadorial task would be easy, particularly so as we of Dexa are of similar physique to Earth people. Yet the mission failed.

"We have learned everything about the people of Earth—except the most important thing. Racial prejudice! I had imagined that the black skin of our race—due to our nearness to our sun—would not, have meant anything. On the contrary it has meant *everything!* Because we of Dexa are all black, and the most powerful races of Earth are white, any possibility of friendship is foredoomed to failure, at least for a long time to come.

"I therefore suggest to Your Excellency that in spite of our many preparations, in spite of our numerous visits to Earth for the purpose of distant observation, in spite of our intention to convey to Earthlings the marvels of discovery in medicine, engineering, science, eugenics, and so forth which our own civilization has perfected, we forthwith ignore this planet and its utilization as one in a chain of friendly worlds. The peoples of Earth are still low in the scale of advancement, unreasonable and bigoted in their outlook. If we *could* make friends with them they would probably reward us by bringing their bombs, power-politics, and insatiable love of conquest to our world. Rather then that happen, let us prepare against them.

"I am aware that all this will be grievous to Your Excellency, particularly as you were so confident that I—groomed for many years in my ambassadorial task by the use of radio and telescopy—would effect a quiet conquest the moment I landed on Earth. It is not to be, Excellency, and for that reason I have withheld the benefits I intended to bestow had the Earth people proven friendly. I met only one who seemed to be at all reasonable. On the other hand I did not commit the supreme sin of wiping many of them out of existence with the weapon I carried, even though I had plenty of justification.

"Forget Earth, Excellency, and let its peoples first learn one of its own laws—'Do Unto Others as You Would Have Them Do Unto You'.

"4617. Ambassador Extraordinary, Dexa."

THE VISITOR

Eric C. Williams

A taxi drew up outside 13 Hanover Terrace and Zaroff got out dragging two heavy suitcases. For a gold coin (filched from the vault of a 29th century museum) the driver picked up one case and carried it to the door of the house while Zaroff carried the other.

"Love us!" puffed the driver. "Is it bricks you got here?" He lowered it with a thud.

"More constructive than bricks," said Zaroff. "Books."

The door opened and an elderly janitor looked out glumly. "Mr. T.T. is it? Mr. Wells said you might come."

"The prophetic old devil!" said Zaroff with a smile.

"Indeed, Sir. May I help with the cases?" He attempted to lift one. "My, my, they *are* heavy." He shut the door behind Zaroff then limped off towards the foot of the stairs leaving Zaroff to handle the cases.

The hall was broad with a flight of stairs at the far end. Standing now on the landing at the top of the stairs was Wells's dumpy shape.

"Hallo T.T.," he called in a shaky voice. "I was expecting you. Bring your stuff up." He raised a hand and went back out of view into his drawing room.

Zaroff rallied his strength and began the ascent with his teeth clenched in effort. He reached the landing, and there was Wells standing in the doorway to a long, book-lined room.

"Come in," said Wells.

Zaroff entered the room with feelings approaching awe. So many books, several hundred being Wells's own works in many languages, and many others being the books that helped fuel his mind over the years. Wells stood by the marble fireplace looking at Zaroff keenly as he dragged the cases in and closed the door.

"Let me look at you," said Wells heartily. "The return of the Time Traveler, eh? T.T., it's wonderful to see you again. I have been thinking about you since all the news out of Hiroshima. Do you remember your visit in 1912 to my place at Easton? What a day that was! What a game we had!" He laughed joyfully and smacked a fist into a palm, then became serious.

"You came to tell me about the Bomb."

"Yes," nodded Zaroff. "You were writing 'The World Set Free': you wanted something horrible to scare the world into seeing sense."

Wells levered himself off the fireplace and went to a table and poured a glass of whisky. "Here, drink this," he said. "I can't take the stuff myself, but you look as if you could do with it. Yes," he continued, "and you chose to give me only half the truth about the Bomb. Why did you do that?"

Zaroff took the glass. "I'm sorry, H.G. I was trying to prevent a Time-Disaster but I wasn't entirely successful. The idea of chain reaction got through. I've found out that Leo Szilard read 'The World Set Free' and it put the idea into his head. The seed was sown. The Time-Disaster went ahead."

Wells dumped himself in an armchair and stared at Zaroff.

"That's nonsense, T.T. Fermi and Szilard didn't work it out from reading 'The World Set Free'."

"Maybe not entirely like that," said Zaroff. "But there's no doubt you gave birth to the idea of dropping the bomb from an aeroplane; that's just as bad."

Wells banged the arm of his chair. "I refuse to accept responsibility for the bomb. I suppose the next thing you will be accusing me of inciting Martians to invade Earth just because I wrote 'The War of the Worlds'. Rubbish: the whole idea is rubbish." He felt in his pocket and produced a bottle containing pills. He shook one out with a shaking hand and swallowed it.

"I'm sorry, H.G." said Zaroff. "Of course it's not your fault: it's mine. I should not have told you in 1912; I must have been trying to warn the world, fool that I am!" He kicked one of his cases. Wells sat a moment or two in deep reflection and then stirred himself.

"Oh, I can't work it out." He looked at the cases. "What have you there?" He gave a boyish grin. "Gold Bricks?"

"Just as valuable," Zaroff responded. He opened one of the cases. "Your books: first editions. I brought them here for you to sign."

"Pshaw," grunted Wells with a sour look. "I never took you for a book dealer."

"Nor am I. These will be the core of a collection I shall donate to the twenty-ninth century."

"Incredible!" muttered Wells. "There you stand, a man from the future, a Time Traveler, and here I sit, a decrepit old wreck from the days of Victoria and Edward: it boggles the mind: it truly does. And although I have spent my entire writing life trying to bring sanity into the hodgepodge of warring nations, all you tell me I have achieved is to plant the notion of the atomic bomb. It is very sad. Is there nothing else?" He looked utterly downcast.

Zaroff went and knelt before him and gripped his knees. "H. G., I come from a World State; I come from a world run by the most intelligent; a world where population is kept at a sustainable level; where towns are severely limited in size, and where Nature is guarded as carefully as our own children. These are things you fought for."

"Utopia, are you telling me?" Wells interrupted sardonically. "What about your Time Police?"

"Yes, the Time Police, they are there," agreed Zaroff. "If you have Time Travel for all, then you must guard against its misuse for it can be as dangerous as, say, giving a child the computer password to the world News network. History can be rewritten over and over without end by the careless. The Time Police have been given total power in correcting these matters."

"Hitler gave the Gestapo total power to correct non-cooperation with his State. Are your police hated like the Gestapo were?" Wells lifted his chin, more like his argumentative self.

"No. Their punishment is disliked, but not them. Their job is too horrible to merit hate."

"In what way 'horrible'?" Wells seemed to take on energy; his moustache bristled.

"Most go mad in the end. They are afflicted with fragmentation of the persona because of their continual moving through all the years this planet has been inhabited." Zaroff halted momentarily, then added: "As you will find out. The experience of arriving in a different age is unsettling."

Wells at up straight.

"What did you say?"

Zaroff stood up, glad to cut the dismal subjects they had been pursuing. He smiled down at Wells.

"If you are a good friend and sign these books, I will give you a ride to the end of the world. What do you say to that?" Zaroff held up a small bracelet-like machine before Wells's bulging eyes.

Wells began to tremble, and Zaroff had a few seconds of apprehension that he had over-estimated Wells's strength, then Wells almost whispered: "This is what I was going to ask you when you came. Give me one minute and I'll sign every book in the British Library. It is a vision I have had ever since I wrote the 'Time Machine.' What was that—fifty years ago? What does it matter if I freeze a few days off the end of my life. I have finished all I had to say."

He reached out for the bracelet. Zaroff retracted it with an apologetic smile.

"Sign first, reward later," Zaroff said, and began piling the books on the table near his chair. Wells picked them up one by one with either a grunt of dismissal or a ho-hum of regretful approval, and then he signed them with his small, neat signature. The work took about ten minutes and looked like a foreign diplomat signing papers fed to him by an obsequious secretary. He flipped closed the last one, 'Mind at the End of its Tether', and waved it at Zaroff.

"I wish I hadn't issued this thing. I haven't really given up all hope that one day Homo Sapiens will become sapient. But I suppose the newspapers will say I died a disappointed man." He tossed the book on to the table.

"Now, T.T., set that bracelet thing and let us get moving." He was suddenly as full of energy as the schoolboy Zaroff had met many years ago in Bromley.

"Put on as many clothes as you can," said Zaroff. "A hat, scarf, greatcoat, gloves. This is no picnic."

When he was finally ready and standing before Zaroff he looked a sad old heap of clothes, round-shouldered with the weight. Zaroff set Wells's and his own bracelet, and gave him simple instructions on their use.

"Take a good breath," Zaroff instructed. "Right? Switch on."

It was foolhardy. The abrupt plunge into that bitterly cold, rarified air might have stopped Wells's heart in an instant, but although he tottered and gripped his chest as if in pain, he held on and straightened up and looked around. They were on the slope of a shallow valley leading away to the distant, ominous, slow-surging sea that Zaroff had described to Wells on one of his numerous visits. The dark red sun hung above the sea, dulled now and again by drifting banks of ice crystals. There was no noise, no movement, only the touch of ice on the cheek in its invisible languid fall through the air. Zaroff had not Wells's layers of clothing and the cold soon struck into his body making him shiver as if he were connected to an electric current. Wells shuffled his feet round to look at him.

"What a miserable end," Zaroff heard him say in a faint voice which was even more scratchy than normal. "So this is all that millions of years of evolution come to! Let's go back. I've seen enough." He was panting. His face looked blue.

Zaroff nodded as best he could. He gripped Wells's wrist to press the return button on his bracelet, but Wells stopped him.

"Let us go to the year million. Perhaps Man will still be on the planet." He leaned heavily on Zaroff. A minute more and his heart might stop, yet, nevertheless, he wanted to see more, and his great fighting spirit held death back.

With chilled fingers Zaroff set the controls, and sent them back. The sky brightened, warmth struck through their clothing, sweet air rushed into their lungs. Wells gave a low groan and sat down heavily in the deep grass. His Homburg hat rolled off, his forehead was wet with perspiration, his right hand made flapping movements towards his breast.

"Bottle," he croaked at Zaroff. "Pocket inside."

Hurriedly Zaroff opened Wells's greatcoat and felt inside his jacket. There was a small bottle containing liquid that Zaroff applied to the gasping man. The action of the medicine was swift, for within a few seconds Wells smiled up and offered Zaroff his hand.

"Give me a hand up. I want to see this. There's no view down here."

Zaroff got him up, and Wells stood holding Zaroff's shoulder and gazed around with complete absorption. They stood in the middle of a herd of strange, hairy animals as big as horses but with curly horns. Those nearest regarded the men peacefully and stretched their nostrils as if testing their smell; those further away continued grazing.

The travelers were in the same valley as before although it was deeper and a river flowed over the level fields. Fields! Yes: in one place a line of hedge on the further bank of the river, and behind it a narrow track trailing inland. There were patches of cultivation on the further slopes, and a cluster of trees that looked like an orchard. High up, on the sky-capped ridge of the other slope of the valley there was a collection of white shapes that were undoubtedly houses.

"Men," breathed Wells, nodding in the direction of the settlement. "Pastoral civilization, hey? You know, I wrote an article about the year million—years ago—a million years ago!" He looked momentarily amused and then disgruntled. "Nothing like this."

He measured the distance with a frustrated eye. "Too far for me to go. How about you, T.T.?" Wells's hand clenched on Zaroff's shoulder.

"What are they like, eh? Giant brains? Greek Gods and Goddesses? Get them to come over here, there's a good fellow; do it for me, T.T. I'll be able to die happy."

"Well . . . " said Zaroff doubtfully and looking at the broad ribbon of the river. "I don't know about the river; I can't swim. Maybe if we shouted they would hear."

"Try it," said Wells. "My shout is no good, but you look as if you have a good pair of bellows."

Zaroff took a few steps downhill and shouted "Hoy!" Birds flew up from the grass, and from across the valley a winged shape lifted into the sky, performed a large circle, then came towards them. It was a glider holding a solitary figure. Zaroff waved, then rejoined Wells and waited. Wells gave him a quick glance.

"Garden of Eden culture. Animals: silent flight. I wonder what language they will speak; Esperanto do you think?" He grinned like a wolf.

"Unlikely," said Zaroff. "More likely to be silent speech: telepathy." Wells clapped him on the back for that.

The craft landed fifty meters away, and its pilot sat looking at them.

"It's human," muttered Wells. "Why doesn't it talk?"

"I am talking. It takes a few moments to get the right wavelength," said (they presumed) the pilot. "Welcome Martin Zaroff and Herbert George Wells to Shorehome." The words came inside their heads without any sense of direction.

"Is that you?" Zaroff called towards the plane. "Can we see you nearer? My friend is curious about you."

"Aren't you?" hissed Wells. "Why implicate me!"

"I will stand, but I cannot approach nearer," said the figure.

"Oh; why is that?" asked Wells.

"You are surrounded by a cloud of bacteria which you have brought from your times. We shall decontaminate the area as soon as you go."

The pilot stood up and showed himself to be a perfect, naked youth.

"Beautiful," muttered Wells. "Better than the Eloi."

"There are no Eloi and no Morlocks," said the youth. "All that terrible prehistory from whence you come was destroyed a hundred thousand years ago."

Wells growled in his throat. "Have you no intellectual activity now: no metropolitan life?" Wells asked this with a distinct touch of asperity. Zaroff guessed that he was annoyed by this negation of his own vision of the year million.

"Have you only this Arcadian existence, this beautiful drift in unity with Nature, this cosy, animal existence? It is not the triumph of the intellect I foresaw."

"Our intellect, as you name it, went away. It exists still, we believe, around the star Epsilon Eridanus. The scientists of the world chose to escape the slow death of the world they prophesized by crossing space to a younger star. We built a happier world here."

"Looks nice," said Zaroff amiably.

Wells was still a bit huffy about the total inaccuracy of his forecast in his 1893 article 'The Man of the Year Million'. He began flapping his arms in annoyance.

"I don't like it: it's decadent. Where's your intellectual curiosity? Where's your drive? Are you content to be controlled by the seasons, like cows in your fields? What about education? What about literature? What about world government?"

Zaroff stopped him by grasping one arm. "H.G.," he said urgently "He's pointing something at us. I think we ought to go."

"But we know nothing yet," Wells complained, jerking at his arm. "What about women; what is their position? Are they still confined to the home? Have we not advanced at all? What about trade, commerce, economics? I want to get to the bottom of this. I don't believe a pastoral culture can be stable indefinitely. What do they do with their exceptional people? Kill them? There's something fishy here."

A puff of red smoke came from the airplane and floated towards the men, billowing and rolling and expanding as it came.

"H.G.!" shouted Zaroff. "Let us get out of here." He took Wells's wrist and pressed the 'return' button.

Wells went with one last "But . . . " The cloud loomed over Zaroff as he followed Wells, and with a gasp he fell six inches and found himself beside Wells on the carpet of the flat in Hanover Terrace. Wells sat up and hit the carpet an enthusiastic blow with his fist

"What an experience! By God! I've seen the end of the world, and I've spoken to an Eloi." He rolled over on his back and kicked his feet in the air.

Zaroff packed the books into his cases while Wells puffed and wheezed himself back to some semblance of responsible behavior. At last Wells lay back in his armchair and looked at Zaroff in a strangely penetrating way, his lips in a sad smile.

"Thank you for that experience, T.T. What things we have seen, eh?" He grimaced. "How much longer have I got to digest it? When do I die? Can you tell me?"

Wells saw Zaroff's look of refusal, and he went on: "Don't answer. My nurse will be calling in soon; she tells me I'll live to a hundred. Better go before she comes." He stood up and offered his hand. "Off you go. Give my regards to the twenty-ninth century."

Zaroff was sad to leave him. He knew this was the tail end of a brilliant life. Almost he wanted to say, "Come with me, H.G. Let us visit Rome, Greece, Egypt in their glory; let us hunt dinosaurs together." But there is no way to cheat death. If he went, Wells might see a few weeks of marvels, and then his ailing system would collapse and he would die in some outlandish place instead of in bed in the flat.

Zaroff picked up his cases and left. The janitor opened the front door for him.

"How is he, Sir?" he asked.

"Cheerful," Zaroff said. "Fulfilled."

THE ELEMENTALS

Philip E. High

The sequel to "Production Model"

Despite the police car at the side of the road and the ambulance on the pier, the scene was peaceful enough. Sunday morning, bright sunshine and the curve of the river almost as blue as the ocean.

There was no sense of drama, one of the paramedics from the ambulance sat on a pier bollard reading a newspaper. The other was leaning against the ambulance eating something from a paper bag.

There was also a single policeman talking to a civilian standing in front of the ambulance.

"You have no right to be here, you know that?" The policeman's voice lacked authority, he was emotionally involved with the civilian's sister.

"I'm sorry, Jack, the paper got an anonymous call and I was sent along."

"What kind of message?"

"The exact call said 'two stiffs dropped in the river off pier two.'"

"Pretty much the same words as ours—look, Andy, if I turn a blind eye, I'm not quoted or seen, eh?"

"You have my word. Know who they were?"

"Oh yes, a kid on a bike threw a plastic bag at us just before we pulled up. He was gone before we could get out of the car but their wallets were in the bag—minus cash, of course. The first victim was Aubrey Munford, known informer—which accounts for *his* end. The other man was Stephen

Shaw—looks as if one of those weirdos has been taken out at last."

"Sorry, I'm not with you—Stephen Shaw?"

"God, you must have heard of 'Wallace's Weirdos'—all sorts of people have been raising hell about them."

"Oh, yes, of course; just didn't ring a bell at the time." The reporter looked about him. "A bit elaborate isn't it? Two paramedics for two corpses? Hell, they must have been submerged for at least eight hours!"

"Got to go by the book now, boy—expert on the spot testimony. Makes coroners happy I'm told."

"Take your word for it, Jack. What are we waiting for anyway?"

"Police launch from up river. It's deep at the end of this short pier, even at low tide. They've got all the tackle, ropes, nets, lifting gear and a couple of experienced divers for luck."

The launch arrived twenty minutes later and they wasted no time once they were secure. A diver fell back into the water and disappeared in a swirl of bubbles.

He was up again in less than two minutes. "I'll need some special gear and Bill there to help me. The poor devils were given concrete boots and some heavy chain which we'll have to clear before we can get them up."

The reporter was aware of change about him. It had been a bright cheerful morning but now it looked bleak and harsh. The sun no longer felt warm on his face and inwardly he had begun to shiver.

It was not two corpses that had been flung into the river but two live men. Two living beings with their feet encased in concrete to make sure they never rose to the surface again.

The reporter knew at that moment that he was not so experienced as he had imagined. He had covered many social and government events and, yes, five murders. However, he had never seen the bodies and the details had come to him second hand. He had hoped one day that his name, Andrew Pearce, would head a column in the paper, but now it no longer seemed to matter.

When the two bodies were finally laid on the warm planks of the pier he pretended to appear interested but tried not to be. Two sodden sacks, water spreading from them, no more, don't look at their faces.

The paramedics came forward and he was not going to look at that either. Cutting the cords that bound the wrists together, tapping away concrete from feet and ankles.

It all seemed to take an incredible amount of time.

Finally one of the medics stood up. "That's cleared number one for the mortuary. Let's see now—Ah, yes, that was Munford, the informer."

The body was carried to the ambulance and the doors shut and Pearce had already decided that one was enough. From hereon he was going to look at the river.

He only discovered that something was wrong when one of the paramedics ran to the end of the pier and was violently sick.

The other one ran to him. "What's up, Harry?"

The first one turned, his face ashen. "Mother of God, Tom, *that one ain't dead*! As I undid his wrists, his fingers moved—his body is still warm!"

"You must be—" The paramedic never finished the sentence; he ran back and knelt down by the soaked body on the boards. His examination was only brief but clearly sufficient. "I need some help here, all of you. *Move it*, for Christ's sake!"

By the time they had turned the man on his side, he was coughing weakly but no water had come from his open mouth.

"He was completely submerged for more than eight hours," The policeman sounded as if he doubted his own words. He did not add, 'it's utterly impossible,' but his expression did.

They looked at one another helplessly; there was no procedure for a situation like this. One of the paramedics made an examination of the man and, seven minutes later, helped him to sit upright but he had no answers.

"He's more or less fit, still shivery—it's bloody cold down there, but he's returning to normality quickly. There's not a single pointer to drowning or anything near it." He paused and exhaled noisily. "What the hell will we put into a report?"

The sub-editor looked up at Pearce and shook his head. "I don't think his Nibs is going to wear this one. I'll try him, of course, when he comes in, but I have doubts—a lot of doubts."

"But, Good God, I've witnesses and their written statements."

"I don't think it would matter if you had an affidavit from the Supreme Being Himself. Mr. Barker is only concerned with the reputation of the paper. In the first place, he will call it a publicity stunt by Wallace and Co. In the second, he will know full well that every other rag in the world will jump on us for faking facts to boost circulation. No one will ever believe us, you must see that; it's too way out. I'm sorry, old son, but that's the way it is."

Pearce shrugged. "Not your fault but its a bit frustrating, you must admit."

"Agreed." The sub-editor steered the conversation away. "What happened when Shaw came round?"

"Well, he was on his feet within thirty minutes, talking normally twenty minutes later. Someone should have asked him how he did it or what happened but no one seemed to think of it at the time. Finally he asked someone to ring a number, no need to leave a message, just calling the number would be enough."

Pearce paused, frowning. "The police had got around to producing some form of restraint to keep him as a witness when this damn great car arrives, no doubt in response to the phone call. A big man got out of it, really big, shoulders like an ox, if you know what I mean. This man knew the law, and he cut the idea of indicting Shaw as a witness from right under their feet. In the long run, of course, he would have to give evidence against his attackers. No, they had no legal right to question his method of survival. In point of fact, new legislation would have to be introduced to make such questioning compulsory. Shaw was driven away almost before the police could draw breath."

The sub-editor nodded thoughtfully. "The big man was Burke, no doubt about that, partner with Wallace. Doesn't look like a mystic, does he?"

"Is he?"

"Don't know, boy, quoting from public opinion but, yes, he must be *something*—but I wouldn't care to classify."

"You wouldn't care to go a little deeper?"

The sub-editor looked up at him tiredly. "Look at me, lad, I'm old, you can see that for yourself. Most of the reporters call me a cynical obstructive old bastard. True in part, I admit that. Nonetheless I've learned a lot in this job and one of the greatest lesson I've learned is to *listen*. Listen to everything, even if you don't like what you hear, really listen before you jump in to pass judgments. About these weirdos now, there's not one scrap of evidence to prove that they have ever *done* anything wrong. Yet half the world seems ready to run forward to condemn them! Fourteen times they have been brought into court on various charges only to have those charges dismissed through lack of evidence. In point of fact there is considerable evidence in their favor, which, of course, only heightens the opposition. This is not new, religious or not—that kind of mentality resulted in the crucifixion and its gone on ever since. I have often wondered where it begins."

"I'd like to follow this up, Sub. I'd like to interview Wallace himself."

"He's never granted an interview. Can't say I blame him, everyone pre-pared to write his own distorted slant to suit editorial policy and no one pre-pared to listen."

"I would listen, I'd even go free-lance if I had to."

The sub-editor managed a cracked but genuine smile. "I've been calling you boy—bloody cheek, you must be all of thirty. What you say makes you mature. My advice, go for it but read it up first. Find out what these weirdos are like and be prepared to bend. Take Shaw, for example: he makes talis-mans."

"Eh?"

"Lucky charms, laddie, think about that and then read on."

Pearce spent a long time in records before he had the information he wanted and he began with Stephen Shaw. The man had been a minor radiologist in a research complex before falling foul of a drunken man in a sports car. The vehicle, completely out of control, had mounted the curb and hit Shaw as he was leaving for lunch. The impact had flung him high in the air and dropped heavily on some iron railings beside a street crossing.

They got him to hospital but his body was a wreck, very few bones in his body remained unbroken and he was kept alive by artificial means. Progno-sis by the attending surgeons was one week—'make the man as comfortable as possible, oddly he is still conscious.'

It was said, but never proved, that Wallace visited him on the third day staying about an hour.

Two months later Shaw walked out of hospital on his own two feet. There were no reports, the attending surgeons could never be found or had moved to another city. Hospital officials had prepared statements of double-talk which tried to blind the recipients with science; real information was non-existent.

Shaw had been brought before the court three times for selling lucky charms. The defense proved beyond doubt that no money had ever changed hands. There seemed no reason why he had been finally thrown in the river.

The most likely explanation being that he was what he was, a weirdo. Pearce was amazed that the venom leveled against them—they were a threat to society, to law and order and to democracy itself. They were agents of a foreign power, they were atheists, they were profane and in league with the devil.

On the credit side, they appeared responsible for some remarkable medical success, Shaw being an example. But such reports, if mentioned, were confined to the back pages at the bottom of a column. Anything thought worthy of attack, however was always given headlines on the front page. Pearce began to wonder what they had *done* to deserve it and just who had it in for them.

There was also a girl, Altha Cheem, very pretty according to her pictures. Spanish-looking, full lips, huge dark eyes, and long, almost blue-black hair. A tragic background: once a classical violinist of considerable promise, she had lost her right arm just above the elbow in a traffic accident. No apparent miracles here, she was still bound up in a huge unsightly dressing. There was a general opinion that she was slightly deranged, she was known to walk around muttering audibly to herself. It was difficult to understand where she fitted in among the weirdos.

All that was left were the two leaders. Wallace was a scientist, a specialist in metallurgy and an all round scientist. Burke had been a car designer of genius. There was no clue in the reports as to how the whole business had begun.

Pearce went through the reports several times before, days later, he dialed a number. "I'd like to speak to Mr. Wallace, please."

"About what?"

"I am a reporter, I'd like to ask you some pertinent questions."

"No doubt, but will you listen to the answers?"

"Look, I'm not prejudiced and I have no axe to grind, this is primarily personal." The voice at the other end paused, considering.

"I feel that you mean what you say. I can spare some time around ten, tomorrow morning. We can go through the introductions then."

Wallace was a thin active man or about thirty-five with pale but astute gray eyes.

He waved Pearce to a chair. "Comfortable and old-fashioned like the house. But what can I do for you, Mr. Pearce?"

"Well I'd like to know how all this—forgive the popular description—all this 'weirdo' business began."

"I won't blind you with science, Mr. Pearce. I, and my partner, Mr. Burke were exposed to a unique form of radiation plus sonic side effects, which stimulated certain aspects of our minds. When we came out of it we had become different human beings with heightened perceptions and new faculties . . . "

"Excuse me butting in there, Mr. Wallace but 'faculties'—what do you mean by the word faculty?"

Wallace laughed softly and apologized before answering. "Mr. Pearce, forgive me, how can I do that? Could you define sight to a man blind from birth or hearing to one permanently deaf? There is no way of describing a true faculty save by experience."

"You go into trance or something?"

Wallace shook his heed. "Sorry, I am not quite sure how to induce such a state and dubious of its benefits if I did. Oh, yes, while I think of it, I read in the papers, yours included, how Mr. Shaw survived his submersion. He induced a catatonic state by means of suspended animation—nothing could be further from the truth."

Wallace paused and looked at the other directly. "You must see, Mr. Pearce, that there are no simple answers and, further, that there are far too many questions. However I will give you an outline. As you know, Mr. Burke and myself underwent an experience; that experience changed us. In a normal world we had become aliens among our own kind but, worse, we saw that we were living in alien world fraught with dangers, which we had never dreamed existed. If this stretches your credulity I am sorry—that's the way it is, but I cannot prove it. I can only raise one possible parallel. Imagine, please, that your vision is limited only to black and white. How could I prove to you the existence of color? Unfortunately, my friend, the alien world visible to *our* eyes, is far less inspiring and, much, much more dangerous."

Pearce was silent for some seconds, his mind racing over the implications. There was nothing here, nothing he could use. If he wrote the article, it would never be left alone. It would be slanted, distorted and dramatized beyond meaning. Wallace and Burke would be depicted as medicine men seeing ghosts in an underworld of monsters.

He said: "You've been honest and helpful but, for me, it's not enough. How can I learn more, gain more answers?"

Wallace looked at him thoughtfully. "There is only one way to do that, Mr. Pearce—join us for a time, three weeks at the very least. There's a spare bedroom upstairs, you're welcome to stay without charge."

They were interrupted by a man arriving with a tray. Pearce recognized him instantly as Burke.

Wallace introduced them and explained the situation.

"Simple things first," Burke grinned. "Tea or coffee, Mr. Pearce?"

As they were drinking, Burke said: "You've heard the domestic arrangements and a few answers to many questions in your mind, but there is a debit side which it would be wise to consider before plunging into anything. Debit number one: as soon as it gets around that you are associating with us you will become a marked man, not from everyone, of course, but from a strident few—usually verbal abuse in a public place. This could well lead to violence as it did with almost fatal consequences to Shaw. Don't ask us why, we're only just beginning to understand that ourselves because it's much stronger than racism."

"Debit two," said Wallace taking up the theme. "To a degree you'll have to participate, join members as a volunteer on missions and all these missions are dangerous."

Pearce felt apprehensions inside him but he had a stubborn streak in his nature. "One question: what would I gain?"

"Well, we cannot depict a faculty but we could perhaps demonstrate its effects—are you quite sure you want to go through with this?"

"Yes, having thought about it—quite sure."

The two partners looked at each other. "Altha first, I think, put him at ease, eh?"

Burke picked him up at nine the following morning but he made no mention of the mission, his main conversation was about cars, a subject which still seemed to fill a large part of his life.

Finally they stopped on a country road. "Think this is the spot. Shaw should have dropped her—ah, there she is, over by the tree there."

It was a drizzly sort of day and she wore a red raincoat, which somehow heightened her Spanish-type beauty. She was far more attractive than her pictures suggested. Pearce had avoided entanglements so far and flattered himself he had become adroit and light on his feet but now he had the uneasy feeling that he had met his match.

She shook hands with her left hand when Burke introduced them. She was still bound up clumsily one side but it still didn't detract from her obvious vivacity or grace of movement. How long did a stump take to heal he wondered and would the experts finally fit an artificial limb?

"Come on," she took his arm, "just through this gap in the hedge, its not far."

"Where are we going exactly, and why?"

"Simple thing really, rich man buys some land but there's a right-of-way passing it. He closes the right-of-way, locals complain, and the local authorities order him to reopen it. Petty really, happens a lot of places everywhere but here it turns nasty. People terrorized, two nasty accidents."

She turned, ducking under a sign which said: **NO TRESPASSING. PRIVATE PROPERTY**. She smiled. "Not to worry, I can handle this."

He nodded, hoping she could because there were sounds in the distance that made him uneasy. Someone, not too far away, had dogs and these were not lap dogs. This was no yapping—this was *baying*.

Ten minutes later, passing through a small woodland area, they came upon a man standing in the middle of the path holding a heavy whip.

"You people are able to read I assume?" He spoke like an educated man but he was grubby looking and had not shaved for several days.

Behind him two more scruffy men, with considerable effort, were each holding back three animals on long leads.

Pearce felt a coldness stir deep inside him like something alive. These were not just big dogs, these were hounds; they were used in some areas of the world to hunt bear.

The man in their way raised his arm and looked pointedly at his watch.

"We keep warning people but they keep coming. We keep warning them for their own safety but they still keep coming. Sooner or later they're going to bring an accident upon themselves."

He glanced at his watch again. "Took you about eight minutes to get here. I'll be fair, I'll give you five minutes to get out of here, after which I'll let these dogs go—an accident, of course."

She stepped forward but Pearce grasped her shoulder. "Don't be heroic, he isn't joking."

"I know," she said, "and his five minutes is actually two, make no mistake about that."

She went forward again. "Do your damnedest," she said.

He looked puzzled briefly then he shrugged. "You want to be torn to pieces now rather than later, lady, that's up to you." He turned to the two men behind him. "Let the bastards go."

Pearce, frozen inside, stood in front of her knowing it was only a gesture. There was nothing he could do to protect her or himself against six hounds.

The animals were about thirty meters distant when they were released literally howling, but within half the distance they began to slow.

Pearce with a choking sensation in his throat and the feeling that his eyes were somehow fixed watched them extend their front feet. They literally slithered, scrabbling desperately by themselves to stop a bare two meters from the girl and himself. They whimpered, they almost wagged their tails, their very posture. conveyed both ingratiation and apology.

"All right, boys," she said softly. "Lie still."

They went limp, their tails beat the ground and they looked up adoringly into her face.

The man with the whip stood stiffly, his face blank as he stared at the dogs with his mouth open.

She went forward and looked up into his face. "You force obedience with a whip. Care to challenge my authority over yours? Or would you prefer to find out just who would be torn to bits?"

She smiled briefly but without humor. "Don't get ideas about that sawn-off gun hidden under your coat. My friends here know about it, you may succeed but it will be the last shot you will ever fire."

She looked at the dogs. "Go home now, go home."

They went, cheerfully, wagging their tails and often looking back.

One of the men who had brought them threw down his lead. "Some other bastard can take them things back. Not me—they're jinxed."

They walked back in silence for some minutes then finally Pearce said: "How the hell did you do that?"

She frowned thoughtfully. "I have asked myself that question many times. The nearest I could get to it is an affinity with nature. I have not always had it. I have always loved animals but I never had this affinity before my accident, before Mr. Burke came to see me in hospital."

"Now, hang on a minute, please." Pearce was becoming confused and a little angry. "You're running way ahead of me. Perhaps you could start with your accident, I know you lost your right arm above the elbow—what happened then?"

"Mr. Burke came to see me, I don't know why. He said he had read about the accident in the local newspaper."

"And he saw you through it, all the trauma and so on?"

She came to an abrupt stop, looking up at him in disbelief. "They haven't told you a thing about me, have they?"

She fumbled with the top button of her red raincoat and let it fall aside. He saw that she had a plastic cover on her right side from shoulder to hip.

"Special snap-studs," she said, "easy to use even with one hand."

"Oh, God," he thought, "she's going to show me the stump."

The plastic covering swung back; she wore a light blue sleeveless summer frock.

There was no stump.

There was a perfect wholly formed right arm to match the one on the left.

There were no distortions, scar tissue, or marks above the elbow to show there had ever been an accident.

He swallowed audibly. "Burke did this? He laid healing hands upon you or something?"

"Mr. Burke did nothing, he merely told me what to do. He pointed out that the human body has the most efficient defensive and repair system in the entire animal kingdom plus the backing of an intelligent brain . . . "

"Don't tell me he gave a course in self-hypnosis plus an advanced line in visualization?" He was unable to keep the sarcasm out of his voice.

She took his question seriously. "Oh no, nothing so complicated as that. One has to consult the psyche within, of course and obey a higher law. If one does this the right way a bonus comes with it, in this case my affinity with animals."

He opened and shut his mouth several times before he finally managed to speak. "This still does not explain your arm."

"Oh that's simple enough, my dear: I just grew another." She hurried on before he could question her again. "It took me eighteen months and, of course, it is still very weak. It will be another two months before I can begin a course of gentle exercise, perhaps two years before I can play a violin again."

He fell silent, realizing at last where his casual enquiries and reporting instincts had led him. He had a feeling there was no going back.

He need not have worried. A phone call, an hour later, informed him that the paper no long required his services.

He caught Wallace first. "Sorry, I'll have to leave, I'm out of a job."

"I wasn't aware we were charging you for staying here. You haven't lost your talent for writing, surely? You could freelance."

"Very precarious, I'd earn a pittance."

"You lack faith in yourself, Mr. Pearce. You could work with us here—might be the basis for an interesting article. Again, consider the ties you are already forming."

Pearce colored and changed the subject hastily. "What was all that business about?"

"Well, for our part, it was a kind of sortie, we wanted to see how far they'd go if we challenged them. Normally it would have ended up in a legal battle. In this case, when it came to us, murder was on the cards."

"One moment, who do you mean by 'they', Mr. Wallace?"

"We are not quite sure of that ourselves yet. Call it the opposition. Now that we can see and perceive things beyond the normal, perhaps we have become visible to them. I do know that within a week of our experience we became the targets for abuse and attempted violence. There was no call for it then, we had stated nothing, done nothing, and our experiences were known only to ourselves. Let me be frank with you, Mr. Pearce. As an associate or friend of ours, you place yourself in a certain amount of danger, verbal abuse and even physical violence. If you joined us, you would become a target. You must see that. Stephen Shaw didn't throw himself in the river, you know. Sure, it was done by a mob—but who paid them to do it?"

Pearce was frowning. "Hang on, am I to understand, that I could join you if I wished?"

"Not just like that, no. We have, as we have told you, certain faculties. We don't switch them on and off, they work all the time. You were assessed when you first rang up and from our angle you would-make an ideal recruit but the ball is in your court. Think about it—think very hard indeed. You are placing yourself not only in a highly dangerous situation but also a terrifying one."

Wallace paused and waved his hand at the window. "Look out there, it all looks so cozy, so safe, so familiar out there with all the dangers carefully listed and written down. Yet I must stress, without being melodramatic, out there is world so alien, so full of dangers it could well haunt your dreams for years."

Pearce made no attempt to hide a scowl. "You're telling me I could actually see this world?" The disbelief in his voice made the words sound grating. "How would you do that—hypnosis?"

Wallace pretended not to notice the tone of the question. "Nothing so easily explained, Mr. Pearce. Just go away and think about what you may be letting yourself in for before you jump in with both feet."

Pearce took four hours but he came back shame-faced and apologetic.

"Sorry about my rudeness, most of it, I admit, was fear. The rationalization of the unknown threw me right off balance."

"But you have made up your mind?"

"Oh, yes, very much so and come to think of it, what's the difference? As a reporter it would have been warfront, famine or earthquake—would I have been any safer?"

The two men met him in the morning at nine o'clock in a large black car.

Burke handed him a short length of polished metal as he climbed in. "Hold that between your hands until I tell you to give it back. Oh, and in case you're wondering, we're heading for a hill just outside of town. We can get a good view from there."

He changed the subject and kept the conversation casual for five or ten minutes, then he said: "You can hand that back now."

"What was it?" Pearce had the uneasy feeling that he was being brought under some sort of control.

Burke sensed it and laughed softly. "Nothing to worry about, these cars are special and you have just attuned yourself to the main computer. From hereon you will not need a key to open the door or start the engine. The car will 'recognize' you and obey simple instructions. Shout 'open' from thirty meters away and the nearest door will open as you approach. This vehicle is a refuge; it is not designed to withstand anti-tank weapons but it will keep you safe from rifle and machine-gun fire."

Wallace, who was driving, pulled off the narrow road and onto a patch of grass at the top of a hill. "Beautiful isn't it? Rolling grassland, dappled with summer flowers. Oak and elm over to the left, and you can just see a willow by the small lake on the right. You can also see a few sheep grazing in the meadow straight ahead. Beyond all that you can just make out the small town of Warrenden in the distance. The yellow roof of the new hospital is clearly visible."

Wallace stopped, his face expressionless. "Have you taken all this in Mr.—no, you're one of us now. Andrew isn't it?"

"Andy will do fine, thanks." He tried to make his voice sound casual but he had the terrified feeling that he had come to the edge of something.

Wallace nodded and smiled quickly. "We've hinted at our past experience in which our brains were stimulated to such an extent that we became attuned to conditions beyond this world, and possibly beyond this dimension. Since that time, almost two years ago, we have been working together to try and. reproduce those conditions—not in full, mind you. In full one is so perfectly attuned that, to all intents and purposes, *one is actually elsewhere*."

He paused then continued, very quietly. "We have made progress. With assistance from Mr. Shaw we have been able to construct a device that activates that part of the brain that controls visions. In brief, Andy, wearing a special helmet you will see as we see the hidden realities of a world not in another dimension *but this one*."

The helmet was round, silvery and unexpectedly light. There seemed to be no trailing wires but to minor contact pads were taped to his skull just behind his ears.

"You have one minute," said Burke, "one minute only."

"Close your eyes," said Wallace, "and keep them closed until we tell you to open them." He counted slowly and steadily up to ten then he said: "Open."

Pearce had expected to feel some surge of power or mental stimulation but he felt perfectly normal. When he opened his eyes the countryside looked the same but it had additions.

"You're not trying to tell me that this is a world of spirits?"

"I'm not trying to tell you anything, but hundreds of primitive tribes still conduct ceremonies to placate them. The Chinese used fireworks to frighten them away."

"Oh, dear God! Not evil spirits, not that hoary old yarn."

"Did I say they were? I don't think they're alien beings either. I think they are just as much part of the scene as flowers and trees but no one could see them."

Pearce stared at the nearest oak tree, bright in the sunlight, but, hanging from the branches were things like huge bats. Bat-like yet, at the same time shapeless, unfinished at the edges and un-solid like black thunderclouds.

There was a huge greenish thing, repulsively translucent and almost as big as an elephant crouched in the middle of a meadow. A flapping thing, like a huge yellow blanket with tattered edges flapped slowly across the sky in a movement that reminded him vaguely of a jelly fish.

Wallace's voice, seeming to come from very far away, reached him as he watched. "Note the black cloud of things hovering over the roof of the hospital, also an opaque cloud enshrouding a single sheep near the edge of the river. Close to you, say eighty K's distant, a thing that drifts close to the ground like an evening cloak without a man in it. Lastly, time is running out, don't miss the column of tiny spheres descending and spreading out, they look like sickly yellow bubbles—time's up, Andy."

Pearce heard a click that seemed to come from far away, then a brief flash inside his mind then everything reverted to normal.

He said: "What the hell do you call those awful things?"

It was Burke who answered the question. "A presumed mystic coined a phrase years ago, it seems to fit. He called them *elementals*."

"They're frightening, but they don't seem real, not solid as I understand it."

"They're not, you probably walked right through several of them yesterday. The fact that you can't see them makes them no less dangerous. The black clouds touching the hospital roof—there are probably more inside—we call them ghouls. They derive sustenance and strength from pain and death. Believe me, battlefields are almost obscured by them."

Burke continued the explanation: "The sheep I pointed out is sick, need I say more? The bubbles you saw descending are probably minor infections like flu or the common cold."

"You know these things." Pearce felt the sunlight could no longer warm him.

"We have classified a number, yes. And before you ask the question—Yes, there are familiar diseases brought about by virus, microbes and various other causes. But out there are things which can so exactly duplicate them that few can detect the difference."

Wallace paused briefly, then: "The thing which looked like a black cloak without a body, we've classified that as a vampire. Don't get me wrong, it doesn't turn into a bat and drink blood, it drinks energy. A man depressed by responsibility, recovery from an operation or sickness, a woman after childbirth or anyone at low ebb. That thing will enfold itself around and drink not their blood but their energy. Victims caught by these things usually fight a losing battle."

Wallace leaned forward and started the engine. "Find a car park in the city somewhere. We'll give you another minute to look at these things and people inside the city."

"Why only a minute?"

"If we give you more than two sessions longer than a minute, you cannot revert to normal. Your sight will stay in two dimensions like our own. You will never be able to shut these things out again."

Pearce found the city worse. Things cloaked down-and-outs, addicts and alcoholics—but some of the people themselves were terrifying, they were no longer human. They appeared normal on the outside but within they were distorted and were virtually monsters.

"Shutting off," said Burke.

"No!" Pearce's rejection was almost a shout. "No you damn well don't. It may be horrible but I'd rather see what I'm up against."

Pearce went out next day, primarily to let his mind settle down and, secondly to get his bearings; this part of the city was unfamiliar territory.

He soon discovered it was a suburban area, almost a peninsular created by the curve of the river. A major highway, Weston Road, almost gave the area a separate status.

When he returned he managed to catch both Burke and Wallace together.

"I've been out snooping, discovered two things I think you ought to know. One, those elementals, they're thick over the city, even infesting streets and hospitals but there are none in this area. How long since your experience or, perhaps, more aptly, since you moved here?"

"Around two years," said Burke. "Why?"

"Because—two—since your arrival, a sort of migration has been taking place increasing with the passing of time. On the one hand there have been people anxious to move out, and an equal number of people, anxious to move in. A council official I spoke to, said, in the last year, they'd had to get in extra helpers to cope with the constant change. The newcomers, incidentally, come from all over as well as from this country. Japanese, Australians, Africans, everywhere. It would appear also that in the process of moving out are the less pleasant members of our society. I am informed, on good authority that even 'the mob' have vacated their premises by the piers and set up headquarters on the other side of the river."

The two looked at him with respect. "You have been busy, this information is of great help and clarifies a great deal."

"I need information myself," said Pearce. "In the first place these lucky charms. It sounds unreal, they don't actually work, do they?"

The two men rose. "You'd better come along to Shaw's place and see for yourself. Shaw worked in a well-lighted studio a short distance away and he seemed to know why they had come. The lucky charms, in the shape of small round disks, were laid out on a long table.

He smiled at Pearce. "I look a bit better now, eh?" He waved his hand at the table. "Not superstitions, my friend, nothing blessed by a medicine man but, in truth, dimensional technology. Yes, they rid victims of vampire infestation and prevent a reoccurrence—but not by magic."

He brought one of the charms closer and pressed the edges with his fingers. "As you see, it snaps open. Inside, as you see is a small mechanism that sets up a high frequency vibration which the vampire can't stand. It's inaudible to us, of course, but very effective. The elemental usually detaches itself within four hours. The mechanism derives its power from a long-life watch battery set in the corner here."

Pearce was over-awed and said so, but he had not finished. "Everything neat and explainable—save for one thing. I'm in love with a girl who lost an arm and has grown herself another. I am speaking to a man who, I know, was submerged for eight hours and lived. What is it—some vast spiritual power?"

It was Wallace who answered the question. "I don't think the word spiritual has meaning any more. It's been used in so many ways that its real meaning has been lost. One thinks of saffron robes, beds of nails, incense, prayers, fasting, and, of course, celibacy, a great asset that, although never fully explained. No, Andy, I can't explain it like that. I can only say that a few weeks after our experience we had a greater understanding of things—it will come to you, too. The application of a few simple laws that can change one's life completely. When our two friends were visited in hospital there was no laying on of hands, no chanting, no magic, we merely told them how to apply the law."

Shaw turned and laughed. "Oh, come on, you two, you choose us because your faculties informed you that we were receptive subjects."

Wallace grinned. "Guilty," he said.

Pearce was persistent. "These laws—they're new?"

"No, they've always been around but too often shunned because they were usually delivered with an implied threat. Do these things, if you disobey dreadful consequences will follow. The other side of the coin was never emphasized—that is, obey from free will and good things will multiply and keep multiplying."

"The more you try, the more it works," said Shaw, "and the more it works the more you learn how to apply it. In the long run one receives something far more than one expects. I was not only healed but something was added perhaps events were foreseen but this extra something saved my life."

He removed his jacket and then his shirt. "Look at my back. On either side of my spine, two parallel lines, slightly longer than the normal finger just below each shoulder blade. They are not scars, Andy. They're gills, I can breathe under water."

The telephone interrupted any comment Pearce could make and Burke picked up the receiver. "Yes? Burke speaking—" He listened for a few seconds then replaced the receiver. "Looks like trouble, tip off from a friend, about twenty louts with banners coming down Sterne Street. Usual stuff, 'down with the Weirdos', that sort of thing."

Strangely it was Pearce who took the initiative. "We'd better go and meet them."

She was waiting by the door as they left the building. "I knew you would need me," she said.

"You're not coming with us."

"Oh, yes, I am, my love. I haven't forgotten how you stood in front of me when those dogs were coming."

He took her hand, his developing faculties told him it was no use arguing.

"They'll come by the pedestrian underpass," said Burke, "too much traffic on the main road this time of day."

The leader of the protesters had been paid well and, at the same time, threatened. "You don't trip up this time, Croyne. I warn you, someone will be around to even things up if you do."

"No need to worry." He had meant it at the time, for reasons he couldn't explain he hated these weirdos. Also he had a score to settle with that bloody woman. His hounds were useless now and, if he tried to enforce orders with a whip, they turned on him.

He plunged into the underpass and flung his banner away, the real statement would come from his machine pistol.

It was unexpectedly cold in the underpass and a chill wind seemed to blowing at him steadily but it was bright at the far end—somehow too bright.

By the time he reached the exit slope it was hurting his eyes and he was curiously short of breath. He knew all the light was perfectly natural. Sunlight reflected from showroom to display window and back again. Where the hell was his supporters? There were no shouts, no pounding feet—he was alone.

He came out of the subway entrance half blinded by the light and found himself facing five figures. Figures that became distorted and huge in his mind, figures clothed in light.

He dropped the gun and ran back but was stopped at the far end. "Hold it! I can explain—" He never finished the sentence. The gun which stopped the words was absolutely silent and the killer a professional. Passers by thought the shabby unshaven man had just collapsed.

On the opposite side of the street, three men were walking back and, behind them two lovers stopped and kissed.

"This is heaven," she said.

"Yes, yes," he nodded slowly, "and I have the strange feeling that that kingdom is beginning, right here, on Earth."

THE PAPER KILLER

Eric C. Williams

Monsieur Delacroix slowly unscrewed his fountain pen and corrected a word in the memo before him. Although punctilious, he was not normally punctilious to the degree of correcting other people's memoranda. He did so now because he was pondering.

The memo was from the office of the Director of UNESCO's French Section and said briefly that the first of the attached threatening letters had been received six weeks earlier, but since then the police had interrogated the occupant at the address given and were sure the address was false, and the occupant blameless. Further threatening letters had been received, and the office would be obliged if Delacroix would use his well-known skill to deal with the matter—in other words, get this crank off this Department's neck. Monsieur Delacroix had read the letters and was impressed by something in them that he was now trying to isolate. They were all short.

The first ran as follows:

At its establishment after the war, UNO declared that they were setting about the formation of a world government. Since then decades have passed, without result. It is clear after all these years that UNO are evading their responsibility and will have to be forced into action. Now I give you this ultimatum. Either you send your accredited representative to my address within two months bearing a treaty for the formation of a World Parliament signed by all heads of Government, or I shall release on the world a germ that will kill all paper. Without paper, civilization will cease. The world will doubtless be a happier place; nevertheless, I would prefer our present technological development to continue within a world-state framework. This ultimatum expires on March 31st.

The second was written three weeks after the first:

I remind you of my ultimatum. You have five more weeks to arrange and present the declaration of intention. After this time I will kill all paper.

The last:

I continue to culture the germ that will kill this paper world. Send me your representative within two weeks or I shall release the germ.

None of the letters was signed.

There was a brief police report giving the name and address of the occupant of the house near the Port de Clignancourt as Gustav Menton, and describing him as a retired sewer-worker living along on a low income. No political record, he had only the vaguest idea of what UNO was. He denied writing letters to UNO.

End of file.

"Strange," murmured Delacroix to his silent office. Mademoiselle Lamaroux looked up from the index of correspondence she was compiling.

Monsieur Delacroix waved the letter he was holding.

"You have read these letters, Mademoiselle. Did anything strike you? In the phraseology, I mean."

"His use of the word 'kill'," said Mademoiselle with the clairvoyance born of many years of working with Monsieur Delacroix.

"Indeed yes," nodded Delacroix. "What an unusual word in that context—'a germ that will kill all paper!' Why not 'destroy' or 'rot' or whatever it does? You cannot *kill* a piece of paper."

Mademoiselle Lamaroux allowed her boss to continue his pondering without interruption.

"There are two possibilities that occur to me," said Delacroix presently. "He is a foreigner with an inaccurate knowledge of the French language, or he is a Frenchman with a flamboyant turn of phrase. The first I would discount because of the construction of the letters, the French conciseness . . . their general fluency . . . The second I find more promising." He thought for some seconds in silence.

"He says he has been watching UNO for decades. Therefore we can say he is a man well on into the second half of his life, and of an idealistic nature. He is given to a literary turn of expression . . . perhaps a journalist: you notice the terms 'accredited representative' and 'Heads of Government?' Now take the address he uses: near the Porte de Clignancourt in a house occupied by this old man. I am sure that somewhere within the neighborhood or facing houses our man will be sitting watching the comings and goings at this address and waiting to accost the representative he has demanded. He is too clever to be taken in by the police: he waits on us, Mademoiselle—UNO—to enter Gustav Menton's home first before he shows himself. Shall we test my theory?"

Mademoiselle Lamaroux immediately rose to her feet. She would not have hesitated if he had suggested a descent into the crater of Vesuvius.

The district of Clignancourt possesses few of those architectural beauties that draw tourists to Paris—although it has a famous market—but it has plenty of reasonably priced rooms and flats, and this draws the less prosperous Parisians, so that the quarter is as busy as the center of the town, even if there are fewer limousines about.

Gustav Menton's address was in a street almost completely lined with small shops and cafes. Monsieur Delacroix halted at the foot of the steps leading upwards between two shops, and looked around ostentatiously. From his pocket he took a card prepared before leaving the office and held it up for any unseen watcher to see. In ten-centimeter letters were the letters: UNO.

"Now, Mademoiselle, let us go up and await the rendezvous in Monsieur Menton's parlour."

The door at the top of the dark steps was opened to their knock, and a small, white-headed man in his shirtsleeves looked at them blankly. Both parties looked at the other waiting for explanations, but as the old man seemed prepared to stand blankly immobile indefinitely, Delacroix said in a low voice:

"We are from UNO. May we wait inside?"

The old man moved aside with a look of humor spreading over his puckish face. "Oh, more on that game, eh? Come in. I want to hear about this UNO thing. Blessed if I know what's supposed to be going on." He bowed to Mademoiselle Lamaroux as she passed him, then moved a chair for her to sit on.

The room was tidily kept and polished like a cabinet-maker's dream. All the furniture dated from about 1900, and the pictures on the wall were engravings from the same period. The lace cover spread across the round mahogany table would have made a collector's eyes gleam. The carpet on the floor was thin but still clean and obviously Persian. An open door revealed a bright bedroom beyond, with a massive brass bedstead taking up most of the space. The old man hopped across the room into the bedroom, plucked a. jacket from the bed post and put it on.

"Excuse my deshabille, Mademoiselle," he said returning with a grin. "You caught me washing my socks. I always wash my socks on a Tuesday morning."

"A commendable habit, Monsieur," murmured Mademoiselle Lamaroux.

Delacroix did not speak. He was waiting for the knock on the door. He was sure that the old man had been paid a sum to allow the use of his room for this meeting, and that he, too, was waiting for the knock of his accomplice.

"Now, what's all this?" asked the old man, standing like a comic gnome between Monsieur Delacroix and Mademoiselle Lamaroux. "First the police talking about UNO, and now you. I'd like an explanation. What is this blessed UNO thing to do with me?"

"You are Monsieur Gustav Menton?" asked Monsieur Delacroix, with the calm of a judge at the beginning of his examination.

"That's me."

"Then you will know that certain letters have been written to the United Nations Organization from your address asking for a representative to call here. We are those representatives. Here is my identity card and passport, which give my position in UNO. If you have to call your accomplice, please do so now. We have come to discuss the demands he has made."

"Oho!" breathed the old man. He took Delacroix's papers and read them with great care. Delacroix, in his turn, studied Menton with greater attention. He had an antiseptic smell about him as if all his clothes had been washed in carbolic acid; his fingernails were perfectly clean; his shoes looked new. His face, intent on examining the many pages of the passport, showed intelligence and determination. He looked altogether a more dynamic personality than one would imagine a low-class manual worker to be.

Delacroix made up his mind. "You are a retired sewer worker?" he asked abruptly.

Menton handed back the papers. "Yes. You learn many things when you have to do with sewers, Monsieur . . . personal cleanliness without which you soon become ill . . . and about bacteria, which are your day-to-day concern, like letters are in *your* work, Monsieur . . . Bacteria that work to save our lives in the sewers under Paris . . . germs that break down effluent and reduce everything to a fertile pulp—even paper. Yes, I have the honor to be a retired member of La Force Sanitaire."

"So!" said Monsieur Delacroix somewhat disconcerted at finding the deductions he had made in the office entirely wrong. "So *you* wrote those letters!"

Gustav Menton chuckled, then bowed slightly and moved over to a cabinet from which he took a bottle and three glasses. While he talked he measured out wine.

"You must excuse the charade in the beginning. I have no wish to waste time revealing my secret to anyone not in a position to bring about what I desire. There are only two weeks to go before the expiry of my ultimatum, so your organization will have to move very quickly, Monsieur. Briefly, and as I will show you, I have developed a culture of bacteria from the sewers of Paris that kills paper utterly and instantly, leaving nothing but sludge. I have this culture in phials in my laboratory where I happened to be working when you arrived—and also hidden about my person. I tell you this in case you or others may have it in mind to arrest or kill me. I have but to shatter one of the phials on my clothing and the deed is done; the phials would certainly break if I collapsed; so if you have come simply to see how vulnerable I am, then let us not waste more time—my plans are unchangeable, and if I have no response before March the thirty-first, small explosive charges will break the tubes I have hidden, and this will happen even if I am in prison.

"Now," he continued, "let us talk about this world treaty I want to see signed." He handed them each a glass of wine and took a sip himself before he launched on what was obviously a rehearsed catalog. "It must bear authentic signatures and the seals of all nations and agree to complete equality of races, to complete disarmament, to complete freedom of movement across all old borders, to the fair distribution of food, to the pooling of resources and knowledge, to the end of speculation, to the end of all trade barriers, to the end of unearned privilege . . . All these things to be immediate. The treaty should promise the formation of a world parliament with a charter within two months, its headquarters to be in Paris. And most important, it must promise to move towards the elimination of money as the system of reward and exchange, and to put in its place the right of everyone to have all the food and possessions he needs just for the asking. Competition as a way of life is to disappear. These are the first things I demand. There may be others later."

Arrant Nineteenth-Century Socialism thought Monsieur Delacroix. Aloud he said, "Agreed."

"Good," said Menton. "Now I will demonstrate that I am not a lunatic, and that the nations had better do what I demand or there will cease to be nations to govern."

He indicated that they were to follow him into the bedroom, Silenced by the old man's fantastic demands and his obvious phobia, they followed him through the bedroom and into a narrow kitchen beyond. At the end of the kitchen was another door, which he opened to reveal a small shelved room stocked with food.

"This is my laboratory," said Menton. "Not perhaps as luxurious as Pasteur's, but I use pretty well the same sort of glassware to breed my children in."

He indicated a row of wine bottles with spigots in lieu of corks in their necks, and a series of what looked like casseroles. There was also a fermentation bottle with an airlock fitted.

"The police saw it all and handled some of it, but they went away satisfied that I did not intend to blow up the Bastille."

Menton laughed and took down one of the wine bottles. "Fools they are! In this bottle there are enough bacteria, to bring their paper fortress to the ground in a few hours. A good wind could spread destruction across the whole of Europe in one night. Let me show you!"

He placed the bottle upon the kitchen table and brought out one of the casseroles. Now that he could see it in the light, Monsieur Delacroix realized that a glass spigot had been fixed through one side of the casserole. Menton connected the wine bottle to the casserole by means of a length of glass tubing which itself had a valve in its length to which was connected a bottle containing liquid. Into the casserole Menton put some pieces of paper, and carefully sealed the casserole with thick grease. He then went to his electric cooker and switched it on.

"I have to take precautions so that the bacteria do not escape before I am ready," he observed, and made one last check on his makeshift apparatus before starting the demonstration.

Despite himself, Monsieur Delacroix was impressed with the cool competence of this maniac. He was acting exactly like a bacteriologist in the field. Was it possible that the bottle that had once held cheap red wine could now hold the doom of civilization? He bent over the casserole and examined the assortment of paper through the glass. "What are you going to do?" he asked.

Menton placed a hand on the spigot of the wine bottle. "I shall turn this tap and allow bacteria to enter this tube, and then I shall open the tap on the side of the casserole. The difference in air pressure between the two vessels and Brownian movement will cause the bacteria to move along the tube and enter the large vessel. There you will see them kill the paper. Then, when the experiment is over, I will reseal the wine bottle and open the tap in the tube. This floods the tube with caustic solution that effectively sterilizes it. I can then disconnect the casserole and put it in the oven of my cooker and sterilize it at a high temperature. Now watch."

He turned first one spigot and then the other. Before Delacroix's horrified eyes, the paper in the casserole turned brown almost at once and drooped into a mess of slime. Menton carefully turned off the spigots and released the antiseptic fluid into the connecting tube.

"It is fast, is it not?" he commented with a chuckle. "Excuse me while I put the casserole to sterilize in the oven."

At last he led them back to the living room. Both Monsieur Delacroix and Mademoiselle Lamaroux were silent, weighed down by the possible consequences of the demonstration they had just seen. If this man could destroy paper at will, then truly civilization would be dealt a terrible blow.

Menton seemed ironically amused at the expressions on their faces. "Do you think you will be able to convince them?" he asked, referring to Delacroix's superiors.

Delacroix shook his head dismally.

"Then take a sample with you," said Menton. "Got them to test it in the laboratory. Wait!" He went back to the kitchen.

"This is horrible!" whispered Mademoiselle Lamaroux. "What can we do?"

Monsieur Delacroix shrugged. "Do as he says," he replied.

Menton returned and handed Delacroix a small, corked bottle. "Be careful with it," he warned with a grin. He opened the door. "I hope to see you before the thirty-first."

Holding the bottle gingerly, Monsieur Delacroix and Mademoiselle Lamaroux left the room.

They had come to Clignancourt by Metro. But Monsieur Delacroix did not feel like risking the bottle in the crowded carriages.

"Get a taxi," he said to his secretary. "We shall go straight to UNESCO Headquarters with this."

He stood there holding the bottle with both hands until a taxi answered Mademoiselle's frantic calls. They got in, and Mademoiselle gave the address. Off they rushed on the long journey to the other side of the Seine where UNESCO had its home in a modern building in the Place de Fontenoy.

Part of it stands on stilts and has innumerable windows none of which open, as the building is air-conditioned throughout. Into this controlled atmosphere rushed Monsieur Delacroix with his bottle of doom: up three floors; into a reception hall; via an assistant secretary, a full secretary; insistent demands for audience, finally led into the office of a high official of the French Section.

Henri Lesage had been a military hero and thereafter a great worker for peace; but he was old now, and a little deaf, and somewhat vague. He had to be reminded of the memorandum written by his department.

"Ah, yes," he said. "I think I remember the man. What is this about a weapon that threatens civilization?"

Monsieur Delacroix placed the bottle in the middle of the desk before the official.

"Monsieur," he said, "before I explain, would you please summon a biologist. We will need him to test the contents of this bottle, and when he has verified the accuracy of what I shall tell you, he must then destroy them."

"Indeed!" said Lesage, mildly surprised. He depressed the key on his intercom, and spoke to his secretary. "Is there a biologist in the building?"

"I beg your pardon, Monsieur?" came the reply.

"A biologist—a medical sort of a fellow."

"I will see, sir."

"Send one up as soon as possible."

The UNESCO official turned to Delacroix, "Now tell me the full story."

Monsieur Delacroix, assisted occasionally by interjections from Mademoiselle Lamaroux, told of his visit to Gustav Menton. A young man in a white coat entered the room quietly while the story was being told, and listened with absorbed attention. At the end the official turned to him.

"Are you the biologist?"

The young man looked confused. "No, sir," he said. "I was told you wanted a doctor up here. I'm from the first-aid unit."

"Sacre Coeur," murmured Lesage to Delacroix. "Never mind," he said to the young man. "Take this bottle and get it analyzed. You've heard the story. See if it kills paper. Then report back to me."

"Yes, sir," said the doctor enthusiastically. He took the bottle from the official, uncorked it, sniffed it, looked into it. "It's empty," he reported.

His audience stared at him in horror.

"You uncorked it!" shrilled Mademoiselle Lamaroux.

"Mon Dieu!" cried Monsieur Delacroix.

"You idiot!" roared Lesage. He jerked to his feet and waved his hand frantically. In rising, he had pressed his hand upon the leather-backed blotting pad before him and it had disintegrated into a brown slime.

Monsieur Lesage revealed then the quality that had made him a military hero. He pressed the button to contact his secretary. "Issue the following emergency instructions to the Security Department: all doors leading to the outside are to be locked and sealed; nobody must leave until further notice. Contact the Maintenance Department as well and ensure that any rooms containing vents to the outside atmosphere are sealed off and advise the Security Department of what they have done. Finally, get the switchboard to connect me to the public-address system. I want to put out a statement."

Even as he released the button, the expensive paper on the wall nearest to where the doctor still stood petrified, became disfigured by brown blotches that quickly ran into each other and then spread round the room. An odor of decay wafted to the terrified onlookers.

The UNESCO official strode across his office and listened at the door to check that his secretary was engaged in making the calls he had ordered. He did not want to interrupt her by using his own connection. His eyes fell on the cases full of books flanking the windows, and he groaned as he saw the brown ooze running from between the leather bindings.

"It's like lightning!" he said to Delacroix. "Pray to God we can contain it within the Building!"

His intercom buzzed.

"You are connected to the public-address system, Monsieur."

"This is the office of the French Section. A state of emergency has been declared in the building and all exits will be kept locked until the emergency is over. A specimen of bacteria that destroys paper had been accidentally released in my office, and until we are sure that all traces of it have been removed, I'm afraid the building must be kept sealed. Don't be afraid if papers in your office are attacked—the effect is not harmful to human beings—but because of the virulence of the bacteria it is vital to our country that it does not get out of the building. Fortunately, because of the air-conditioning system, it is possible to ensure that air leaving the building is subject to ultra-violet radiation that will kill the bacteria. The windows cannot be opened, and if the air-tight doors are kept locked, we will be able to let our biologists work in confidence that the bacteria will not spread before they have found a way to kill it. There is plenty of food in. the building and stores in the basement. Please keep calm. I promise that you will be kept informed of progress, and that you will be released the instant the building can be declared clean."

The room looked like a dank cellar with wet, stained walls. The door burst open, and the secretary staggered in, her face white with horror, her hands brown with slime. "Monsieur, your report to the Director-General, it's . . . it's . . . I went to the safe and it's . . . there's nothing but filth!"

"Don't worry, Madame," said Lesage crisply. "I'm afraid everything will go, my report is the least of our worries. Please contact the Director of UNESCO and all senior medical personnel in the building; ask them to come here at once for a council of war."

He turned to the wilting junior doctor. "I think perhaps you will find a lot to do amongst the more hysterical members of the staff, doctor. Get along with you—and let this be a lesson to you to use your head as well as your nose when diagnosing."

The young man fled.

"What a catastrophe!" Lesage whispered. From the rooms around, faint shouts could be heard. The telephone rang. Lesage picked it up and listened.

"If anybody tries to smash their way out of the building," he said, "shoot them. It's as serious as that! If this bacteria escapes, the whole of France—the world—will be infected. So use every means at your disposal to ensure that the building remains sealed." He put the telephone down.

A group of medical men came quickly into the room followed closely by a tall, lean-faced man who was the Director-General of UNESCO.

"In God's name, what has happened?" he greeted Lesage. "Henri, you've turned loose a devil!"

Delacroix surreptitiously removed his wallet from the inner pocket of his jacket—it was full of slime—and dropped it into a wastepaper basket. There was not a thing in the wallet that had escaped destruction.

"Messieurs," said Lesage, "Sit down. We must make some plans. What we decide now may or may not mean the end of civilization."

He introduced Monsieur Delacroix and Mademoiselle Lamaroux to the gathering, and then explained the business of Gustav Menton.

The Director-General was the first to comment. "Does anyone outside know about this, Henri? There must be a crowd of people trying to get into the building already. We ought to issue a statement. Get in touch with the Prime Minister's office. I'll do it, If you like, while you work out the scientific side."

The medical men were chiefly concerned to get back to their little laboratory at the top of the building where they could start to isolate the bacteria and then discover how to kill it on a wholesale basis.

"Our difficulty is going to be that we hold such small stocks of the usual antiseptic materials that we couldn't possibly sterilize the whole building," said one.

"Then sterilize the entrance hall and bring in some more stocks. Lock the doors again and complete the job," said Lesage, and sent them away. He looked at his watch. "Time for lunch. Let us see whether the canteen is still functioning."

Monsieur Delacroix and Mademoiselle Lamaroux followed, although they had not the least desire to eat.

The walk through the building to the canteen was an eerie experience. At first glance, the corridors were unaffected as their walls and ceilings were, of course, unpapered, but here and there were notice boards disfigured by brown patches. Doors on each side of the corridor had little brown smudges in place of cards showing the name of the sections, and from the offices came shouts, curses and shrieks of disgust. In one office the staff were frantically emptying the slime into wastepaper bins and throwing water about in a frenzy. In another, where the decaying process was still sweeping through the filing cabinets, the girls were snatching files out of the mess and holding them high in the air to escape defilement. Through another door, they saw a man laughing hysterically as he pulled open drawer after drawer in his desk and found only mess, and another man farther on, sobbing over years of work dissolved into mire. The typing pool was deserted, the girls having fled to the lower floors, leaving their machines choked with slime.

The canteen was a desolate sight. Some of the staff were still there but were doing nothing. An assortment of clerical staff were there, but had congregated more to assuage their panic than their hunger. The arrival of Monsieur Lesage slightly reduced the excited discussion.

Lesage raised his voice. "Where is the canteen manager?"

A man elbowed forward.

"Have you a meal ready?" asked Lesage brusquely.

"Yes, Monsieur . . . But . . . " The Manager spread his hands.

"But nothing. Get your staff to serve it. Everybody in the building will need to be fed, and you had better start planning an evening meal as well, and a breakfast for tomorrow. We are liable to be locked up in this building for some time."

The manager looked frantic. "It will be difficult, Monsieur—every label has gone; we don't know what half the things are . . . "

"Fiddlesticks!" interrupted Lesage. "Open the containers and find out! Do I have to tell you how to do everything? Now order the meal to be served."

Over the meal that was, at last, placed before them, Lesage quizzed Monsieur Delacroix about his work. Mademoiselle filled in the gaps. Monsieur Lesage finally held up his wineglass and asked Mademoiselle to toast with him the health of the man who had in the past done more to save his countrymen from disaster than anyone else in the world. "And may he, too, save us from this latest one."

"He will," promised Mademoiselle Lamaroux.

Monsieur Delacroix's glance expressed his disapproval at such levity. "It is a pity the young man pulled the cork from the bottle, but he merely precipitated, I am sure, a situation that would have arisen sooner or later. I fear we may leave this building only to find the world ruined despite our sacrifices, or with Menton still waiting to release the germ if his impossible demands are not met."

"Could we deceive him with a forged treaty?" asked Lesage candidly.

"Not for long. He would merely break his bottles when he found he had been tricked and that no world parliament existed. There is no way out of the impasse. He has his phials hidden on his person and elsewhere, and if we do not give him his treaty he will allow the phials to break. There is only one hope, and that is to form a world parliament with a charter as he wants it."

Lesage sighed heavily. "I've worked towards that end for twenty-five years and I can assure you we wont get a world government in two weeks." He ruminated for a few moments, and then rose. "We'll have to put our hope in the doctors."

He beckoned the hovering canteen manager. "Come to my office. We must work out how long your stocks of food will last."

He turned to Monsieur Delacroix. "Pray come to my office whenever you feel so inclined. We shall welcome any idea you may have."

Two dreary days passed. Outside, the early spring dashed icy rain against the windows, and inside the doctors could give no early hope of success to those who waited in the stink of decayed paper. Although every particle of paper in the building had been transformed into slime, the bacteria were still active under the microscope. The only contact with the outside world the 400 imprisoned people had was the daily telephone call they were allowed to make to their friends or relations.

Delacroix spoke to his wife, who reminded him that she needed money for the weekly shopping. "The bank manager won't accept my signature," she said. "Paul, I must have money. Can you speak to the bank?" He spoke to the bank manager who was incredulous and suspicious, and at last he gave up. In desperation he went to Monsieur Lesage.

Lesage looked ill. He had not been eating or sleeping properly, and he looked an old man. "Hallo, Delacroix," he said. "Any ideas? We have no more."

"Yes," said Delacroix loudly. "Let me talk to Menton, he trusted me. Let me plead with him. I'll make him see that he can't go on with this thing."

Monsieur Lesage leaned back in his seat and waved towards the telephone. "You are used to dealing with maniacs, Monsieur. If you think it will produce some result . . . "

Monsieur Delacroix gave the exchange Menton's number, and in a few moments he was talking to him. "In the name of God, tell us how we can kill this bacteria of yours!" he pleaded. "This was no part of our bargain, and it is, in fact, stopping any arrangements being made. An object lesson has been given on the reality of your threat, Monsieur Menton, now show us the reality of your desire for world peace—tell us how to get out of this building."

"Why should I?" asked Menton. "I am a prisoner myself—the police are all around my apartment. They follow me everywhere."

"I am sorry about that," said Delacroix desperately. "It was no order of mine. But, Monsieur, if you want to know why you should reveal any way of killing your bacteria, it is because there are four hundred people here in misery, facing a possible death from starvation as a sacrifice to the safety of the world."

Menton laughed in real delight. "Is that all that is worrying you, Monsieur Delacroix? With anybody else I would let the joke go on, but you, Monsieur, were polite and honest with me, so I will tell you. The bacteria, once it has converted all the paper in its environment, changes to another form that dies in five days. You will be able to emerge at the end of five days."

"Thank you, Monsieur Menton," said Delacroix. "On my part, I will try to have the police taken away from your apartment."

"And what about the world treaty?" demanded Menton earnestly. "I still stand by that. If you do not produce it within twelve days, I will cause the bottles to break. On that I stake my life."

Monsieur Delacroix laid his hand on his heart. "I swear to you, Monsieur Menton, that every man of goodwill here at UNESCO Headquarters is working towards the same end as yourself. If goodwill counts for anything you will have your treaty in twelve days time."

"Good," said Menton. "I trust you, Monsieur."

Delacroix replaced the telephone sadly.

The promise of release in three days' time was announced just in time. A militant unionist was at that moment leading a column of malcontents into the entrance lobby to do battle with the guards at the doors. They intended to disarm the guards and smash down the doors. The announcement that came just as they were descending the last flight of stairs and the guards were unbuttoning their revolver holsters, weakened the dissidents' resolve, and the battle was joined only in spoken curses. The insurgents retired to their offices to drink and gamble. Only the pipe-smokers were able to enjoy the tobacco vice, as cigarettes were sticky cylinders of brown grass.

Monsieur Delacroix had another telephone conversation with his wife on the fourth day. She told him that most of the local shopkeepers were giving her credit, but that she was entirely out of money.

"Go to de Lith," Delacroix told her. "He will give you all you want. We shall be out tomorrow."

He finished the call, doubly thankful that the bacteria had not got loose into the world to consume all the paper money. Mankind—at least half of it was conditioned to believe that life could not be lived without money in the pocket. If money and ledgers vanished, there would be nothing left of wealth, nothing left to prove it ever existed. There would be instant, roaring confusion. Men needed money as a warm coat against the hard, primitive world in which the measure of wealth was the possession of a fast right arm and a sharp weapon.

At which point Monsieur Delacroix turned in his tracks and hastened to Lesage's office.

"What is our greatest problem now?" demanded Delacroix, standing before Lesage's desk.

"Why . . . the . . . er, smell, I suppose," said Lesage. Delacroix shook his head impatiently.

"The threat Menton holds over us of releasing the bacteria on March the thirty-first if we don't give him the treaty," said Delacroix. "It is no use arresting him or even killing him. He has timed devices pre-set to explode in various unknown places. How can we possibly stop him from doing what he threatens?"

"Indeed, that is so. I have been thinking of nothing else for the past four days."

"There is only one person who can stop him," said Monsieur Delacroix leaning forward.

"And that is?"

"Gustav Menton himself."

And before Lesage could put the question, Monsieur Delacroix explained his plan.

At seven in the morning, before the district of Clignancourt was fully awake, an armored vehicle drew up before Gustav Menton's apartment. Six men emerged from the rear carrying large sacks and two men with revolvers guarded the party. At the loud knocking on his front door, Gustav Menton opened it and then retreated at sight of the crowd on his threshold. The men filed in and deposited their loads in the middle of the Persian carpet. All but one withdrew. He gestured to the sacks with his revolver.

"Five hundred million francs, Monsieur. There is no need to return the sacks."

He pocketed his pistol and shut the door on the flabbergasted face of Gustav Menton.

Two days later Monsieur Lesage said to Delacroix as they stood watching the decorators repaper the office, "You must have a profound knowledge of madmen. There is no doubt of it—he does not intend to forgo that fortune. It was a cheap victory for us."

"Menton was not a madman, if I may be so bold as to contradict you," said Monsieur Delacroix. "He was merely poor—a man of pride who had once been comfortable and had been deprived of his comfort by our terrible inflation. I deduced that he hated money—or, at least, the indignities that lack of it brings—and that hate he had transferred to the physical aspect of money, namely paper. When he was given a sufficiency of money, the hate disappeared."

"But how could you deduce that, Monsieur?"

Monsieur Delacroix inclined his head modestly. "It was largely a guess, and the incessant worrying of my wife about money turned the key in the lock, so to speak, but from the very first I was troubled by his use of the term *'kill'* paper. What a peculiar word to use! I saw, suddenly, that it was an expression of personal hate for paper and nothing to do with the action of the bacteria. The insistence in his world-government plan that money should be eliminated pointed to the type of paper he hated. So we gave him more than he can ever spend, and suddenly he loves money! I am perfectly confident that Menton has baked every one of his bottles of bacteria to death in case they ever destroy his money."

Monsieur Lesage smiled and produced an oblong piece of paper from his inner pocket.

"I trust you like money, too, Monsieur, because your grateful Government would like you to accept this—in strictest confidence, of course, as it is not usual to reward public servants, you understand."

Monsieur Delacroix looked at the check and his heart warmed with gratitude. The Department had granted him one whole month's additional salary as reward.

BOUGHT ON THE INTERNET

B. J. Empson

The house was hidden by a low hill from the rest of the sea front cottages. In fact the tarmac road terminated abruptly at the beginning of hill, leaving only a shingle track to reach the unseen building on the opposite side.

Wainwright stopped before driving into the garage and looked at his purchase. He had, of course, checked it out before but now he was actually moving in.

MODERN SEASIDE VILLA. Yes, it certainly looked good and, as far as he was concerned, exactly what he wanted. **FULLY FURNISHED TO THE HIGHEST STANDARDS**. No doubt about that, certainly it had been a bit pricey but things thrown in without charge had made it almost a bargain. **SOLAR POWER, ADVANCED SECURITY SYSTEM, INTERIOR CLIMATIC SYSTEM, COOKERY UNIT, UNDER ROAD PASS TO PRIVATE BEACH. LARGE TENDED GARDEN WITH LARGE LAWN, SMALL, COVERED SELF-PURIFYING SWIMMING POOL FOR WINTER USE.**

Peter Wainwright grinned to himself and stepped out of the car. A bargain—no doubt about that.

He reached over and lifted the carrier from the passenger seat. "This is your new home, chum."

The cat's green eyes expressed nothing but it said "Yow" in a minor key as if agreeing.

He opened the rear door. "Out, you!"

The dog lollopped out, wagged its tail and sat down waiting. Domestic, wasn't it? While he lasted he could be happy here.

He closed the car doors—drive it in later—bent down to pick up the carrier and stopped himself in time. Wrong arm! Left arm and left leg were subsidiaries and painful.

He approached the front door of his new home with a distinct limp but he had almost become used to the nagging pain. He was not going to let it spoil his enjoyment now.

In the carrier, the cat's fur rose in spikes, she arched her back and hissed. The action was only brief—she settled down almost immediately and, as if assured, began to purr. Once released from the carrier she made her way to the biggest chair and curled up in it.

The dog's only reaction was a half-hearted cough that never quite made a proper bark. He began to wag his tail almost before the sound was ended. It was clear that the animals liked their new home.

Later Wainwright put the car in the garage and made survey of the kitchen. The agent had stocked up well and he had even remembered a comprehensive supply of animal food.

Wainwright took a Meal-For-One and put it in the Self-Cook installation. The device would strip the packaging, cook to perfection and ring a bell when the meal was ready.

Lazy, he thought, he'd like to teach himself to cook later but not now, while he was settling in.

He lowered himself carefully into one of the easy chairs, wincing as he did so. Somehow he had never mastered the art of sitting down without a sharp twinge. Of course, the damn magnets didn't help, tightening the muscles.

Wainwright was an ex-policeman or, more aptly a high-ranking officer, although he had begun in the ranks. He had been Area Commander North, and gained several awards for bravery.

He gained other marks of battle as well. A rifle bullet had passed completely through his body resulting in six month's hospitalization. In later engagements he had taken three slugs, two in the calf of his left leg and one in his left forearm.

A slug was not propelled by a firearm, it was released by a low velocity weapon. An air pistol, a blow pipe, a special bow, and, with an experienced marksman, even a catapult.

The slug was not intended to hit a vital organ but to penetrate the flesh just below the skin.

It was designed both as a terror weapon and one of revenge. Revenge was obviously the reason why Wainwright had become a recipient. He had broken up several crime mobs and had become a thorn in the flesh to hooligan organizations.

The slugs were special, poison would have been easier and immediate but that would hove been almost merciful—mercy, however, was not the object of the exercise.

The slugs were splinter missiles containing a minute and timed explosive charge. Any attempt to remove it surgically caused it to detonate. Detonation, in any case, caused the slug to splinter and penetrate the nearest blood vessel. Eventually the tiny splinter would be carried to the heart. Here, although they might not be immediately lethal, they would become so as they had been designed to coagulate, forming a fatal clot.

The victim, therefore, had not only to suffer an agonizing wait but also endure the inflammation and possible major infection set up by the missiles embedded in his flesh.

In Wainwright's case, the police experts had almost found an answer which, it was hoped might provide a solution. Since the missiles were metallic, magnets had been fixed to his limbs between the slugs and his heart. It was hoped, when the missiles finally detonated, the metallic fragments would be held in one place without being carried by the blood to its fatal destination.

There was no telling when the slugs might blow, some took years. It was also known that some could be activated by remote control.

Wainwright had not learned to live with it, he had become resigned. He often studied himself in the mirror; he was thirty four but, on some days, looked fifty. A thin face, not without humor, deep-set dark eyes. At least his hair was still thick and without a trace of gray, not that it mattered. Here he was, invalided out of the service on a full pension, a false name and background. In this house he was Ernest Poole, business executive suffering from a recent road accident.

This fact was born home to him only two days later when the door chime disturbed his meditations.

"Mr. Poole—Mr. Ernest Poole?"

The man who stood at the door was thin and was dressed somberly in black and looked, thought Wainwright, like a pallbearer at a funeral. The eyes, however, were astute; this man was an official of some kind.

He was correct; the man presented an authorization card in a plastic holder.

"Department of the Environment, sir, Estate Section. I am Claude Selby."

"What can I do for you, Mr. Selby?"

"Well, sir, there are peculiarities about this property which worry my department a great deal."

"Perhaps you'd better come in and explain them."

"Thank you, sir I appreciate that. I must stress, however, that although I must ask many questions, you are not, at this moment in time, obliged to answer—I make myself plain?"

"Certainly—if I do not answer, you will obtain a court order for me to appear before a committee."

Selby shifted his feet uncomfortably, unhappy that this man knew the law. "I'm sure it will never come to that, sir. My enquiries concern the property, not yourself."

"Good." Wainwright smiled. "Do sit down, Mr. Selby—Oh, mind Hogwash, please—perhaps the other chair."

"Sir?"

"Oh, sorry, that's the cat—Hogwash. While on the subject, that thing in the corner there is the dog. I call it Fleabag."

Selby stopped himself scowling at the animal with an effort. The damn creature was nearly as big as a pony and looked as if it was wearing a doormat. A thought occurred to him: was this man an eccentric, or was he secretly laughing at him?

He sat down and produced papers hurriedly. "If we may begin, sir."

He hurried on without waiting for an answer. "The first thing which troubles my department, sir, is the existence of this property. A survey was made of this small seaside town only nine months ago. There were then twenty-seven properties on this part of the sea front, no more. Now there are twenty-eight—you have that number on your front door but, officially you do not exist! The local council has no application for planning permission in their records or deeds of construction. The postal services knew nothing about until you rang up and told them. The same applies to newspaper delivery and like suppliers. Several of them confess that they never knew that this house existed."

Wainwright shook his head slowly. "I'm sorry, Mr. Selby, but I can't help you. I only moved in here three days ago. True, I came down and inspected it a month ago, but I know nothing about its past history."

"I take it that the property is yours, sir—it's not rented?"

"No, not rented or even mortgaged, I bought outright. I bought it on the internet. I've all the paperwork here—excuse me a minute, I'll go and get it for you."

Selby went through the papers carefully but everything seemed legitimate, Faber Construction Company, Moyle Transport and even the legal side was in order: Shalwood, Souter and Brice Ltd. There was, however, one glaring error, construction date was only five years in the past. No such building had existed there five years ago and, come to think of it, less than a year ago. He distinctly recalled that he, and his family, had had a picnic on the cliff, less than eighty meters beyond this property and there had been nothing visible then.

He rose and handed the papers back. "Thank you for your co-operation, sir, much appreciated. I do understand that you acquired this property in good faith."

When he returned to his office, however, he wondered if he had spoken too soon. He was unable to find a single reference to the transaction nor any of the firms involved in it. Poole had issued a bank draft to the tune of one hundred and eighty two thousand but the money had not been deducted from his account. As far as Poole was concerned, the property had been handed over to him free of charge.

As a conscientious official, Selby couldn't leave it at that—further investigation was definitely called for.

It was not a rewarding task as, four days later, he received a letter from Internal Security which said in four verbose pages "lay off, or else."

He was not intimidated by the implied threat but the folder with the letter did bring him to a dead stop. Selby was impressed by documents and this one had so many tabs, seals, and double signatures that he almost cringed. Nonetheless, his curiosity had been aroused—no harm in keeping his own eyes and ears open. In his absence Wainwright had a visitor of his own. It came howling along the coast, so close to the water it dragged a long plume of mist and spray behind it.

The noise when it touched down near his home spraying grass, pebbles and sand in all directions was appalling. As a boy he had once seen one of the ancient helicopters at an air display. Compared to this, however, a chopper made a bearable noise. Vertical ascent craft sounded like thirty police sirens shrilling away on different keys.

The sound didn't last long, a brief stop then up, howling even louder in ascent.

A few seconds later the door chimes sounded and he frowned. This was official, no doubt about that.

He opened the door. "Yes—what can I do for you?"

"Commander Wainwright?"

"Ex-Commander." He looked her up and down. She was in full uniform and wore high status symbols. She was also pert, pretty, red haired and, he thought, undoubtedly bossy.

"I'm clear of the Service," he said. "I believe I stressed the ex-commander."

"Not entirely, sir, you're using department medical equipment which under Section 72 gives us medical inspection rights."

"Oh, I see—you're from the butchery department." He regretted his words almost immediately. "I'm sorry, not fair to take it out on you, but your presence does not raise my spirits. I'm quite sure you have not been sent here with good news."

He stood to one side. "Please come in, I'll try and remain civilized—coffee, or something a little stronger?"

Ten minutes later, sipping her coffee, she said: "This may come as something of a shock, Commander, but the medical committee sent me."

She paused and he said quickly: "You don't have to tell me, your visit is enough—bad news."

"I'm very sorry." She shook her head. "We're worried about the slug in your arm. Photo-analysis suggests that is not all metallic which means, if it blows, that the fragments can not be controlled by magnets."

He poured himself another coffee with a steady hand and said: "if this is a death sentence could you be a little more specific please."

She became practical and clinically detached. "My name is Ruth Keel, Techno-Medical, first class, and I have been specially trained for this assignment. To do it and, if possible save your life, I must be at a minute's call at all times."

"I take it that the solution is drastic?"

"Yes, I'm afraid it is: drastic, crude and very brutal. If the slug blows, I must amputate the arm within one minute, that is before any fragments reach the blood stream."

His hand was still steady but his face paled. "The equivalent of a saber blow?"

"Yes, I have a special instrument. Some of the fragments, although probably plastic, have still coagulating properties."

She paused and put down her cup. "You will, of course, have an alarm button by your bed at night and a similar button on your coat during the day—"

Selby knew he could not follow up official channels but, as he told himself frequently, casual questions did no harm or, come to that, just listening.

The man in the pub had had a few but not too many. "Don't care what you say, call me mad if you like. People keep saying that there must always have been a house there and I'm telling you that there bloody wasn't. It's only nine weeks, nine mark you, that I took the dog for a walk right past the place and there was nothing there then but bloody grass."

Selby nodded to himself, probably find out a lot more later if he kept on listening.

He turned his attention back to his work and switched on his audit file, a lot of unpaid rents still outstanding in Goodge Street.

As he worked, music became audible from the street below. Of course! The carnival. There were only two thousand inhabitants in the village, but they kept up the old traditions.

He rose and glanced out of the window. Of course, the lead float with the carnival queen.

He frowned. Hell of a lot of people for a local carnival wasn't it?

Too many!

Dear God! Hooligan raid?

Surely not here!

He punched the town warning button savagely and then his own.

"Mary, we've got a hooligan raid—yes, *here*—don't argue, girl. Move! Grab the kids, punch the shutter switch and get down into the hideout. Don't come out until you hear from me or receive an official all clear over the radio link."

Alarms were going all over the town now but it was far too late. Hooligans, posing as summer visitors had already started individual fights with the locals and the fighting would turn into an engineered riot. Windows would be broken, premises looted and vehicles set on fire.

Every open building would be invaded and its content stolen—secure buildings would be vandalized.

A heavy brick bounced off the safety shutter of his office as he lowered it over the window.

There was nothing more he could do but pray; it was suicide to go out on the street. His family should be safe with hooligan shutters and a secret room downstairs. The rover bands of louts seldom wasted time on protected homes. They were out for easy pickings—the open shop, the small supermarket, contents and tills.

Selby knew that looting would not stop on the main street. Cars would be stolen and the unshaven tide would wash out to the very limits of the town. An unshuttered house, frightened girls, even an unprotected hospital.

Macron was one of the louts, unshaven, unwashed and high on alcohol he was ready for anything.

Bryer, his companion, was beginning to lose interest in this part of the town. "All the bloody places are shuttered," he said. "Twenty-seven, reckon it's the last one on the front."

"You never know, there might be one more just over the rise."

He drove car to the top of the rise and stopped. "Look at that, wasn't I right? Bright new villa, wide open, no bloody shutters."

"You're damned right, boyo." Bryer climbed out of the car and picked up a large heavy stone. "Look at that lovely wide window! I'm going to put this chunk of rock right through it."

He swung his arm and they watched the missile sail towards its target but when it hit there was no crash of breaking glass. Instead the substance seemed to bend inwardly and there was a curious twanging sound.

Dazedly they saw the stone coming back. Bryer was too stupefied to duck and the stone hit him full in the face.

Macron only half understood what had happened. His companion was lying on the ground with both hands pressed to his face.

"Get up, what yer playin' at?"

Hell, Bryer was hurt, blood was running out between his fingers. Macron had just enough humanity left to help his companion into the car and speed away.

On the way back he made a call. "Macron here. I want Eddie and Paul to hang on, meet me on the way to the War Memorial. I got trouble here, Bryer is hurt bad. Nose proper flattened, cheek bone fractured too, I reckon—Yeah, you'll have to get him to a medic—eh?—Oh, gimmicked house, something new, that's why I want the boys—we'll torch the bloody place as soon as it's dark."

Macron was a hooligan but he did not know that his dynasty was over a hundred years old and had humble beginnings. It had begun as trouble makers began to stir resentment between rival fans at sports meetings. Fights developed in which premises were badly damaged and nearby shops looted.

As the number of hooligans grew, their attentions spread. If, for example, there was a large peaceful demonstration, it was infiltrated by the hooligans who quickly turned it into an aggressive demonstration.

Over the years the cult had not only developed but had become organized with various sections divided into 'chapters.' There were 'The Bikes', 'The Sports', 'The Looters' and 'The Vandals' to give only a few examples.

The worst aspect of organization, however, was its vast army of secret members. Many hooligans were public exhibitionists, well known to the police but for each of these were twenty or more unknowns. These unknowns came from all strata of society. Working men, students, doctors and, in two highly publicized cases, a lawyer and a county judge. On legal holidays, sick leave or like occasions, they discarded the mantle of respectability and for a day became hooligans.

No one knew why, psychiatrists admitted they were at a loss and even the hooligans themselves were unable to give a detailed explanation. The captured unknowns only confessed to getting a kick out of it and the moronic said they were out to destroy the 'Establishment.'

Time-wise the entire riot was over in less than an hour leaving the residents to clear up the mess and lick their wounds. Usually there were one or two fatalities and several rapes. On average, four to eight business concerns completely cleared out by looters.

In due course police would invade the city but there was little they could do. The hooligans would have dispersed in all direction long before they arrived.

In fairness to the police, they had a difficult task. Hooligan riots, real or staged, were timed to occur in several parts of the country at once. Picking the active one was a whole time problem. Village or city suburb? Protesters peaceful demonstration or funeral cortege—riots could occur anywhere.

When the all clear went in the town, Sid Mappin, with many others, breathed a long sigh of relief. Attempts had been made to break into the

Ship Inn, which he owned, but without success. Not only had the shutters held, but the new steel door had defeated them completely.

He was not alarmed, therefore when the bell rang soon after the all clear. No doubt a customer—or several customers—urgently needing drink.

He pressed the release button and the door slid back.

"If you want to live," said the unshaven man on the door step, "make no sound, man—understood?"

He pushed a short but cannon-like weapon painfully into Mappin's stomach. "And don't, just don't even think of touching any alarm." He jerked the gun painfully again. "Get back and when the three of us are in you lock the door behind us. After which, my friend, you will illuminate the 'Closed' sign outside the building. No one will question it after a day like this."

He patted his gun gently. "Never forget, old chum, one shot from this will smear you all over the wall in bloody fragments."

"What do you want?" Mappin's voice was hoarse but firm. Damned if he was going to show terror in front of these louts.

"Fair question, chummy boy, you will hide us and feed us until darkness. In short, anything we ask for you will cough up without question—drinks, cigars, chocolate or whatever. If you've done it right, with a smile, mate, you might survive without even a bruise."

At number twenty-eight Wainwright did not even know there had been a hooligan raid. Possibly because the building was set in a hollow, the warning alarms had never reached him. He was not even aware that a heavy rock had been thrown at his front window.

His attention, too, had been taken up with contradictions. It was now four days since Ruth Keel, the medical officer, had arrived with her dire news—but he felt that his own reactions were totally out of keeping with the information.

Since he had first been shot, his sleep had been broken and disturbed by unpleasant dreams. This condition had been doubled when he became a carrier for three splinter missiles. The longest periods of sleep he had learned to expect was never more than twenty minutes and often less. After which he would lie staring into the darkness until sheer exhaustion forced him once more into brief unconsciousness.

The cheering news that his arm might be struck from his body at any moment would, he thought, cut his periods of rest to less than ten minutes.

EDITED BY PHILIP HARBOTTLE AND SEAN WALLACE

On the first night his inner prediction was true but, on the second night he was shocked to discover that he had slept without waking for almost three hours. He checked both his watch and the wall clock but there was no mistake. Stranger still, he not only felt rested but less worried. What the hell, there was nothing he could do about it in any case.

It was on the day of the hooligan raid that he awoke after five hours unbroken sleep only to punch the alarm with a sense of darkening despair.

She was in almost instantly, the nuclear scalpel like a tiny sun in her gloved hand.

"Stretch out your arm."

He did so and then surprisingly, the bright light went out. "Let me have a look at that." She leaned forward staring at the small wound in his arm.

"Dear God, surely this is not possible." She was speaking half to herself, her face pale. She put on magni-spectacles and adjusted the side stud.

"Get back, well away from the bed." She strode forward and pulled back the sheets. "There! Look there!"

He found himself staring at a small black object about the size of a grain of corn lying close to the pillow. There was no need to ask what it was: he had seen two many pictures of it while in the Service.

"It didn't blow?"

"No, for reasons unknown, your body ejected it. I've checked the wound and there is no sign of fragmentation."

She left the room and returned a few seconds later with a small cup-like instrument on a rod.

"The sooner this thing is out of the way, the better."

It was clear she had been trained to use the instrument for the missile was contained within a few seconds.

"There's an automatic shutter inside, no need to worry—not that it could do much harm clear of the body. Nonetheless I'd prefer it elsewhere."

She left the room and he sat heavily on the edge of the bed. His legs felt weak and he was shaking all over. God, he might have died or, at the very least, lost an arm.

His thoughts, however, were with the woman. As he had first suspected she was bossy, and detached, but beyond that, he didn't know her.

She had checked him over three times a day with instruments, but beyond that he had barely seen her. All three bedrooms in this luxury villa were self-contained with all facilities so they had not even eaten together—a truly professional relationship. On reflection, he was not sure that he cared for it. Not that he had intended to make a pass but conversation and company would have been nice.

He'd thought of her as clinically cold but now he was not sure. When he had banged the alarm button she had come in virtually fully clothed.

Only her regulation tie had been loosened. It was quite clear that she had spent nights in the next room, fully clothed in readiness.

She came in a few minutes later with a tray. "I thought we could both use a cup of coffee" She was strangely pale.

He took the cup of coffee and then, quickly, the tray. "Sit down—you're shaking."

"I know, Commander, I'm sorry. I shall have to resign—I failed in my duty."

"Oh, come on. I'm safe!"

"I still failed, it was my duty to remove your arm immediately and without question. I could have caused your death."

She put her head in her hands, now shaking visibly. "I'm cracking sir, no doubt about that. I was poised, ready to strike but, I swear, a voice in my head shouted 'stop!' just before I did so."

"But you saved my life and my arm."

"Not from a professional decision, sir, not from intense training but from stress and it could have cost you your life."

"I don't see it like that." He was looking at her in a new light. He had seen her as an efficient and somewhat bossy official. Now he was seeing her as a woman, almost a girl, vulnerable and in need of support.

She shook her head. "Thank you, but the board won't see it that way. Inefficiency, dereliction of duty, I should have amputated first and asked questions afterwards."

"In which case, I would have lost an arm for no purpose."

"That is true but, as I say, the board won't see it like that."

He resisted a temptation to put his hand comfortingly on her shoulder. "You are sure this is due to stress?"

"When one hears voices, what other explanation can there be? In my mind I heard, or should it be felt, the voice distinctly."

"And you are convinced it was stress?"

She looked into his face. "Dear God, sir, do you think this assignment has been easy? Do you consider that severing a man's arm from his body is a simple task? Oh, yes, amputation with the patient unconscious is one thing but to strike off a limb in cold blood is another. Yes, I suffered stress, I hated the idea and should have withdrawn from it in the first hour."

This time he did put his hand on her shoulder. "Please, don't blame yourself too much and do me a favor, just one favor. Give it a couple of days."

"Heavens, sir, that will put the final nail in my coffin."

He was glad she had accepted his hand on her shoulder without a reaction.

"Maybe it would," he said, "but, using your own simile, they'll probably bury you anyway."

She nodded slowly. "You're right, of course. They will, but I can't find reasons for putting off the inevitable."

"You may not, but I can, I asked the favor, remember? I, personally, need you here. I have two more slugs stuck in me which the magnets may, or may not, render safe. I have seen and noted your dedication. I don't want anyone else around whatever happens." She laid her hand briefly on his—on the one still laid on her shoulder and he was aware of a sudden happiness inside him. He didn't feel like that about her did he—did he?

He said: "There is one other reason, since you have brought up the subject of stress. Perhaps I am suffering from it, too. You see, I bought this house on the internet. It's a lovely place but I can't help feeling there's something downright strange about it—"

The inside of the Ship Inn had been designed to look 'period.' The bar, the paneling, the chairs and tables, although plastic, looked like very old but frequently polished wood.

Above the bar was a large picture of a steamship. Printed beneath it were the words S.S. MERETON. **Argos line 1910**. Obviously a passenger liner, she boasted four stacks and the painting depicted her broadside on.

Macron had helped himself to a beer but now sat at one of the tables grinning. "Dinner time, eh? Fancy a steak, I do, yeah, steak and chips—jump to it, barman."

Mappin shot him a look of complete contempt but said; "I'll get it and, for your information I'm the owner and the licensee of this place."

"So what, old chum, as far as we're concerned you're part of the Establishment, no more."

His two companions laughed, nodding in agreement. They were sprawled in chairs with their feet on the nearest table.

Eddie, nearest to Macron was red faced, unshaven and little-eyed. He giggled frequently for no obvious reason.

Paul, on the other hand, was probably one of the unknowns. He was clean-shaven and neatly dressed. His face was bleak and almost wholly without expression.

They ate, they drank and became almost convivial and it was not long before Macron began boasting.

"'Spect you wonder whey we're 'ere, eh, barman? Well, I'll tell you this, no one crosses us. Queer place up on the front there—one of me mates got hurt bad. So tonight, my friend we're going to torch the bloody place."

Mappin kept his face expressionless but he saw a chance to get in a word which although it might not alter the situation, would disturb and, perhaps, cause a mistake.

"Reckon that would be number twenty-eight," he said, "sooner you than me."

"What do you know about it?"

"Nothing really, only what I've heard, people talk in a bar, y'know."

"What have you 'eard, mate? Tell us—an' quick!"

"Well, people say the place wasn't there a few months ago, sort of appeared like. It's got lights on at night but its not connected to the main grid. A man from the water board went up there to read the water meter. There ain't one, nothing's been laid on—yet they're getting water just the same."

"Give us, a whisky, mate," Eddie's red unshaven face had lost some of its color. "I don't like the sound of this."

"Oh, come on!" Macron's voice was jeering. "Bloody old wives' tale. No one believes that rubbish!"

"Ain't all rubbish, mate. My old gran', she came from central Europe somewhere. She told me some strange things and she didn't think they were rubbish."

Mappin saw a chance to get in a final word. "Queer fellow up there, too, they say. The man from the Electricity said he had damn great bandages round his legs. Queer, too, got a huge great woolly dog called Fleabag and the cat, of all things is called Hogwash."

Eddie held out his glass. "Fill it up again, mate." He was grinning broadly but his hand shook.

At number twenty-eight, they had settled in the lounge and were drinking coffee.

"You were telling me about the house," she said.

He nodded. "Well, consider. There had to be water to make this coffee, where did it come from? I'm not connected to the mains. I have light and heat but I have no cable to the grid. More to the point is the psychological factor. When I came here I slept in snatches and, inwardly I was keyed way up. With each passing day and night, however, I slept longer and grew calmer. Despite the imminent danger I began to feel assured."

He paused and looked at her uncertainly. "You underwent an experience which you put down to stress. I underwent an experience that made me calmer—shall I put that down to stress? Don't answer that question yet because I only told you a part." He hesitated before continuing.

"I have developed, or acquired, a rather wild theory but, mad as it may sound, hear me out, please. In the first place, I think this house is a mechanical entity, a sort of advanced computer, maybe, and I'm damn sure it didn't originate on Earth."

She took him seriously. "I accept that, as a theory. Much of what you tell me supports it but where do we go from here?"

He laughed uneasily. "Well this is the awkward part—fancy yourself as a psychic medium?"

"Pardon!"

"I'm sorry, I put that badly. Speaking personally, I've felt pressures in my mind but I've shut them out. On the one hand I thought I might hear something frightening and, on the other, I thought I might be sort of taken over if you know what I mean?" She looked at him wide-eyed. "You too! I thought it was part of my stress. What, exactly, had you in mind?"

"I thought we might go to separate rooms and just listen, give way to pressure as it were. If you are not prepared to join me, I'll understand and go it alone."

"No way," she said. "When?"

"'It's now fourteen hundred—give it an hour.'"

"Fine." At the door she turned. "I have to confess I did listen—feel—something. I know your feelings about me and, yes, I feel the same."

An hour later they looked at each other knowing that no qualification was necessary. They had listened and learned.

"It's not a machine, but it was created."

"Yes, grown for a specific purpose. Somewhere, way out, a highly advanced race grew her, and thousands like her, as part of their civilization—"

"Her?"

"Oh, yes, she's organic and female despite the fact that she began life as a seed."

She said: "She's lovely, I can feel it, warm and caring; we'll always be absolutely safe. Last night, she was seeding, not at random but specifically. The coast of Maine, clearly, yes, an island in Japan. I think also Norway, but I am not sure of that. She settled on Earth because she could fulfill herself here, caring for intelligent life. On the other hand I never found out what happened to her original creators."

"Oh, I got that part clearly—they advanced so far that they became pure thought forms, no longer requiring material homes."

He smiled. "Oh, yes, one other thing, there was a physical response. Half way through the session, a couple of splinter-slugs were ejected—painlessly—from my legs . . . "

In the Ship Inn they were still demanding food and drink with Eddie concentrating on the drink.

Macron kept glancing at his watch. "About forty minutes to darkness, then we'll pay a little visit, eh? Could have done it in the day, of course, but it looks better at night, like a bonfire. Couple or three petrol bombs should get it going."

Eddie stood up and stretched out his hand but the demand for another drink never came. Instead he said: "What the 'ell was that?"

"What—what are you talking about?"

"That noise, sort of a muffled explosion, like. It wasn't outside, it was in here."

"You're dreamin', mate, we heard nothing. A whisky belch, that's what that was . . . "

"I 'eard it, I *know* I 'eard it!" He held out his glass again. "Whisky, fill it up."

When it was full, he fell back in his chair heavily and belched. "I know what you lot are thinking, but you're wrong, mates, I could drink the whole lot of you bastards under the table. I could—" He stopped, they saw the color drain from his face and his mouth fall open stupidly. The glass of whisky slipped from his fingers untouched.

"Its an omen," he said, "a bloody omen." His voice was oddly cracked and he was dribbling slightly.

"What the hell are you babbling about?" Macron shouted the question angrily.

"The ship, the bloody ship in that picture, can't you bloody see it—*she's down by the stern!*"

"You're mad—trick of the light." Paul's voice sounded as if he was trying to convince himself.

Mappin, although he was unable to see the painting from where he was standing, saw a chance to undermine their morale even more,

"She was torpedoed in 1916," he said.

"I told yer! An omen that's what it is." Eddie strode towards the door. "You can count me out of this, you do the job yourselves." He stopped and pointed. "Look at the bloody thing, waves breaking over the stern and her bows clear of the water! She's going down stern first!" The door slammed behind him.

The two remaining men stared, probably some sort of trick. Macron produced his gun. "You want me to blow your head off, barman?"

"Nothing to do with me, it's a painting, you touched it yourself when you came—I saw you. Think I'd be mad enough to play tricks with you lot?"

Macron scowled at him. "Man, if I ever find out that you did, I'll be back and I'll blow you to bits in pieces. I'll start at your feet and work my way up—clear?"

He glanced at his watch. "Time we got moving, Paul."

As they left, Macron glanced back but the canvas was virtually empty. There was water but no steamship. For the first time Macron felt a coldness rise inside him, but fought it down desperately. A trick, that's what it was, one of them clever electronic gadgets; he'd go back and do that barman.

They found their way to the hidden car without fear of being seen. Vandals had accounted for the lighting system and most of the townspeople were making temporary repairs to ruined houses and premises.

When they reached the sea front a curious mist had arisen, thick, but only waist high. When they got out of the car near number twenty-eight, they found it disconcerting. It was like wading in dark water and they were unable to see their feet and legs.

Paul, who was only wearing a thin shirt, found it cold but he had very little time to shiver. Before he had taken ten cautious paces, something leapt out of the mist and landed on his back. He felt something land just above his shoulder blades and sink what seemed to be short blades into his back.

He screamed, the pain was ripping downwards and he sensed instantly what it was.

"What's up, mate?" Macron's voice was beginning to sound frightened.

"It's that cat, that Hogwash, the barman told us about. It's ripped my back to shreds and I can feel the blood."

"Hang on, I'll go back to the car and get a couple of torches."

He made his way painstakingly back and removed them from the back seat.

"Here you are, Paul, over here, I got 'em." He waved the beams up and down to attract attention. "Can't you see 'em, mate? Why the hell don't you answer?

With a sinking feeling inside Macron realized he was alone. Another thought occurred to him, if a cat could conceal itself in the mist so could a damn great woolly dog . . .

His nerve cracked, he had forgotten why he was here. Had to pull out—stumbling through the mist he ran downhill and away from the house—

In another part of the town Welby was talking to his wife. "Number twenty-seven on the sea front has become vacant. I'm thinking of putting in a bid for it."

"But isn't it near that funny place you kept talking about?"

"It is, but a lot has happened favor then. I know, I *feel* different about the place. I don't know why, I just do. I know, if there is another raid, up there, close to that place, we shall be absolutely safe."

THE DINOSAURS OF LONDON

David Redd

I was sketching on a balcony; high above the ruins of London, when I heard a shout from below.

"Whoa! Easy, you stupid dino!"

My hand jerked in the middle of drawing the picture. Consequently my charcoal stick went skidding ruinously over the pad, leaving a thick black line across a promising rooftop sunrise. And I'd come up here especially to draw this, instead of finding breakfast.

"Hold still, you varmint!"

Before I had time to get annoyed, I heard an odd clattering, scratching noise behind the unfamiliar voice. I knew that noise. Everybody here knew it. We had heard reptilian claws in a paved street far too often.

Instinctively I dropped my sketchpad, jumped to the railings and looked down.

Muffled curses floated up at me from the street. Their source seemed to be an enormous brown hat, its wide round brim rippling with buckskin style fringes. Sticking out from underneath this hat I saw two huge clawed feet and a long yellow-green tail.

Next second, the hat tilted up. A stubbly gap-toothed old face was grinning up towards me, a human face—and beside it, a hissing reptilian head.

I saw a man in brown leathers, laughing, his arms wrapped around the long ostrich neck of a struthiomimus.

A dinosaur, and the madman down there was trying to ride the thing.

104

I stared. The creature shook itself wildly and managed to dislodge its rider, who somehow was still laughing even as he fell. "Yipes!"

The old man sat down heavily and suddenly in the empty road. Tins from a burst ruckshack rolled everywhere. I saw the dinosaur scuttle away along the empty street, while the old man squatting in the road simply went on laughing. Out of everything, it was the laughter in his face and eyes that I saw.

What a picture the old man mad! The round hat, the wide-opened mouth, the upturned eyes screwed up tight with his laughing . . . The charcoal stick, I realized, was still in my hand.

Charcoal was good for line and contrasts. I retrieved my pad, settled back and and begun sketching rapidly, far more rapidly than usual. My madman appeared on the paper as a wide grin framed by that round hat. The bristly chin, the missing teeth, the insane joy, yes: I put them them all into the face I drew. Not an ugly face—I hated ugly things—but a face full of character. Whoever he was, I enjoyed drawing him. I worked as fast as my ancient hero the old-man-mad-about-painting would have worked.

Naturally I added a snakelike head lower left, to give the necessary hint of menace.

Absorbed in creating the picture, I never thought to wonder where this madmen had come from, or why he had tried to ride a dinosaur. I just accepted him as one more isolated survivor wandering through the ruins of London, as indeed he was.

The face came alive on the paper so quickly that I hardly realized I was drawing it, until it was finished. Then I gazed at my creation in amazement. The lad who would rather sketch than eat had never drawn anything this good before.

I went over the railings.

"Hey! Mister! Come and see what I've drawn!"

The stranger was filling a torn rucksack with scattered tins, the ones spilled onto the road during his lizard ride.

"Hi!" he called upwards. He gestured at the fallen tins. "What a mess! Thought I'd try walking on someone else's feet for a change. It nearly worked!" And he added half an explanation, "Just looking for someplace new. My name's Happy Gumption."

Anybody calling himself Happy Gumption had to be an aged hippy, or a crazy, or a guy who liked reading dictionaries. Somebody weird enough to need no further explanation.

I held up his portrait.

"Look! I've drawn you! I'm Timothy Stedding, and I'm an artist!" My name was only a borrowed one, like my claim of being a genuine artist. I couldn't actually remember what I'd been or done before.

Old Happy squinted up. He clearly had trouble focusing on the sketch, but he seemed to like it anyway.

"Why, that's a nice picture, son."

I looked at it again, feeling more pleased with myself than I had felt for months, while Happy gathered in the last of his dented food cans. Then I heard him call up again, more urgently this time.

"Timmy boy, anywhere tidy to live round here?"

Normally our secrets stayed secret, for safety, but in my rare satisfaction at the sketch I forgot to be cautious.

"Sure," I told him. "This block is as good a place as any."

"Fine! Anyone mind if I pick me a room?"

A speck of common sense penetrated my dreams of artistry. I had to warn him about the others.

"Look, it's not up to me. You'd better go down the steps—ask the Basement Gang. They might like you."

"Huh? What if they don't like me?"

Good question. The Basement Gang were keen on black leather and lethal weapons. They tolerated a few harmless neighbours like me or the two girls on the second floor—possibly because neighbours could be fed to dinosaurs first—but their tolerance had narrow limits.

"Just hope they like you," I said.

He gave me a tin which was hardly rusted at all, with a faded picture of peaches still visible on its label. I went down to the door of Du and Sylvia's flat, and gave the usual knock.

"What's wrong?" Dusanka opened the door a fraction. I could just see the ghostly outline of her face, the large round-framed spectacles, and lower down the pale muzzle of her gun.

I held out the tin. "Look, I got some peaches. Thought you and Sylvia might like them."

Du said, "Wait." My tin disappeared, and the door closed. I wished Sylvia had answered, but Du was so protective of the pale blank-eyed doll she had found and nurtured back to life that Sylvia never did answer while Du was there.

Suddenly the door opened again, and it was Sylvia herself, blonde curls and khaki dungarees, handing me back my tin with just a few peach slices left in the bottom. She looked brighter again thanks to Du's continuing efforts; she had been speaking whole sentences for weeks now. I reached forward, but she pressed a finger against my lips and stopped me.

"Thanks, Timmy. Come round again soon." The door closed.

I stood outside the door, fishing out the bits of peach and eating them one by one, breathing the air she had breathed, wondering when Du would go out scavenging next.

This was another kind of hunger. Recently I was discovering something missing from the solitary separate lives we led.

After I finished licking my fingers, I remembered that the man who had given me the tin was seeing the crowd downstairs. Maybe he would be all right.

I needn't have worried. Happy Gumption negotiated successfully with the Basement Gang, introduced himself to Du and Sylvia with old-fashioned courtesy, and chose a couple of cleanish first-floor rooms below us, all this in under half an hour.

Then he spent two days looting other buildings to furnish his new home.

Afterwards, Happy told me what had decided him to stay. Me. He had not cared at all about most of the people he'd encountered since everything happened, but he felt he could well like me. He had been amused by my sketching away as though London had not died, and by my naïve honesty to a total stranger, not even pretending to be pointing a gun at him. If someone as impractical-seeming as myself could survie around here, he'd thought, anyone could.

Later I confessed the truth to him—it was all pure luck rather than a safe neighbourhood. I wasn't really a survivor, only someone who had happened to stay alive.

He just laughed at me. Happy laughed about most things.

Happy himself was certainly a survivor. While I spent most days on my balcony and went on sketching—dreaming all the while of my ancient hero the old-man-mad-about-painting—Happy Gumption was merrily reorganising his world. For the first time since Sylvia arrived I had a new neighbour. I liked him, I found. He brushed away the horrors of his summer with a real enthusiasm for his new life.

(The summer? The deaths, of course. Sylvia's nightmares were of reptilian jaws, mine were of gunmen. Would things have been better if people had co-operated with each other? We would never know.)

For his first weeks, I was too busy improving my art to welcome Happy more than briefly. I was even eating from my hoard rather than going out for food, not that I would have seen more of Happy if I had, since our food searches were all independent. He had given me more than that one peace-offering can of fruit; he had given me a new dimension of my art. Once I'd had that magical glimpse of him riding the lizard, I found that I could draw the figures of people without trouble, without drawing them dead. I had a real dream to replace the nightmares.

I was a genuine artist at last.

So I drew everyone in our territory.

Happy himself first, then Sylvia, my little Miss Pears with her schoolgirl pink cheeks and blonde curls. Even Dusanka who looked on herself as someone above foolishness allowed me to sketch, her too: a long firm face framed by dark straight hair with those round glasses, and instead of being a cartoon character Du came out strong and capable and alive. Happy liked the picture too. This unexpected success sent me back to painting Sylvia. I captured her in water-colours, and pinned the picture unframed to the wall. While Du was out foraging Sylvia and I made love, on spread-out artist's smocks I would never wear, while her portrait smiled delicately down at us like someone else's painting.

All this happened during that long hot autumn while the world was ending, while great dinosaurs prowled the deserted streets, and we small people pretended that London was still our home.

From water-colours to acrylics (I raided art shops as often as I looted foodstores), my next portrait was old Happy in full colour. Again, head and shoulders and that brown hat like a halo, around him. It worked. I'd managed to soften the texture of his stubble and it made him look years younger. This was something else I had to show him.

As soon as the painting was dry enough I tacked a frame around it, went downstairs and knocked on his door. (We inheritors of London always locked our doors. Not so much against things which might slither or stomp in, but against other people, the ones who looked after only themselves.) After the usual rattles of home security devices Happy let me in, and motioned me towards the table.

It was only my fourth or fifth visit. Suddenly nervous of what he'd say about the picture, I pushed it into his hands without a word, and looked away.

His room was incredibly full after only a couple of weeks, its former emptiness crammed with chairs and boxes and rolls of blankets he'd scavenged from other buildings. On the table were six different brandy bottles—all empty—which he'd scavenged from other buildings. Probably there were similar junkyard rooms all across London where wanderers like Happy and me had built ourselves little nests before moving on.

I heard him laugh.

"You're doing good, Timmy. You ought to paint someone prettier 'n me, like your Sylvia say, but it's a good picture, right enough. Like the one in the galleries."

He laid down the painting carefully enough to make me feel important, then went to a tall upright refrigerator—-useless of course without electricity—and got us a couple of warm cans to celebrate the picture with. I sat down on his table and sampled sugary fizz (non-alcoholic, but not too stale) while he went on studying my portrait of him.

"It's all right," he said. "You're a real painter."

I shook my head. Bubbles tickled my nose inside. "Just learning. I do want to be a painter one day though, I really do."

"No future in it."

We both laughed.

Happy leaned back in an antique carved chair which would have cost him a fortune if he'd had to buy it. "All you want to do is paint, Timmy? Right?"

"Right, Happy." I didn't want to say why.

"Not get out of London, Timmy? Not try to save the world?"

Me? Try to save the world? How?

We didn't know what had hit us, or where the dinosaurs had come from, or why the rules of life had changed suddenly. That summer, people had got crushed and eaten, and then the dinosaurs had eaten each other. Eventually both dinosaurs and people had become few. If the country's great leaders had failed to save us, and failed to save themselves, then one half-grown apprentice painter couldn't save anybody. Better to be myself—whoever that was—and carry on with my art, rather than throw away what little life I had. I tried to explain these feelings to Happy, but he just grunted strangely at me.

"Rage, rage against the dying of the light," he said.

"You what?"

"Old age should burn and rave at close of day."

I said, "But Happy, I'm not old."

He took a drink of out-of-date fizz from his faded can, and sighed in my direction.

"No, you're not old, Timmy. I guess that makes the difference."

He looked at my portrait of an idealized Happy, his expression thoughtful for the first time since I'd met him.

"Sure, go ahead and paint. If we're not co-operating or rebuilding, at least we're not working against anyone else. It doesn't matter that we're all dying slowly here. You make art out of us, young Timmy, whether someone sees it or not. You might as well."

And that was exactly how and why I'd built my refuge here. We understood each other a little, this old-man-mad-about-living and me. In fact he'd brightened my life simply by arriving, by changing my art. Thanks to Happy there were people in my pictures now.

I gave him the painting.

So that was the first time that Happy changed my life, showing me by accident how to draw faces when he rode that ostrich lizard up the street. He could have been killed so easily.

The second time he changed his life, he nearly got *me* killed. Him and Sylvia.

One morning I was drawing her hair in pencil, trying to make the highlights seem bright yet soft, doing my sketching down on the front steps for a change. It was too early for the Basement Gang to be up. Around us in the silent gutters I saw green fronds sprouting. They didn't look like any plants I remembered. On other days I'd sketched these strange primitive growths, filling whole notebooks in a few hours, just as the old-man-mad-about-painting had done, but today Sylvia was here for me. Sylvia was small and pretty and quiet (still too quiet really, especially when remembering her summer), and she was patient enough to sit for me any morning Dusanka was away. Our being in love in a friendly sort of way helped, and I wondered if we might stay together in future, in spite of everything. Sometimes I did want there to be a future. Today I just wanted to catch the sunlight in her hair.

Unfortunately today Sylvia wanted to talk.

"Timmy, what'll we eat in the winter?"

I shrugged, not really wanting to answer since it might break my concentration. "Dinosaur steaks. First catch your dinosaur "

She took me seriously. "What'll we cook them with?"

"Oh, camping gas I suppose, if it lasts." Suddenly I realised that my pencil was doodling aimlessly. My usual two problems: trying to be too precise, and not concentrating.

I started again.

So did Sylvia.

"But Timmy, we don't see dinosaurs around here so often now. Not like it was. Don't you remember?"

"Sylvia, I don't *want* to remember!"

Just the little flashes of memory from her reminding me were bad enough. Everybody fleeing, dying the outer zones disintegrating, martial law, the centre fortified and then collapsing, only the outer suburbs still habitable by us few drifters. All that summer, great scaly monsters had roamed across the ruins of London. But now there weren't so many people around, and there weren't many food caches still unplundered either.

It was unlike Sylvia to express concern about this, my sweet impractical Sylvia. Her flatmate was the one who monitored the situation and made recommendations. I asked, "What's Du been telling you now?"

"She came back last night with practically nothing. She was very tired."

Du must have been very tired indeed, to let Sylvia sneak out to me unchaperoned.

I'd had problems finding food myself lately. We solitary scavengers tended not to give away trade secrets to each other, but the growing shortage of findables was no secret. Certainly the Basement Gang had been everywhere before me, everywhere that wasn't guarded. Any day now someone commodity-oriented might abandon the unspoken truce about the water-tower and seize it. Pity I couldn't think of anywhere better to move to. There was nowhere better, of course.

I said, "Well have to eat those dinosaur steaks I mentioned—raw."

I made a joke of it again, but Sylvia's unusually earnest mood was beginning to needle me. My sketching suffered.

"Hold still a moment, Beautiful."

Another new sheet. Try her hair another way. Shading the curls, breaking into dots at the highlights? Not with a 2H pencil. Maybe I'd better do a bunch of quick sketches in different styles, to see if any of them worked

Then we saw the baby triceratops.

It was wandering down the street. It hadn't noticed us. Probably it wasn't a true triceratops, since it had only one stubby little horn, but otherwise it had the bony rough scales and the general heavy build of one of the family. I saw it approaching behind Sylvia quite slowly, like a giant turtle-shelled hippo, pausing to graze the ferny weeds along the road. I put down my pad for a better look.

Beside me, someone else materialised.

"See that, you kids?" Happy Gumption put a broad and not very clean hand on my shoulder. "You two wanted dinosaur steaks, now's your chance."

How long had old Hippy Happy been listening to us? I waved my 2H at him severely, and then his comment "now's your chance" got through to me. The small mountain ambled nearer towards us. I realised what Happy meant me to do, and I wished I was back up on my balcony, or preferably on some other balcony several miles away.

"Steaks? That?"

I was an artist not a hunter. (The young-man-mad-about-sketching, not any young-man-mad-about-killing.) I told Happy that to his wrinkly old face. He might have listened if Sylvia hadn't interrupted me.

"Timmy, can't you see he's right? We've *got* to start hunting proper food now, before we all starve. You'll have to catch it!"

"She means kill it," said Happy.

I didn't need the translation. Kill that? A monster with enough meat to flatten any little human being who came within leaning distance? I wished Dusanka (now sleeping all innocently after last night's safari) had kept her worries to herself. But Sylvia was looking at me with her baby blue eyes at their widest, and Happy's great hand was squeezing my shoulder meaningfully, and even me myself . . . well, I'd been wondering lately how soon I'd have to start killing food instead of merely stealing it.

All this time the baby triceratops was nibbling away at green stuff, nearby, not comprehending that we were discussing impending doom for it. The very slowness of the monster made refusal of the idea difficult.

"All right," I said, without hiding my reluctance. If this was co-operation, what people had to do to survive in the modern world, I didn't like it. Co-operation meant the nearest able-bodied sucker got the dirty job, as far as I could see. But I still loved them.

They both beamed at me. I warned them, "I've never done this before."

"We ain't asking you to be a brain surgeon or anythin' technical," said Happy.

"I'll help you," said Sylvia.

She was about the same size as one of the beast's legs, only slimmer. I was lucky the triceratops wasn't full-grown. Some baby. Although, when I looked properly the creature did seem slow and clumsy compared to the big bipedal dinosaurs, the real killers. Surely I could tackle it on my own. It was very slow. Should I call out the Basement Gang for extra manpower? No, they mightn't be interested, and anyway I needed to learn to do this myself.

"Here goes," I said.

If I told myself loudly enough that I was ten feet tall and invulnerable, I might just believe it.

The armoured herbivores did tend to be slow. I had enough time to go indoors, collect ropes and knives and stuff, and come back to find the monster still only just past our block. Somehow I wished it had gone faster down the empty street. I definitely didn't want to do this.

If I live long enough, I'm going to paint some pictures about **How Not To Kill A Dinosaur**. How I tied a rope to a street lamp column, and tied the other end around the dinosaur's neck. The dino kept moving. The column bent and fell over.

(The crash was what woke up the Basement Gang.)

Another picture: how I stabbed my longest and sharpest kitchen knife into its throat, and the knife broke.

How I chopped at the scales of its neck with a meat cleaver, my whole body tensed to run as I hacked away, until the dark blood came pouring out all over me in warm horrible stickiness, and the dinosaur didn't notice. (Other than moving slightly, as if to get away from whatever was tickling under its chin.)

How I jumped up and down, and kicked and swore at its legs.

How the Basement Gang found me sawing off the monster's head with a timber saw, or trying to.

Perhaps I won't paint the pictures. The memories are still too vivid, too awful. As I stood there sawing frantically I finally penetrated the neck armour, and reached tissues which contained nerve endings. Then the triceratops did notice me.

It jumped!

While Sylvia shouted helpfully from the doorway, and the Basement Gang lounged on the steps sadistically enjoying the show, the triceratops displayed a bizarre talent for dinosaur tap-dancing. It twiddled its feet in a peculiar sideways shuffle, probably the way it dodged charging tyrannosaurs, but more importantly it whipped its massive head round towards me faster than I'd thought possible, and butted my stomach—hard. Luckily for me its nose was only that small bony bump, not a full adult horn. Even so I still folded up, winded. A scream like an old steam train nearly deafened me. Evidently the triceratops was annoyed. When I could receive sound again I heard someone shouting at me.

"Go it, Timmy!"

I glimpsed Happy Gumption dancing with excitement, but I shouldn't have looked at him. Next second, the baby triceratops was shoulder-charging me. I nearly got away despite the distraction from Happy, but found myself tangled up in a loose rope, the one which still
dangled from the beast's neck after the street lamp episode.

I ended up tied tight to the shoulder of one demented and very furious dinosaur.

Everything got confused and blurry around me. I remembered my earlier thought. I was an artist, not a hunter. This shouldn't have happened to me. Trapped against rough dinosaur scales, I pushed and struggled with the rope. Of course I'd dropped the saw. Desperately I tried to hold myself back to stop the neck ruff crushing my chest.

The Basement Gang saved me.

They shot it.

When I'd stopped shaking and rubbing my bruises and persuading Sylvia to patch up my messier injuries, I hobbled around to face Happy Gumption.

"You got me into this! You nearly got me killed!"

"The only way to learn, Timmy boy. That's how to get fresh meat!"

"But I'm an artist! I don't want to bother with eating!"

Of course Happy was right and I was wrong, although several days passed before I would admit it. Eventually I scavenged myself a rather businesslike gun, a rifle from an old Army checkpoint, and found I felt more comfortable with it around. Then I realised that Happy Gumption had changed my life a second time.

But meanwhile, the Basement Gang cut up the carcass with

petrol-driven chainsaws from their toy box. They liked that bit. Generously they let Du and Sylvia and me and Happy join in. This was rare neighbourliness for them; maybe Happy's little lectures about co-operation had been having some effect. I discovered a strange feeling of almost enjoying working with them. Together we took the meat off the bones, picked out the bullets, dried the chunks and salted them and locked them away in our freezers which didn't freeze. Happy said he admired the way Dusanka organised us to tackle all the jobs properly. This was the first time we neighbours had really combined this closely to tackle anything, and I wondered if we ever would again.

We carried the bones and offal ten streets away, dumped them, and heard distant growls and crunching all night afterwards. I barricaded my door solidly for a week in our own street, seagulls and foxes mopped up the small scraps, but the bloodstains stayed, as without running water we had no way of washing them off. (Without running water we had other problems too, mainly sanitation, which was why we drifters generally changed houses so frequently.) So our road had large fading bloodstains which we scuffed over with dirt, and I had three sketchpads full of people chopping up dinosaur meat. I had an uneasy feeling that I might be doing more chopping than drawing in the future.

We were living on borrowed time, as Du kept saying. She was a worrier. Happy called on her most days, I gathered, because he thought she needed cheering up. I went on drawing and painting Sylvia for several more days. From the balcony we would look down on the Basement Gang draped across the pavement like black lizards sunning themselves, but otherwise we didn't see people much. I restarted my scavenging trips and did meet a few other folk, had friendly words with some and had to dodge bullets from the rest.

With everyone the message was the same. London was running out of food.

I took time off from painting. From the military cache I'd helped myself to that high-powered rifle, and I started doing target practice in a sound-proof basement.

Happy claimed I was becoming more normal.

The empty husks of buildings felt even emptier, while the strange plants were growing higher in the street. It rained. Occasional carnosaurs would snuffle at the doors and perhaps hang around all day before moving off at night. The bloodstains in the street hadn't been hidden well enough. A few of the Basement Gang emigrated, and most of our less visible neighbours went missing. I suppose they tried to get out into the countryside, although life out there was rumoured to be even worse, with more dinosaurs and fighting, and less food. But me, Timmy, still hoping somehow to become an old-man-mad-about-painting, I stayed on in London. Dry hard-to-chew triceratops meat became intensely boring and repulsive to eat, but it was better than nothing.

Dusanka came calling.

Seeing Dusanka at my door was an omen of bigger troubles ahead. Du had no social smalltalk and her only conversations were about Serious Problems. She regarded the time Sylvia and I spent together as a Medium-Serious Problem.

"Come in," I said dubiously. It was evening and she was alone. She'd never visited me in my room before, despite my saying she could call any time.

I closed the door behind her and lit an extra candle. (Sylvia thought I was romantic using candles, but really I just couldn't stand fiddling about with paraffin lamps.) Dusanka stood in the middle of the floor, surrounded by my easels and cartons and piles of art books, clearly disapproving of my lack of Sensible Furniture.

She said, "You're seeing too much of Sylvia."

Which was clearly a crime to Dusanka, whose particular obsession was that the blank-eyed waif she had found needed protecting and bringing back to normality.

See too much of her? I was actually seeing less of my sweet Pre-Raphaelite angel, now that I'd started target shooting. I bristled where normally I would have shrugged.

Harsh words on both sides.

Then a calm period when I managed to speak.

True (I said), I might be distracting both Sylvia and myself from the Important Business of surviving. But Sylvia and I really did care for each other very much, and I was trying hard to become more practically-minded. I offered my gun as proof.

Du hadn't realised that I could go in for self-analysis. She didn't understand artists. She certainly wouldn't have understood the old-man-mad-about-painting who occupied my thoughts, a man of astonishing genius, yet who at seventy years old had wished to live longer, that he might start achieving something worthwhile. I was still only sixteen, probably.

At least I was old enough inside to know that loving Sylvia might not last.

To my amazement Du simply nodded.

"I see, Timmy."

She did look very tired, I noticed. She must be older than I'd thought.

"I'm going out to find more food," she said. "Do you . . . Do you want to come?"

The thought of roaming the night with someone else sort of scared me. I didn't realise just then what it must have cost Du, fiercely independent Du, to ask me along. "Er—No, thanks. Got a couple of sketches to finish off."

I thought she was going to explode, but instead she made a vague wave over my scattered artwork, nodded again, and murmured, "How can you keep on doing this?"

The art was my own Serious Problem, not Du's. I was a young-man-mad-about-painting. Without that, I was nothing. How else could I stand being one small insignificant boy about to vanish from the ruins of London? But I couldn't say that to Du.

"I like my sketching and painting," I told her. I looked at her face, all thin cheeks and short grave lines of her eyes and lips emphasised by the candlelight. "What do you like to do, Du?"

"Survive," said Dusanka.

I couldn't answer that. I let her out, and lay awake thinking half the night.

I was hungry.

Under my blankets and coats, I kept thinking about me and Sylvia.

Where we were going. Where we couldn't go, in the emptiness that was London and our future and our lives.

Du didn't approve of us, but she had stopped disapproving, I thought. None of my thoughts helped. In the middle of the night I made myself put aside thoughts of Sylvia until tomorrow, but that only left me alone to face the nightmares. I didn't want that. I pushed the nightmares away in the only way I knew: by looking up at the dark ceiling and picturing a face there.

A wrinkled, aged face. A kindly, lively little old face.

The face of the old-man-mad-about-painting.

He had been a real person, best known by the name of Hokusai. He had lived in nineteenth-century Tokyo, then called Edo. He was a compulsive painter and illustrator and sketcher of everything he could see or imagine.

His art was full of contrasts, of emotions, ideas, people, and that Oriental sense of the frailty of human hopes. When some of his pictures appeared in the West, the old slow evolution of representational art here was shattered forever by a sudden explosion of new colours and forms. I thought of him as the greatest artist who had ever lived, and I knew that the mass-produced colour prints which struck the old fossilised European art like something from another planet were by no means his most perfect work. His friends had gathered his cast-off sketchbooks into published collections, in the same way that friends of Shakespeare had collected and printed Shakespeare's scattered playscripts (or so Happy had told me once.) I would meet this old man in my dreams and be humble,

Yet Hokusai had thought of himself as a perpetual student, with so much to learn even at the end of his long life. And his wisdom was almost forgotten. I'd been unable to find any decent book of his pictures anywhere in my scavenging of the suburbs. Van Gogh's brief year or two of insane daubs everywhere, but Hokusai's lifetime of exploring humanity nowhere. Perhaps my ideas about him were only half truths, picked up from picture captions and bits of magazine articles, but he was still surely an immortal for those creations of his. Red Fuji. The immaculate duck and the sinking melon rind. The Great Wave.

I wanted to be like him, or wanted to *be* him.

Surviving was just a way of getting there. So was Sylvia.

The trouble with Sylvia was, I loved her.

And the trouble with surviving was, it was going to get much harder.

Half awake and half dreaming, I could listen to the old-man-mad-about-painting whispering in my head, telling me things I couldn't have thought of for myself He would tell me that everything was impermanent, and every ambition was impossible to achieve fully. One might only achieve at best a compromise, which might for a time look like success.

This was a dreadful thing for me to think in the middle of the night, alone, aged sixteen, but having lived a long nightmare lifetime last summer. It must have been just as dreadful a thing to think on a sleepless night in ancient Edo, alone, aged seventy or more, having lived in this night-mare world where the best of everything always died.

The only thing which could make it bearable was painting pictures.

Pictures did not *have* to die.

Eventually I fell asleep, still only sixteen, still in the ruins of London where drifters squatted amid emptiness, and dinosaurs prowled.

Morning came.

Sylvia called me down to her room.

In the shadows Dusanka sat hunched in a chair, notebook in hand, look-ing like a pale-eyed ghost out of Munch. She saw us together and nodded strangely. "We need more food," said Du.

What else could I have said but, "I'll look for some?"

Sylvia spoke to me outside. She said, when I came back we would face the winter together. We'd find a well for water, and seek out food stores. Collect seeds. Find dinosaur eggs and raise baby ones for meat, perhaps. (Sylvia's eyes were bright and alert as she spoke. I could see that she wanted to *learn*.) She talked of hunting, of making pit-traps in drained swimming pools, of incubating eggs with heated bricks in cloths. Sylvia seemed to think I had a day job ready as a dinosaur farmer. "But that's for the future, Timmy. We've got to get through the winter first. I'll be waiting for you "

With my head buzzing from her chatter, thinking dazedly that my world was still changing, I went out through the cobwebby gloom of our bottom corridor (the one the Basement Gang didn't use). My future started here.

I took about two steps along the street before a familiar shout came from above. "Going some place, young Timmy?"

I called back to Happy that I'd told the girls I'd get some food.

"Hang on a minute! I'll come with you!" Happy vanished from his bal-cony. When he reappeared beside me he explained, "I heard you talking to Syl is down there. Reckon you could use some company

today."

"No," I said. "I never have company."

"Don't be like that, Timmy! It's daylight! You're not mad at me 'cause I overheard you?"

So what he'd been eavesdropping? All survivors did. That wasn't why I didn't want him to come.

I'd have spent all day there arguing with him if Sylvia hadn't come out. "Go along with him, Timmy. I'd be happier if you did."

Something I'd noticed about our little group: Happy always backed up Du, Sylvia always backed up Happy. Between them, they always got me putting down my brushes or charcoal and doing what they wanted instead. Come to think of it, I always did what Sylvia wanted. And Du hadn't complained when I preferred sketching to going scavenging with her . . .

I realised the four of us had become a group.

It felt right.

"You go with him, Timmy. I'll look after Du."

So that was how I headed north with old Happy Gumption. Both of us wore combat jackets with webbing and all sorts of weird gear attached; I had a pistol at my belt and the rifle slung behind my shoulders. We looked like guerrillas or freedom fighters out on patrol, which in a way we were.

I was here patrolling into my future.

Was this better than sketching the present?

The streets were sunlit and weedgrown. Down a number of roads I saw that the strange vegetation had pushed up through the paving blocks and grown tall. A few old cars had been pushed aside by browsing dinosaurs, but otherwise everything had stayed the same between my expeditions. It did look different in daylight, though, sort of starker. Happy kept glancing on all sides for watchers. So did I. We should have been doing this on a soft moonlit night, not in the glare of midmorning brightness, and not together. But it didn't feel as bad as I'd expected, this working as a team. Of course, I'd come out here because I wanted to help the others.

Happy was here because he was crazy.

We spent a long time just moving outwards, trying to avoid any place which might be inhabited. The first building we decided to investigate, over two miles away, was a former clothing factory. Its canteen had been looted.

"Somebody beat us to it," said Happy.

"Better see if they missed anything," I said, although I doubted it. I stared unhopefully around the dusty shambles, the broken plates and the dried-out woodlice, the ad poster of a girl drinking a milk shake—a good painting, but badly torn. A musty damp smell made me breathe carefully. In the general debris I recognised the trademarks of several individual scavengers. The way drawers were pulled out and smashed here, the way a pile of excreta was left in the corner there. All the drinking glasses gone.

Hints someone had slept here. Floorboards ripped up by someone else. But the different personalities responsible were familiar to me from other looted sites, even if the people themselves were unknown. Some of them might be in the Basement Gang. One of them was almost certainly Du. All of them—us—had simply taken food and left only wreckage. It was all so ugly, so empty of meaning.

I sighed. Sylvia was right. We weren't meant to live like this. We could find a better way.

As I'd suspected, Happy and I found nothing edible in those dusty corners. We moved on.

Twenty minutes later.

We tried a large executive house, a clean building of neat modern bricks where the furnishings were relatively undamaged. Happy and I practically trod on tiptoe not to leave marks. Only the front door was broken. Everything else seemed unnaturally new and tidy, like illustrations in a brochure. The people must have moved in only a few months before the dinosaurs arrived. Other looters must have respected its newness, for they had searched it without causing much damage. Former neighbours, perhaps. Someone might have guarded it for months before giving up.

Of course all the food had gone.

As we left the neat house, trampling over the ferns and horsetails spreading across its empty lawn, Happy grew thoughtful.

"A nice place, Timmy. That was the way the future was supposed to be, only it didn't last." He glanced up at the sky reflectively. "All our future gone. No fireside, no books, no wine or music. No information highway. No pilots of the purple twilight, drooping down with costly bales—"

I shook my head. "I don't think the last helicopter drops got this far."

"Never mind, Timmy boy. Just—hey, when I was young, the future was meant to be better than the past. Only, it didn't work out like that."

I had my own picture of Happy's past, possibly an English professor somewhere, probably a good father to someone. All smashed to pieces. I felt really close to him now. His determination to enjoy his present life was his way of painting out what he'd lost, just as those posers in the Basement Gang had chosen to act out their lasertag fantasies rather than live with their memories.

I hacked my way through a smashed security gate into a garden of feathery cycad trees, and thought of the food we weren't finding.

It occurred to me that clinging to buildings was wrong, that Sylvia's new plans were right, and our future lay among these cycads and fronds and other new growths filling the emptiness around us.

We spent the next couple of hours going through lots more homes, shops, even offices and depots. All ransacked. Not even spoilt food on the shelves or in the deep-freeze cabinets. Tumbler-stealer had been here, and Drawer-smasher, and others. Pets had vanished long ago, picked off by people or by hungry reptiles. Nothing was left for us.

As we emerged from someone's garden fallout shelter, empty like everywhere else, Happy remarked, "Times is getting hard, Timmy. Say, you tell me boy, why are we like those old dinosaurs millions of years ago, when their nuclear winter started?"

He meant the cometary-impact winter which had wiped them out, I thought, but I wasn't sure enough to correct him. Was he attempting a joke?

"Don't know, Happy. Why are we like those old dinosaurs?"

"Hah! 'Cause we're all dead too, only we don't know it yet! Haw-haw!" Some joke. At least it pleased old Happy.

I knew how the old dinosaurs had gone, but not how the new ones had come. The government hadn't told us. Probably nobody knew. A slice of the late Mesozoic had landed on us somehow, but in all the panic and dying the details had got lost. Now there were just a few drifters around picking up what was left. Us and the dinosaurs. The dinosaurs of London.

I said, "Let's head for the park, Happy. There's bound to be a park."

"Sure there is, Timmy. I know these parts."

I'd heard him chanting street names but they hadn't meant anything to me. Still, the two of us were a team now. He had the knowledge, and I had the guns. I said, "Just lead me to a park, Happy."

Where there was green stuff growing, I thought, there would be something else eating it. Something we could eat.

I was right.

The park was totally overgrown. The new plants had shot up quickly, and were spreading out past the park wall—what I could see of it—into the street. The whole place looked like a jungle of giant ferns. Rather than plunge straight in we climbed up to a nearby roof, using the fire escape because the inside had a worked-over appearance, and we found ourselves a good viewpoint. I lay near the roof edge, on weathered concrete amid chimneys and ventilation shafts, feeling hungry but ignoring it. When I looked down I saw the thing we'd come for.

The green jungle seemed high and solid, except for a couple of missing strips like trial mowings through an overgrown lawn. The strips were the paths left by grazing dinosaurs.

The strips meant food was here.

Happy pointed to the nearest gap in the fern trees. The creature cutting the gap was far too massive for us to think of attacking it, mach less think of carrying it home. I saw a broad grey back between a long neck and an equally long tail. It stood within the fast-sprouting fronds and swung its little head through the greenery like a razor slicing through stubble. Before long it had eaten everything within reach. Then it took a plodding step forward so it could reach some more.

"Too big for us, Happy."

"Keep looking, Timmy. A big one means little ones somewhere." I looked, but my eyes kept coming back to that big one.

What a simple life for a dinosaur. Surrounded by food, it simply moved forward every few minutes and kept on chomping away. So easy. Until, back at the end of the Age of Reptiles, dinosaurs found themselves in a world where the rules had changed. They stepped forward as usual, but there was nothing more within reach.

So they died.

Somehow I didn't feel like drawing the dinosaur. How would the old-man-mad-about-painting have portrayed it? As a monster? Or as a frightened lost giant?

In my hand was a sketchpad. I still wanted to draw, to be immortal. I wondered if I could draw Sylvia from memory, here on the roof.

"Timmy boy ! You're not watching for meat!"

"Anything coming?"

"Nope."

I gazed down at the greenery for a while, trying to look beyond the colours and the textures. All Happy and I had to do—as simple as what a dinosaur had to do—was wait until something smaller moved down there.

Then kill it.

Not just for me, for Sylvia and Du and Happy as well. I liked to think that Du, at last, trusted me.

The day had become very hot and steamy, up above the new jungle. A seagull landed beside us. It eyed me calculatingly, its webbed feet planted on the very edge of the concrete rim. Swiftly I drew it on my sketchpad, but couldn't quite convey the immense emptiness it was perched beside. Then it gave up on us providing any tit-bits, and flew away.

I hadn't even thought of shooting it, although one day I might be very glad of seagull for dinner.

The sketch showed only the seagull. Not the great gap of the world below . . . I tore off the sheet, crumpled it and tossed it over the edge.

"Timmy! Look there!"

Far beyond my failed sketch floating from the roof, I saw a small yellow head appearing between the fronds.

"See it now, Timmy?"

"Yes!"

For an instant I saw it clearly. A relatively small dinosaur, an upright biped like the one I'd seen Happy riding down the street on his first day with us. Struthiomimus, perhaps. I only knew a few dino names and used them for anything which looked about right. But I knew this dinosaur whatever its name was just the right size for us.

Picture the two of us rushing down the fire escape. The team. Old leatherfringed Happy and young Timmy the artist, both trying to run light-footed down iron steps so no clatter would frighten off the struthiomimus. Sylvia should see me now, I thought. I'm doing this for her. For all of us. And I'll do whatever she wants later. Down we go

Then we were at ground level, heading for the gateway into the green forest which was sprouting within our silent London.

I pulled the high-powered rifle from my back. It was already loaded with the very latest armour piercing bullets, courtesy of the Basement Gang. I didn't want to waste too much ammunition since I might never get any more.

As we peered around the pillar of the park gates Happy held me back. Before us, emerald tree ferns were almost sparkling with colour, bright and glossy, while behind us was the grey dust of an abandoned street where fernlike things were sprouting higher.

"Careful!" whispered Happy. "Might be other hunters!"

I shook my head. I'd sketched London too many times not to feel the difference people made. There were no people here.

Just dinosaurs.

"We're on our own, Happy. Come on."

We went in.

Through giant green trunks and fronds we stepped along warily, caricature white hunters in a Douanier Rousseau dream jungle. I should have been drawing pictures, not being in them, but drawing was a luxury left over from a previous age. Ahead of us, sooner than I expected, was a caricature tiger with zigzag yellow stripes, except that this tiger had no fur and no tiger head. From its shoulders grew a black-eyed snake. Its tail was the tail of a striped dragon. It was huge.

How could I ever paint the big stripey monster, the warmth of the jungle, the glowing greenery, the brown furry tree trunks, the glitter of insect wings? Even the rich greenhouse smell of the place was overwhelming.

I blinked myself into being a hunter not an artist. The scale changed. Now I saw the tree ferns and cycads as only medium-sized, the struthiomimus stooping down as only small. I'd looked too closely into the picture.

But Happy Gumption was running forward already. He held a wadded-up fishing net, scavenged from some nautical theme bar along with his brandy bottles, and had raised the net ready to throw it to entangle the lizard—but he was crashing clumsily through the ferns, and the crisp stalks were smashing under his feet. Noise! Maybe I was too slow and he was too fast—

"Happy! Wait!"

It was all going wrong. Happy in my line of fire, blocking my aim. The rifle too heavy for speed and accuracy together. The saurian moving swiftly, its snake head darting round. I could see teeth flashing as its jaws opened, and wicked claws outspread on its forearms. It wasn't the sort Happy had tried riding at all.

Of course his net got tangled in the long primitive branches, and fell short. He was too old for these games. The dinosaur grabbed at the moving figure it could see approaching. It could see food.

I knew what to do.

I watched my hand pulling the trigger, I sketched myself in my head as I fired. From the gun barrel to the lizard forehead I painted in the line of armour-piercing bullets. I always had a good eye for line.

Happy and the dinosaur went down together.

The dinosaur wouldn't die. Its head was blown away and still it went on tearing and kicking at Happy. He hadn't had a chance to defend himself, the dino had turned on him so fast.

I reached the tangled mass of scales and Happy among the impossible ferns. Its arm twitched as I chopped it away to release Happy. Was that the thing's blood or his own everywhere? I felt sick as I pulled him free and laid him down. I'd seen too many people like this before, this summer.

In that second the whole world changed again around me. Happy lay stretched on trampled greenery, and the dying monster went on twitching and jerking. I could have painted my whole future from that second on.

How I buried Happy under the floorboards of a neat house, because I didn't want him trapped under an alien jungle.

And how I carved the lizard body into joints of foul meat. And carried it home.

And found a note—"Sylvia and I have left. Dusanka."

And lived the rest of my life on a balcony, painting and not eating, growing thinner and emptier and weaker until I could no longer hold a brush, but merely imagined the pictures I was painting, pictures in my mind, pictures high above the dinosaurs of London.

I saw all this as I stood there among the ferns, every frond and branch bright green and shining around me, the twitching of the dinosaur slowing as it died. I bent down over Happy again.

He looked up at me and winked.

"I was snapping its neck, Timmy. You could've saved your bullets."

"Now you tell me! Get up, you old fraud!"

Afterwards we cut up the lizard meat, and we discussed how we start ranching dinosaurs, right here in our jungle which had once been London.

LOVE IN LIMBO

Dan Morgan

LIMBO [L. ABL. OF LIMBUS.] The borderline or uttermost limit of Hell, the abode of souls to whom the benefits of redemption could not be applied.

Nancy was the best thing that had happened to me since my execution. When I met her she was fresh out of her orientation period—what we call a Limbo virgin. Slim, blonde, with deep blue eyes and the delicately boned face of an angel she was the fulfilment of a long cherished dream. Even more of a miracle was the instant empathy that grew into a steadily burning flame of love during the following months.

Normally we were completely content with each other's company, but on that evening we decided to go along to the observation lounge for an hour before she went on shift. It was a special occasion; her first experience of Fiesta in Limbo. It was a first for me too in a sense. This time I would be able to watch the sordid transactions from a newly detached viewpoint, almost—God help me!—one of superior disgust.

Nancy's viewpoint? It was easy see that she found the Bacchanalian scene fascinating. In her innocence she had yet to understand its obscene implications. The lowest, dirtiest, ugliest crew member from the maintenance ship was king for those four days and nights. Showered with drink, food and sexual favors he was debauched with all the unearthly delights Limbo had to offer. The crew could take nothing back to Earth with them apart from their memories of satiation. But that was sufficient to make men—and women, of course—queue up to sign on for what would otherwise have been considered a boring milk run.

Every six months we, the inmates of Limbo, pleasured ourselves in the novelty of these different bodies. But that was only part of it. Without exception our number one obsession was our search for the selves that had been stolen from us through the scrambling effect of *Mattertrans.* The presence of these visitors gave us the opportunity to gorge ourselves on the fresh fruit of their minds, devouring every last trivial detail of life on Earth. Through them we tried to reach across the void and touch a world we had lost.

The observation lounge was a huge dome laid out like a tropical garden. Tall palms grew there, healthy vines that bore purple grapes, profligate bougainvilla and the fairy bells of pink and blue fuchsia cascading overhead. *Everything* grew there in profusion—except the human soul, which shrivels . . .

Normally we would sit for hours, drinking too much, popping whatever lifters were available and watching the vast panorama of space wheeling majestically past. Most of us would be searching for the distant blue marble that might be Earth . . . and our lost selves. Later we would retire in groups of two or more to find further oblivion in the sad pleasures of our bodies.

Not me, not now . . . Nancy was special and we were too much, too exclusively in love to share with anyone. So much in love that for the time being at least my own preoccupation with the search seemed to have faded slightly.

But tonight was Fiesta. A million-watt sound system pounded out a mindless jog ditty sung by Happy Girl Blaze and a piping chorus of clockwork mice. The music was a fitting accompaniment to the scamperings from table to table and the chatter of propositioning and counter-propositioning between my fellow halflings and the lordly scum of Earth.

Nancy noticed him first. He sat alone at a table about five meters from us, unheeding of the chitterings of proposal in his ear as a pink marble statue. Both of his hamlike forearms rested squarely on the tabletop and he was staring at us with pale, bulging eyes. The shiny pinkness of his skin made me think of one of those bugs that fasten themselves into the flesh of their victims and suck their life's blood.

But my natural feeling of revulsion was overlaid by a curious sense of familiarity. I found myself staring back at this strange creature, trying to remember where I had seen him before. The last Fiesta, perhaps? Or—my stomach lurched sickeningly as the uninvited thought arrived—*back on Earth?*

"Why is he staring at us that way?" Nancy's hand moved to clasp mine.

I shrugged. "Maybe he fancies one of us and isn't quite sure of the form."

"One of us?" Her eyes widened in puzzlement.

I smiled my appreciation of her naivety. "Well, *you,* obviously. You're the prettiest."

She shuddered. "Bob—don't even say it. Those eyes . . . and those hands—like bunches of pink sausages."

"Hold on now," I chided. "Aren't you the girl who talks about all human beings as God's creatures, no matter how they look?"

Two parallel lines etched into the creamy smoothness of her forehead as she tried to concentrate on looking at me. She was having trouble avoiding the horrible magnetism of those protuberant eyes

"Bob, don't laugh at me." Her voice was husky with fear. "But I have a feeling that he *isn't* one of God's creatures."

"I'll admit he's not about to win any beauty contest, but he looks human enough to me."

Nancy sighed. "You're right, of course. I'm just being silly. Perhaps it's the sight of all this . . . " She waved her hand, taking in the scene around us, with its seething, flesh-market atmosphere. She glanced at her watch. "I think I'd better be going now, anyway. I'm on shift in twenty minutes and there are a couple of things I have to do first." She rose to her feet.

I pushed my chair back "I'll walk along with you."

"No—you stay here." Her voice was suddenly precise, definite.

"When shall I see you? Maybe I could meet you when you come off?"

"No—I don't think that would be a good idea," she said.

She was right, of course. Six hours close to the subsonic organ bass growling of the *Mattertrans* generators never failed to shake and scramble the very structure of the mind leaving your head at the end of a shift filled with a dull despair. The only way out of that was to take a strong jolt of Euphoprine and that wasn't always entirely reliable, sometimes pushing the psyche to the edge of mania.

"I'll call you tomorrow," I said.

EDITED BY PHILIP HARBOTTLE AND SEAN WALLACE

"Yes—do that."

I watched proudly as Nancy's long-legged figure walked swiftly out of the lounge ignoring a spattering of hopeful solicitings. I was very conscious that she had brought something new and fresh into my life, a relief from the endless, hopeless search for my lost self.

The people of Limbo have no past. Sometimes there remained a few tatters of what might be either real or pseudo memories. To make sense of such poor materials was like trying to rewrite **WAR AND PEACE** with the help of only a few shredded pages, a word here, and a sentence there. Hopeless . . . That was why I, like every other person in Limbo, was obsessed with the desire to discover the identity of that other person I had been back on Earth. The person who no longer existed, whose atomic structure had been destroyed by the action of the Mattertrans field as it sent me into Limbo.

"Hallo there, Chuck. Mind if I sit down?"

The pink, bug-man was standing by Nancy's empty chair. His body filled his light grey off-duty uniform to bursting point and there were dark patches of sweat spreading from beneath his armpits. His red, wet lips were stretched sideways in a smile and as he spoke again I caught a glimpse of greyish teeth that were very small and pointed like tacks.

"I said, mind if I sit down, Chuck?" he repeated.

So it had been *me* he had been watching, after all.

"Suit yourself, but I may as well tell you from the start you picked the wrong guy," I said. My inclinations have never run down that particular branch line, but there were plenty of people around who would have been pleased to accommodate him.

Come to think of it, there seemed to be a larger than expected percentage of queens on Limbo. Perhaps the homosexual aspect of their personalities was so strong that it was capable of surviving even the scrambling effect of *Mattertrans.* On the other hand, it could be just another example of the implacable benevolence of the Welfare Department; an attempt to remedy the sexual imbalance of our community, which seemed to maintain a constant 70/30 male to female ratio.

"I don't think so, Chuck," he said, putting his drink on the table and easing himself into Nancy's chair.

Those teeth should have prepared me for the carrion reek of his breath. "Now look, feller, we like to make you people welcome here, but there are limits . . ."

"Take it easy, Chuck." He leaned even closer, smoothing one pink hand over his hairless, sweating scalp.

"What's the matter with you? Don't they teach you bums back on Earth to read anymore?" I tapped the yellow tag over my left breast pocket. "My name is Robert Morris."

"Maybe that's what they call you now," he said, with a broad wink. "As far as I'm concerned you're still old Charlie Radmeyer from downtown LA."

It took some time for the significance of his words to penetrate my annoyance . . . And another long pause before the pounding of my heart slowed down enough for me to be able to make a reply.

"You *knew* me back on Earth?" I managed at last.

"Sure, I knew you. We were like brothers, you and me. Grew up in the same neighborhood, played together, went to school, dated the same girls . . . "

Me, and this pink-shelled bug—the same girls? It was difficult to believe, and yet why should he lie to me? What possible advantage could there be to him in doing so?

"I've got a couple of home videos and a whole stack of holos back in my bunk on board the *Charon*," he said. "Brought them along just in case I struck lucky." He surveyed me appraisingly, his pink pumpkin of a head canted to one side on its stubby neck. "Can't get over finding you first shot like this. I mean you could have been out on Thule, Alpha or any of those other terminals away to hell and gone . . . "

I sat very still, my mind trying to cope with the idea that the key to my personal obsession had somehow dropped into my lap.

Limbo had once been a simple hunk of rock, an asteroid, but they bored out its interior like a Gouda cheese to provide anchor points for a honeycomb structure of tubes and bubbles proliferating in all directions. Seen from an approaching ship I guessed that it must look like a gigantic web spun by a demented spider. None of us inmates had ever seen *that* view of our prison. We had travelled by a swifter route, along the beam of the *Mattertrans*.

We had suffered Capital Punishment without Death. Or at least that was the way it was supposed to be. The distinction between cutting a human being off from his past and killing him outright was one which had been argued in tedious detail over the years by the inmates of Limbo. Was I, the Robert Morris who sat here at this moment, really that other man who once lived on Earth? Or was I just a kind of paraphrase, a creature molded to his matrix out of random atoms?

Mattertrans was a perfect, economical means of transferring inanimate objects, metal, even foodstuffs from one corner of the solar system to another. But its effect on the complex organic computer of the brain ruled it out as a means of human transportation in the normal course of events.

It hadn't been easy to find people willing to man the isolated terminals like Limbo which acted as massive warehouses and distribution realize for the products of a score of Federation worlds. Then some genius in the Welfare Department hit on the idea that instead of executing its murderers and traitors, Earth could send them through the *Mattertrans* and put them to useful work. The scheme worked well—apart from the unfortunate ten percent who were seldom mentioned. They were the ones whose minds were so scrambled in transit that they had to be mercifully destroyed on arrival.

Hardly surprising that the inmates of Limbo should develop a common obsession about a past that lay behind the curtain of oblivion. Driven by an inner conviction that a man without a past could be no more than half a man, we sorted endlessly among the shards of memory and dreamstuff for some clue to the human beings we had once been.

And now—*here and now*—sitting at the very same table was this man who had apparently come here with the express purpose of giving me back my past. He had made a beginning with the gift of my true name and he promised a great deal more. I was confused. When the impossible happens it is not easy to accept it calmly.

"You mean you were actually *looking* for me?" I said.

"Why sure, Chuck. What else would a pal do?"

"But I don't even know your name."

"Of course—stupid of me," he said, with a brief high-pitched giggle. "How could you remember? That's the whole point, isn't it?" He held out his hand. "I'm Billy Goulson."

His hand was pink and wet, like the living internal organ of some animal. But I shook it. It was the hand of my pal.

"So I'm Charles Radmeyer." I rolled my tongue round the unfamiliar syllables. I still felt like Bob Morris, but then what else had I expected? In time, when the right catalysts had been provided Charles Radmeyer and Bob Morris would meld together into a whole man. That man would have a past, with memories stretching back, way back to that other life . . .

"Tell me more." I was driven by a feverish impatience. "I lived in L.A.? What did I do for a living? Was I married? Did I have a family?"

"Hold on, Chuck, hold on! You're going too fast." He giggled again.

"Too fast?"

"Way too fast," he said. "There are a few details we have to discuss before going any further."

"Details?"

"Sure. You've got to understand that it wasn't easy getting here. And I'm probably breaking all kinds of laws even talking to you like this."

"Limbo makes its own laws. In any case, as far as I know this situation has never arisen before."

"You'd better believe it, Chuck," he grinned. "How many people would go to the kind of trouble I have to help a condemned criminal?"

"Billy, I'm grateful, I really am. But you have to realize I've been waiting to hear the answers to so many questions for over four years. When can I see those tapes?"

He nodded. "Sure, I appreciate that, Chuck. But it isn't that simple. I can't go get the tapes just like that. If I go back now I shall have to stay aboard until 15.00 hours tomorrow. Look, why don't we just sort out the details for now, and then tomorrow . . . " He left the word, the promise, dangling seductively.

Details . . . It filtered through the haze of my eagerness that this was no free gift he was offering me.

"I don't think you understand the way things are run here," I said. "We live comfortably enough, but none of us owns anything. No money, no goods. How can I possibly pay you? In any case, whatever I gave you, you wouldn't be able to take it back to Earth."

"Oh sure, the captain gave us the standard lecture before we disembarked. You've got me wrong, Chuck. Would I take money from an old pal? But a favor deserves a favor, wouldn't you agree?"

I frowned. "*I'm* in a position to do *you* a favor?"

He nodded. His pale, bug eyes took on a milky tinge as if he was staring at some inner vision. His mouth opened further and I could see his pink, wormlike tongue moving over the top row of his grey teeth. God—he was an ugly looking bastard!

"All right—what is it?" I said sharply.

His eyes flowed back into focus. "*The girl,*" he said.

My gut turned to water.

"I watched the two of you here at this table. The way she looked at you all the time. The expression in her eyes . . . She loves you a lot, doesn't she?"

"Nancy has nothing to do with this! What are you trying to pull?"

"Nancy . . . " he breathed wetly. His eyes were going milky again. "Nancy . . . "

"Cut it out!" I shouted, my anger growing at the blasphemy of that sweet name in his foul mouth.

But he was too deep in his waking dream to even notice. His breathing was quick and harsh, his mouth open in a foul rictus, the whole of his squat, sweating body quivering.

"Loves you a lot, Chuck . . . Loves you so much she'd do anything for you . . . if you asked her." The words oozed from that disgusting mouth.

There was no need for him to explain himself further. I thrust my chair back with such force that it clattered to the floor. "You bastard! You dirty filthy bastard! I'll see you in Hell first!"

"But we *are* in Hell, Chuck." His bulging eyes were alert with a new cunning. "And I'm the only one with a round trip ticket. Like I said—a favor for a favor. You want those tapes and holos, don't you?"

Of course I wanted them. I wanted them with a desperation that was eating away inside my head, clawing lumps out of my sanity. But his price was too high.

I leaned forward over the table, my hands flat on its surface. "Look, Billy . . . There are other girls. I could fix it for you. Two . . . maybe more, if that's what you want."

His pumpkin head moved slowly from side to side, grinning up at me. "But I don't want any other girls, Chuck. Just *that* one. Just Nancy."

"She's not even here," I protested. "She just went on shift and I shan't see her again until tomorrow night."

"I can wait," he said. "They say hunger is the best sauce."

"No!"

"Don't be hasty, Chuck," he said. "Think it over. I've got the whole story—the answers to the questions you've been dreaming about for four whole years. I'll be back here at 20.00 hours tomorrow. I can make you the only real whole man on this goddammed spider web. Think it over . . . "

It was a long night. I lay sleepless in the overheated darkness, breathing the yellow acid smell of the universal deodorant that was the dominant stench of Limbo. Goulson's proposition was ridiculous. The idea that I might be prepared to pay such a price for the information he offered was stupid. I was *Robert Morris*. What did I care about the life of a stranger named Charles Radmeyer who had existed once living on another world? What difference could information about his life make to me?

Who was Charles Radmeyer anyway? What kind of man? A criminal, perhaps a murderer. I thought about some of the other inmates. There was no blanket answer to such questions. Who could imagine the nature of the crime that had resulted in Winny Goldman being sentenced to an eternity of exile? Winny, about four feet nine inches tall, with her silvery hair and mild little granny face. Winny with her everlasting solicitude for all of her *boys. What had she been back there on Earth? Did she kill some erring husband with an icepick through the eyeball? Or maybe she poisoned him?*

Then there was old Dennis Calthrop, bony and stoop shouldered, with the nit-picking conversational manner of a cleric. Could you imagine him as a murderer, a child molester? On the other hand, take Jarvis Orne. It required a much smaller effort to imagine him with his great bull shoulders and dangerous dark eyes as a potentially violent man, capable of killing in a fit of rage.

And Nancy? My sweet, naïve Nancy, with her gentle ways. Nancy who had arrived to fill my heart with a new tenderness just at a time when I had been in danger of hardening permanently into the shell of a long term inmate. Nancy who by her example had convinced me against all reason that such a thing as Love existed and could survive even here on Limbo. A murderess? The idea was unthinkable.

Charles Radmeyer . . . It could be the name of a successful man, head of a large corporation, with a beautiful, expensive wife and all the other things money could buy. Could it be that something happened one day in the life of such a man capable of breaking up the desirable pattern of existence? What emotional storm? The discovery of a long-standing infidelity, resulting in a sudden madness of rage that cleared at last to find him standing Othello-like, the broken image of love in his hands?

Or had he been something less respectable, this Charles Radmeyer? A criminal sociopath driven by lust and greed, peddling filthy drugs to ruin minds and bodies, debasing human beings for his own twisted ends?

Or did the reality lie somewhere in between, with an average, everyday sort of guy caught up in some extraordinary situation that led him to commit an isolated act of violence?

I tried a thousand masks on Charles Radmeyer that night, tossing alone in the sweating darkness. And in the morning I was no nearer to a solution.

On shift after that. Six hours of subsonics grinding at the edges of reason as I carried out routine tasks. Two hundred refrigerators to Mars terminal, a thousand gross of men's' jockey shorts to Venus, twenty-five Snocats to Pluto and a wedding cake (for God's sake!) to Luna. Charles Radmeyer . . . Good old Chuck and me, pressing the buttons, feeding in the right tapes, getting the goods there on time. The two of us working together *and we hadn't even met each other yet . . .*

But we were going to. We *had* to. By the time I came off shift that doubt at least had been cleared from my mind. A double sized shot of Euphoprine rinsed away the silted misery left by the generators and gave me the boost I needed to ride the treacherous tide of rationaliszation. I managed to convince myself at last that the concept of sexual jealousy was ridiculous. Any idea of exclusivity was just a stupid convention invented by a society that no longer existed for us.

"Loves you a lot, Chuck . . . Loves you so much she'd do anything for you . . . if you asked her . . . " I wondered just how good a judge of character my old pal Billy really was?

At first Nancy thought I was orbiting too high on Euphoprine and trying to make some kind of sick joke. When she realized I was serious her lovely face went very quiet and pale.

"You're sure that's what you really want, Bob?" Her deep blue eyes twisted my heart despite the idiot chuckling of Euphoprine inside my head.

"Of course I don't *want* it, baby. But this is the only way, don't you see?"

She was silent for a long time. When she finally spoke her voice was different, as if something inside her was broken.

"All right, Bob. Let's do it. Let's get it over with."

Goulson was waiting at the same table in the observation lounge, a frosted glass in front of him. He stood up as we approached, his pink face bursting into a grin of triumph.

"Well, hello there, Chuck. Nice to see you again. And Nancy—how are you? Sit down and have a drink."

We stood side by side facing him. Neither of us had any words for such an occasion. Nancy's slim body was very upright, her pale face frozen. As she looked directly at Goulson I could see a vein pulsing in her right temple.

"No?" he said. He picked up his glass and poured the remaining contents on the floor. "Who needs it? Let's go."

As we walked out of the lounge with Nancy between us I could feel the touch of prurient eyes on us, speculating the significance of the trio. Somebody, I think it was Orne, made a lip-sucking pussy noise.

"Nancy's apartment, I think," Goulson said. "She'll feel more at home there—won't you baby?"

Nancy made no reply. The pale mask remained in place as she walked stiffly onwards turning automatically down the corridor that led to her quarters.

I swear if she'd have stopped then and there and said : "Bob, don't make me go through with this." I would have called off the whole deal and to hell with Goulson and Charles Radmeyer.

But she didn't. She just walked. The only sound coming from the three of us was Goulson's liquid, panting breathing.

Nancy went into the apartment first, closely followed by Goulson. He was sweating badly now. God! I never saw a man sweat like that. And he stank.

"Nice . . . very nice . . . " His bug eyes took in the décor of the room. "Nothing like the feminine touch, eh Chuck?"

I glared back at him in silence, the hate inside my head screaming like a stripped gear.

Nancy stood in the middle of the floor. She was looking at Goulson too. Her blue eyes were glazed with a horror that I couldn't bear to watch.

The worm tongue moved over his wet lips. "All right, baby. Take it off—all of it!"

All was a lightweight jump suit, a pair of briefs and a bra. Goulson's eyes grew milky as she stripped the garments off one by one. She stood there looking more naked that I had ever seen her, hands falling instinctively to cover her pubis.

Please God don't let her look at me! I prayed silently. I knew that if she did I would lose control and blow the whole deal.

It was Goulson's turn to strip. He peeled the uniform from his pink bug's body. His lips were drawn back from those grey tack teeth as he looked and looked at her. His body was completely hairless, eunuchoid—except where it counted. His scrotum was bull-like and the flaming red pole of his erection was like a cruel bludgeon.

"On the bed," he panted urgently. "No . . . not like that, you stupid bitch! Get your knees up . . . and take those hands away. Yes . . . yes . . . that's better . . . " His obscene pink body began to move towards her.

My stomach rumbling the sickness of cowardice I scrabbled for the door handle, eager to escape.

He paused in the act of mounting Nancy, looking back at me over his shoulder. "No! You stay—*and you watch! That's part of the deal!*"

I watched, compelled by a dreadful fascination. Occasionally I managed to close my eyes, but that was no escape from the sound effects that accompanied the activity on the bed. And then, at last it was over. The echoes of his grunting, babbling climaxes still ringing in my ears, I saw him grab a sheet and cover his slimed body with a curious, quick modesty. It was as if he was ashamed of the totality of his detumescence.

Nancy lay with her face towards the wall. Her defenceless female buttocks were marred by weals inflicted by his clumsy paws and her pale shoulders shook with agonizingly silent sobs.

"Nice stuff, Chuck." He winked at me as he began to dress. "Like I said before, you're a lucky fellow." He glanced at the wall clock. "Well, it's been a load of fun, but I've got to go now. You can stay, if you like."

Stay . . . Stay with Nancy to remind her of the shame of what she had done for me? Stay and face the contempt I would surely see in those wide blue eyes? I didn't have that kind of courage.

"Suit yourself," he said as I closed the door of the apartment and joined him in the corridor. "I thought you might want to cut yourself a slice."

He seemed brisker and even more confident now, as if the squalid encounter had boosted his ego. His back was straighter and he walked with a sharp, almost military step.

I grabbed his shoulder. "Just a minute! We had a deal, remember? Those tapes and pictures . . . "

He shrugged my hand off without breaking his pace. "Sure, sure, all in good time."

"What do you mean—*all in good time?*" I had to step out to keep up with him.

He stopped, his round face looking at me in genuine astonishment. "You didn't think I meant just the once, did you? We don't leave for Earth until Friday, you know."

I should have killed him then and there, twisted his bug's head off his obscene body. But I didn't, because I knew that if I did the whole thing would have been for nothing. The tapes would remain in his locker back on the Charon and I would never have the chance to find out the truths my whole being ached to know.

I found Nancy the following morning sitting alone at a table in the coffee shop, staring dull-eyed into a cold cup. It took a lot of nerve to go and sit down opposite that pale, haunted face.

Her eyes regarded me briefly, then slid away again like blue, opaque buttons. I made to reach across the table to touch her hand, then hesitated and drew back, unable to face the rejection of her inevitable response.

I began to speak to her, my voice low and mumbling as I tried to explain my reasons for using her body as currency in my sordid bargain with Goulson. My words were falling over themselves into incoherence as I tried to justify the power of my obsession with identity. Begging her, pleading, explaining that now, so far into the situation, it was not possible to draw back. Eventually my voice staggered to a halt and we sat opposite each other in silence. She was still staring down into that bloody cold coffee.

"Nancy, I . . . "

"All right, Bob. All right!" The harshness of her voice, echoed the pain that was inside her. "If this thing means so much to you I don't see that it can make much difference now."

On that second night Nancy's whimpering spilled through the closed door of her apartment as I walked away down the corridor with Goulson.

"No . . . No more," I said. "It's not worth it. *Nothing's worth it!*"

He stopped and turned to me, his pumpkin face grinning confidently. "Ah come on now, Chuck. You're not going to back down now, are you? I've been meaning to tell you about that other little package I brought along to help you. You've heard of Abrectol?"

Abrectol was the latest wonder drug, used in the treatment of amnesia patients to re-stimulate the pale shadows of memory left in damaged neurones. In combination with the other material he was offering it would enable me to come face to face with Charles Radmeyer and his entire life down to the smallest detail.

"You know it's too good to miss, Chuck," Goulson said. "Tomorrow night I'll give you the whole schmeer. Just think of it! No more doubts. All the blanks filled in. You'll know *all of it.*"

"And you'll bring it all with you?"

He grinned, his foul breath enveloping me. "Why sure . . . Would I welsch on a pal?"

"All right—tomorrow," I said and stopped suddenly as an idea flashed into my mind.

"You Okay, Chuck?" Goulson's grin faded.

"Yeah, yeah. It's nothing," I mumbled. "Tomorrow then." I turned and walked away from him.

It wasn't going to happen again! All through that third night, inside my echoing skull I was promising Nancy that she would not again have to suffer the humiliation, the degrading agony of submission to his bestial coupling. I dared not tell her in reality, for fear that she might betray my intention by some unguarded word or gesture. But she would understand afterwards, when my plan had succeeded. My Nancy *always* understood.

The next time I saw her was at 20.00 hours the following evening. She was already sitting at our regular table in the observation lounge. Goulson was there too. Nancy didn't look at me, or even acknowledge my arrival. There was a strange fixity about her eyes and she was staring at Goulson. I wondered if she had taken some drug to dull her sense to the horror of yet another encounter with that gross body.

Goulson was in great form, confident of his grip on the situation. He handed me a compact little videocam. "Tonight you take pictures," he said. "Souvenirs for the long cold nights back on Earth."

I accepted the camera without demur. There would have been no point in refusing. In any case I had made up my mind that tonight there wasn't going to be anything to take pictures of.

"The tapes?" I asked.

"Sure, Chuck." He patted a bulge in his right hand jacket pocket. "Don't worry about a thing. Everything you need is right here. Let's go."

Nancy remained mute as the three of us began the ritual walk towards her apartment. But this time I was determined that it was going to have a different ending.

That was my mistake. I was too anxious. I grabbed for him clumsily as soon as the door closed behind us, but he slipped away from my fingers. Moving with surprising agility his hand dropped to a jacket pocket and re-appeared holding a small needle gun.

The weapon spat once. I felt the instant coldness of paralysis begin at a point near my navel and race sweep through my body. I tumbled to the floor like a deflated rubber doll.

His pumpkin head hovered over me, leering. "I had a feeling you might try something like that, Chuck," he said.

"You bastard! You filthy bastard!" I wheezed painfully.

"Now is that the way to talk to an old pal?" He put his hands under my armpits and dragged me across the floor. "There . . . now you got a ringside seat," he said, as he propped me up against the wall in a sitting position.

Nancy had watched my abortive rescue attempt without the slightest sign of emotion. Now, as if going through a long established routine, she was taking off her clothes.

Goulson had produced a small tripod and was sighting the Vidcam towards the bed. "Fine . . . Right on the button," he said, satisfied with the view.

Slumped against the wall, my body dead from the neck downwards I watched the familiar scene begin yet again. The bitter acid of frustration burned into my sanity. Even so, it was not long before I realized that to-night *something was different.*

On the previous occasions Nancy's response to Goulson's lovemaking had been at most minimally co-operative, designed only to save herself from a certain amount of pain. She had been little more than a lax figure, a piece of warm meat on which he had performed his obscenities.

Tonight that was changed. Maybe the degradation forced on her over the past two nights had finally penetrated through to some primitive need deep in her female core.

The savagery of her response at first astonished then delighted Goulson. She was no longer the unwilling, grudging partner, acceding to his demands with deliberate clumsiness. The near frigid figure of the previous encounters had been transformed into a writhing female animal that squealed with pleasure as it rocked to shuddering multiple orgasms. Begging for more she clawed at the shining pink flesh of Goulson's body.

In frozen helplessness I watched an endless series of couplings that were like a monstrous re-enactment of a Heironymous Bosch painting. And when even Goulson's lust began to cool, it was Nancy who took the initiative, coaxing him into a renewed virility in a way that would have brought a blush to the most hardened whore. She sobbed with joy as he entered her yet again.

Eventually Goulson was satiated beyond hope of recovery, but she still clung to him, begging him not to leave her, to stay a while longer, just a little while . . .

He thrust her brutally from him and struggled wearily into his clothes. The old jauntiness returned somewhat as he picked up the vidcam and slipped it back into its case.

"This one will be the pride of my collection," he grinned. "I may even send you a copy. Well so long, old pal. Been nice knowing you."

He moved towards the door.

"The tapes!" I shouted. "Our deal!"

Goulson's shoulders began to shake, his gross body quivering as he enjoyed the cream of the jest. "The tapes? You poor dumb bastard, *whoever you are.* Did you really think they existed?"

"But you said you knew me from back on Earth. You said . . . "

"I never saw you before in my life until that night in the observation lounge. You and your Nancy, looking so gooey-eyed at each other that you just had to be in love. *LOVE,*" He spat the word out like a piece of rotten fruit and turned to look at Nancy. "There's your love."

She was crawling across the floor towards me, naked and drooling. Her eyes were red-flecked pinwheels of lust. With scrabbling, frantic fingers she began to tear the clothes from my unfeeling body . . .

This was no longer Limbo. I knew that from now on I would be in the true Hell . . .

THE MULTIPLEX FIXATIVE

Barrington J. Bayley

No emulsion could have come anywhere near it. Photochemical reactions might as well be measured in geological ages. Charged-couple cameras are equally useless: electrons are much too slow. Only my new quantum camera made the astonishing discovery possible

My father died from falling into the blades of a harvesting machine. His blood stained the stubble for ten yards, though most of his sliced-up entrails, bone and muscle were bound up in bales of harvested wheat. Twelve years old at the time, I was unlucky enough to witness the accident. A month later my mother was hacked to pieces by farm marauders who were active in the area, believed to be a gang of refugees from the Balkans. Although elsewhere when she was murdered, it was I who discovered her butchered remains in our farmhouse kitchen, divided into several parts, her abdomen gashed open, her internal organs strewn across the floor tiles. For a year after that I suffered from what is termed 'hysterical blindness' and was unable to see. Once I recovered my sight I resumed my education, in the care of an aunt now, but since then I have been a semi-recluse, forming few friendships, and none that are close.

My parents' farm was sold and the money invested to my benefit, allowing me to live modestly on the income. Consequently I have been able to pursue my personal interests, of which photography is one, and electronics another. Fortunately electronic apparatus of all kinds is inexpensive nowadays. In early middle age I purchased a rundown Edwardian house in the Chorlton district of Manchester, and have lived quietly there ever since. In the end, I have been able to counterbalance my childhood misfortunes, by my discovery of the multiplex quantum fixative.

My house is one of those tall, narrow terraced buildings with high stuccoed ceilings and bay sash windows. There are five floors, including attic and basements. Until one gets to know it, the house seems to be a maze of rooms, levels and little stairways. I have never redecorated any part of it, and the furniture is mainly what was abandoned by the previous owner. There is no carpeting whatsoever, only abraded and holed linoleum, a relic of previous times when carpets were too expensive for most people. The wooden stairs are bare, with only patches of once-applied dark brown paint clinging to the margins. The upper reaches of the house are near to mephitic, with blackened, obfuscating linoleum, dark wallpaper further darkened by age, and grimed windows which admit hardly any direct light, so that the narrow corridors are like forgotten trails in a sunless forest. At night there are one or two low-wattage light bulbs, dimmed by dust and dirt, which offer the feeblest of yellow glows. My domestic needs being satisfied by a single room on the first floor, plus kitchen and bathroom, there is plenty of workspace. It is on the upper floors that I have installed my studio, darkroom and laboratory.

Throughout the ages superstition has invested pictures with magical power. Modern times have far from discarded the belief, though the idea has retreated into fiction. *The Picture of Dorian Gray* and M.R.James's *The Mezzotint* are but prime literary examples of pictures which have assumed the power of life. The invention of photography could only intensify the mystique. A picture made by crystallising light emanating from the scene surely captures the essence of the subject, or so the imagination tells us. Photographs therefore seem to open the way into a secret dimension. Many are the fanciful but compelling stories of people drawn into the emulsion and trapped there, or of characters in motion pictures stepping out of the cinema screen to become flesh and blood.

There are people who claim to have photographed thought. And many claim to have photographed ghosts which remained otherwise unseen.

Ghosts. That's what I thought they were at first. Phantoms trapped between the visible and the eternal.

My aim in life has been to achieve the shortest possible exposure, or to put it another way, the shortest possible DIN number—DIN being the logarithmic expression of the speed of a photographic film or plate. Such an exercise in science has generally been for the purpose of recording chemical reactions. My purpose was different. Not microscopic, but to display the large-scale world in an interval so brief that light is almost frozen. What would such a world look like, I asked myself? How could one reduce the frozen moment of a photograph still further, to produce an irreducible atom of reality?

In one nanosecond (10^{-9}) light travels a distance of one foot. In one femtosecond (10^{-15}) it travels the diameter of the average cell or bacterium. Conventional techniques can achieve these exposures, though I may have been the first to apply them to the everyday world. A femtosecond exposure produces a curiously flat, sketchy, washed-out effect, in which people and objects seem suspended in a gelid sub-reality. At such short exposures colors cannot be distinguished—a femtosecond allows time for but a single wavelength of visible light to impinge on the reacting medium. A femtosecond, however, was too long for me. I felt that I had come to a threshold, and I longed to cross that threshold into a different world.

I purchased a quantum tunnelling microscope which I converted to wide-angle vision, and got to work on what I call 'the fixative'. Another term would be a 'quantum raster', sensitive enough to detect events on the level of Planck's constant, h. There is no need for a developer. The role of fixative is to record evanescent events on memory chips, or, my preferred method in the early stages, on a suitably prepared glass plate.

It may sound contradictory to speak of photographs with exposures shorter than the frequency of the electromagnetic medium they are taken by. Not at all. The fixative can respond to half a wavelength, a quarter of a wavelength, or extremely small fractions of a wavelength. Light, I have discovered, is more complex than physicists have believed.

It was when I passed this threshold that that the 'ghosts' began to appear. The wraiths were no more than vague shapes when I first projected the plates on to the screen, so that I was able to dismiss them as artifacts of the photographic process. It was to eliminate these 'smudges' that I experimented with tuning the fixative. To my surprise the ghosts became sharper the more I tuned, until they took on definite form. It was no longer possible to dismiss them as flaws or blurs.

It thus became my belief that the house was haunted. The belief did not last long. As the tuning became more precise, I was forced to search for some other explanation.

I took all the earlier photographs in my studio. On the projection screen the room appeared, outlined in the curiously flat and motionless light, but the fittings I had installed failed to show. Instead, furniture could be seen. The room had become a bedroom. In it stood a man, bearded and moustached, wearing a starched white shirt with a stiff detachable collar, and stovepipe trousers held up by braces. Five plates are from this session. In another a woman appears, wearing a long white gown with her hair pinned up in a bun. Two more plates see them undressing, revealing underclothes which cover them no less completely. Finally they are naked on the bed, the man lying on the woman, engaged in sexual intercourse. The woman's face is extraordinarily passive for such an occasion, expressing no enjoyment but only blank resignation. The scene fascinates me and repels me at the same time. The idea of marriage is something that has never occurred to me. Guilty at having intruded on the couple's privacy, I moved my experiments out of the studio and into my living quarters. There I found myself photographing the same man and woman, but in more decorous circumstances. My living room was their drawing room. The husband wore a frock jacket and buttoned waistcoat, the wife a long-sleeved gown with a bustle. Once their maid was present. Mostly my 'snapshots' chanced to catch them in formal poses, even looking straight at the camera as though aware they were being photographed, never smiling but always wearing serious expressions. The archaic atmosphere of the pictures made me think I had plucked images from out of the past. But once more I was wrong. The next day the quantum raster became detuned. With care, I tuned it again to the same interval as before; upon which the 'ghosts' again sharpened and took on definition.

But these were not the same people as before. There was a different married couple and different servants, joined by three young children whom I snapped scampering about or reading. The clothing was old-fashioned in appearance still, but more Edwardian than Victorian. Had I photographed the past at a slightly later time? To test the hypothesis I purposely detuned and retuned the raster. Yet another set of inhabitants appeared, this time spanning three generations: grandmother, parents, and five children. I failed to recognize the period by their apparel. It was vaguely Victorian, vaguely Edwardian, but not really identifiable as either. The hair styles, too, were decidedly odd: coiffed close and short for the women and girls, but shoulder length for the husband and eldest son.

Repeatedly I detuned and retuned, using up all my stock of glass plates. At each retuning, the house was populated anew. Conservative dress styles predominated. But in one case the fashion appeared to be for garments even more skimpy than those in the 1960s, both males and females scarcely being covered at all. I cannot explain why this embarrassed me as it did. At any rate I was forced to abandon my theory that I was photographing the past. Even if the house had changed hands at regular intervals of five years—which was most unlikely—it could not have been the home of so many different families, not even in a century.

Slowly it dawned on me that something else, not history, separated the people I had glimpsed. All of them were in the house *at that very moment*—impalpable, inaudible, and were it not for the quantum fixative, invisible. I thought and thought, until I arrived at the truth.

Time is atomic. Consisting of indivisible instants. Which are separated from one another.

Even in the ancient world the atomic idea of matter was well-known, though it belonged as much to India as to Greece. Buddhist philosophers added the supra-logical assumption that atomicity must pertain to duration as well as to spatial extension. In their doctrine every atom is recreated anew billions of times per second. 20th century physicists also toyed with atoms of time, which they called 'chronons', though tending to associate them with space rather than with material particles. J.J. Thompson calculated the duration of the chronon as being $10\text{-}21$ of a second; R. Levi as $4.48\text{x}10\text{-}24$ of a second.

I can aver that chronons exist, and that they share another property with material atoms. Atoms are not atoms only by virtue of being particulate. Their other essential feature is that they are separated by a void. This is just as true of chronons. They are separated by a void of timelessness.

There is more. Our reality consists of a sequence of chronons. *But not of consecutive neighboring chronons.* That would produce a time flow so creeping and cramped that nothing could ever happen. Time, as it turns out, is more complex. Our reality is multiplexed. It selects every nth chronon, skipping the others. On that, continuity and causality depend.

What does this mean? It means that there are other multiplexed realities interleaved with our own, which we cannot touch or—up to now—see. How many? I do not know. Perhaps thousands, perhaps millions, perhaps—

How crowded is my house! How crowded it is!

There are two fundamental temporal constants:

1. The duration of the chronon, or time-atom.
2. The multiplex interval.

Physical causation acts over the span of the multiplex interval. No causation occurs within the interval, which is the region of non-causal quantum events.

As a photographer I cannot be sure of the exact values of either. Tentatively I have put the duration of the time-instant as the time it takes light to traverse a distance equivalent to the fifth root of the diameter of an electron. One does not need to know the multiplex interval, even approximately. It imposes itself on our experience. So one has only to tune the quantum raster to the chronon interval or shorter, and an alternative reality will appear. Any exposure longer than a chronon, and our local reality appears.

In all the pictures I have taken, the house remains curiously the same. Bricks and mortar are unchanged. The furniture varies—though even that not always! What is always different is the people. One gets the impression that people are like gas and smoke; only stone and brick are substantial. A different idea as to the order of things emerges; as though we are exuded by the houses we live in, instead of being the agents which build them.

Today my cousin Tarquin came to visit me. I had not seen him for twelve years. When I lived with my aunt Tarquin was the nearest thing I had to a playmate, though I was unresponsive to friendship at that time. Knowing of the ordeal I had gone through, he was always patient and understanding with me. He lived about a mile and a half from my aunt's cottage, and would sometimes take me wandering through the Worcester countryside.

One day he conducted me on a small adventure. We walked through a lane with high banks, and then through a stand of trees on whose far side stretched rolling meadows. In the middle of one of these we came upon a dense thicket to which clung the mist of a late autumn afternoon. It looked impenetrable, consisting entirely of close-set shoots and saplings. Tarquin, however, knew a way in. Slipping into an invisible aperture, he led me through a maze of slight gaps, until we came to a space large enough for the two of us to sit down in.

"My den," he said with a grin.

I looked about me. The outside world had disappeared. The light was fading. Only scraps of sky showed overhead. Tarquin leaned towards me.

"Bet you can't find your way out."

Taking the challenge, I stood up and set off. It was to no avail. The copse was too thickly packed. I could not push through it, neither could I find the invisible trails. Laughing, Tarquin took the lead. I lost all sense of direction. He led me round and round and back and forth, till the thicket seemed a secret land all of its own. When we finally stood outside, I gazed in wonder that so much could be compressed into so small a space.

Tarquin, it seemed to me, had been sent by my aunt, now in her old age, to ascertain that I was all right. I conducted him on a tour of the house, showing him the laboratory, the studio and the darkroom, doing my best to explain my discovery of the licenseiplex as we went. Adjourning to the living room, I projected some of the glass plates as a demonstration.

Either he had not listened properly, or he had failed to understand me. He chuckled at the sight of the seemingly posed portraits.

"Victorians never smiled when they were photographed," he commented. "They wanted to show that they were serious people, and expected to be taken seriously."

"These aren't Victorians," I corrected him. "They are our contemporaries. It's just that their fashions have changed little, as compared with ours."

He seemed not to have heard me. He pointed to the screen as I slid in another plate. "I see you have some Victorian pornography, too."

I had accidentally projected one of the plates which displayed a family of adults and children clad in only filmy strips of gauze. Hastily I removed the plate. Turning to Tarquin, I delivered a more deliberate lecture on atomic time and the multiplex.

He listened in a silence which lasted some time after I had finished. When he spoke, it was in a strained voice.

"Well," he said slowly, "This time you have shown me the way into the thicket, I would say. But is there a way out?"

Following Tarquin's visit I have hit on the idea of making motion pictures of the other multiplexed realities. The multiplex fixative, or quantum raster, proved easily adaptable to the project. As I have said, the multiplex interval imposes itself. I had but to connect the fixative to the memory chips of a digital motion camera, and theoretically it would take a frame every 10-n of a second.

Except of course that the flow of real time—that is to say, multiplexed time—is much too rapid for electronic recording equipment to respond to. I therefore installed a sampler to take a frame every twenty-fifth of a second, the standard rate at which television pictures are displayed.

The arrangement worked well. I could store sequences up to the camera's memory limit, and also watch these same sequences on the camera's viewfinder as they took place. I confess it did weigh on me a little that this was tantamount to spying. But I found a way to salve my conscience. The chronon interval so nearly converges on the infinitesimal (at which light is next to motionless) that one never finds the same reality twice. To watch people for any length of time one would have to keep the raster running until it detunes spontaneously (by experience I have learned to delay this for up to two days). So I took to detuning and retuning every twenty minutes or so. In addition I began to use the monitor viewfinder only, not bothering to record what I saw. Thuswise, as I perceived it, invasions of privacy were kept to a minimum.

Soon I must find time to write down everything about the fixative. How it is done. How to piece it all together. I do not want to be a Nikola Tesla, who died with half his inventions unrecorded. God knows who might rediscover the fixative independently. Likewise anyone examining my equipment would likely fail to discern its purpose. It is like the 'bent beam' navigation system German bombers used in World War II, whose receivers were disguised to look like ordinary radios.

Yesterday I purchased a large notebook with a tooled leather cover in which to begin my exposition. I have not entered a single word into it as yet. Something has happened to delay me.

The raster has been running for six hours, much longer than I would normally allow, but I have been unable to tear myself away from the scenes it delivers.

During the last month I have elaborated the motion picture arrangement. The tv output is now relayed to a tube projector whose beam falls on the screen once used by the old magic lantern. I have moved both screen and raster; the viewpoint of the room projected on the screen is the same one I gain from my chair. The correspondence is eerie, like a set of Chinese boxes.

Only two people occupy the house: a middle-aged woman and a boy. So much does the woman remind me of my mother that I cannot take my eyes off her. Apart from the same roundness of face there isn't really much of a 'family resemblance'. But her placid, pleasant expression, the gentle way she moves, draw me irresistibly. She is dressed in a simple smock-like gown, the boy in short trousers and a pullover. I can't say whether the boy resembles me at that age or not. Years ago I destroyed all photographs of myself as a boy, in a bid to forget my early distress.

It will be something of a relief when the raster spontaneously detunes, for I cannot bring myself to do it manually. In the peculiarly transparent, sketchy white light, the boy reads a book while his mother busies herself with household tasks. She is clearing ornaments from a cluttered mantelpiece. She wipes the mantelpiece carefully with a dustcloth, then patiently polishes and replaces everything she has removed. She cocks an ear and speaks to the boy. He looks up from his book and replies, concern on his face. There is no sound, of course. It is like watching an old silent movie without subtitles.

Putting down the duster, she makes for the door. Before she can reach it, it opens. Three men enter one after another. They are dark of face, unshaven, unkempt. They look vicious, evil, foreign. They peer about themselves insolently, not in the least ashamed that they are intruders.

The boy is killed straight away. The woman is raped first, her gown ripped off, her flannel bloomers yanked off, before she is butchered. Her plump, stretch-marked abdomen is slashed open. Blood, black blood—there is no color—splashes on to the linoleum.

Her intestines pour out.

I am off my chair by now and screaming, arms flailing in the air as I attempt to intervene. Everything goes black. I am in darkness. I lurch into an obstruction and hear the projector crash to the floor.

I can't see!

I can't see!

I'm blind!

Editor's note: the partially decomposed body of Quentin Dodson was found at the foot of the staircase on the ground floor of his home. A search of the house revealed that he was a collector of antique cameras with slow shutter speeds and glass plate negatives. An album of Victorian photographs, mostly consisting of portraits or of posed domestic scenes, was also found. A 'magic lantern' for projecting glass slides on to a cloth screen lay on its side in the living room, which also contained theatrical props—i.e. proscenium surrounds—and a rack of glass slides on which Dodson had copied some of the photographs in the album, suggesting that he liked to stage Victorian shows for his own amusement. The room he termed his 'laboratory' contained a modern digital motion camera on which nothing was recorded, and miscellaneous items, including a quantum tunnelling microscope, purchased from a specialist electronics retailer in Manchester's Soho district. It is unclear what use, if any, Dodson made of this equipment. The above account was pieced together by his second cousin Tarquin Dodson from scattered notes scribbled on scraps of paper and on the backs of used envelopes, also found in the living room. Tarquin Dodson, who admits to having allowed himself a degree of interpretative license—while strenuously denying he invented the story outright—adds the comment, "Subjective reality is more valid than the shadow show of external appearances." The coroner's inquest returned a verdict of accidental death.

COLLECTOR'S CHOICE

Ron Bennett

He'd take up the challenge.

The anticipation was already quite delicious.

He caught sight of his hand as his reached for the glass of fifty-year old malt. The skin was mottled and the veins stuck out like the half-concealed pipelines in the Northern deserts where he'd seen Persuvian writhe and die from the poison he and Xantina had poured down the Arcadian's throat.

Yes, he thought, they can do so much. Hadn't he had the best and most expensive organ replacements? Hadn't they replaced the joints with the best and most expensive plasticized moldings? Hadn't they pumped him full of the medication necessary to slow degeneration and renew vitality? Hadn't they pepped up his libido to unimaginable heights?

Yet, they could do nothing about the hands.

When they were old, they looked old.

Yes, to all intents, he was a twenty-five year old. He could act like a twenty-five year old. He could love like a twenty-five year old. He could possess the appearance of a twenty-five year old. As long as no-one looked at his hands.

The glass was empty. He had tossed down the contents while his mind was preoccupied, tossed down the smooth, well-aged liquid without taking pleasure from its smooth, rare taste.

Ah, Xantina, the beautiful raven-haired Xantina! He thought of their lying together, of their love making. Xantina, whom he had introduced to collecting, whose tastes he had nurtured and honed, Xantina whose collection now almost equalled his own.

Xantina with whom he had shared so much. But who now wished only to be a rival.

Yes, he'd accept the challenge.

Its arrival had been inevitable.

But thinking of Xantina was one thing. Letting his mind dwell on her escapades to the detriment of enjoying the malt was another.

He poured another measure and held up the glass so that the diffused light shone its ochre beam through the hand-cut crystal and the smoky liquid itself. Yes, one should take the time to appreciate such luxuries. Hadn't that always been his philosophy? After all, what was Time if not the means whereby one could enjoy, one could exult? Ah, Time! Time to feel the young, renewed blood rushing through the rejuvenated body. Time enough to achieve all one wished to achieve, all one might wish to achieve.

He sipped at the whisky, aware of its age, appreciative of its silky taste. Ah! This was how to enjoy a malt. This was how to enjoy Time, how to enjoy Life.

Yes, he'd accept her challenge.

Wasn't he High Marshall of the Collector Caste? Wasn't this exactly what he had been waiting for, sitting here in his luxurious, cosseted Antarctic penthouse, surrounded by the trophies of past exploits?

Were not the very walls of the Great Hall in which he now sat faced with wood from the Temple at Amritsar, inset at eye level with as many of the Elgin Marbles as could be accommodated?

To his right was the entrance to the gallery which housed a dozen of the larger Rubens that had once graced the painter's Flemish home, to his left the small exclusive gallery, with this week's specially chosen centrepiece, Renoir's Sur la Terrace.

He walked idly across the Cretian mosaic floor to the piano on which Gershwin had composed his Rhapsody, allowing his fingers to stray along the perfectly pitched keys.

The slight draft from the movement ruffled the sheets of paper on the small desk which had once stood in the isolated parsonage on the edge of lonely, windswept moors, the eight surviving sheets of manuscript from Pushkin's Queen of Spades.

Yes, now it was time to change the Renoir. In storage on the floor below were dozens more, not only Renoir, but Dali, Takasawa, Matisse, Tissot, Botticelli, Emptcarte, Titian, Rembrandt . . . so many from which to choose. Perhaps this month a sculpture, possibly one of the Kellermann bronzes or the Donatello Mary Magdalene.

At first it had been the Liberators, those who were sufficiently lacking in attention to their own well-being to risk the sorties into the Dead Zones in order to plunder whatever art treasures had taken their fancy. All too soon the supply had been exhausted.

The crystal he had obtained from the dark, curtained dining hall of the Oberschloss by the Rhine, its drapes closed, an unsuccessful barrier against the inevitable maelstrom. The whisky . . . ? Ah, who remembered the plunder of the distilleries amongst almost thirty years of gathering together what was already rarely matched and would one day be the greatest collection of them all?

Admiration. and jealousy. of another's acquisitions had resulted in challenges, at first small, insignificant contests, with some minor treasure the trophy. Why, wasn't that how he had come to own the crumbling print of *Intolerance?*

Over the years, both the contests and the worth of the trophies had escalated, the contests mounting in ferocity and finality, the trophies absolute. Eliminate the collector and automatically his collection became yours. Gradually, the collections grew in size, the number of collectors ever fewer.

He laughed as he remembered once again the face of Abdul bin Suleiman screaming his pathetic entreaties not to be left at the bottom of the dry well into which he had been enticed, screams that had turned quickly to a torrent of cursing as the heli-pod was taking off.

He straightened the sheets of manuscript and stood looking absently at the spidery script. How had he won this one? Ah, yes, the encounter at what once had been Tashkent.

Cheng Yee had tried a double bluff there, he remembered.

The camels hadn't even looked real. And the herd driver! A last surviving peasant in such a toxic area! And so close to the ruins. What was he supposed to have done? Assessed and ignored the artificiality of the pageant laid out for him and wasted his weaponry on the ruins where Cheng was supposedly hiding in wait?

And he the High Marshall!

He'd come in low and fast with the sound-distorters echoing from the north, confusing the man waiting in ambush. He'd burnt the camels and their driver, the high-velocity smoke beams enveloping and shielding his craft as he thundered the hillocks beyond with his new Hy-Rockets.

In addition to his taking possession of Cheng Yee's collection of some three thousand items, of which the Pushkin manuscript was but one, Cheng's family had been generous in their praise for the manner he which he'd caused their son the minimum of suffering. They had shown their appreciation by insisting he also took a unique pair of Chou dynasty peacock vases.

And now, the challenge from Xantina.

Ah, the lovely Xantina, casting her green eyes about her when he'd escorted her through his deep carpeted room, with its jewelled crowns once worn by royal heads from Stewart to the Romanoff, those green eyes sparkling in unbridled envy, sparkling in unison with the display of Faberge eggs and other exquisite trinkets.

Trinkets! Riches heaped upon riches such as the world had never seen! Gold, silver, rubies, diamonds, jades of every color, every shade . . . ducats. doubloons, guineas, shekels, thalers, napoleons . . .

Where could he begin to describe such a collection, such a hoarding? With the Rosetta Stone? The seventeen Gutenberg bibles? With the Tutankhamun mask? With the Aztec heads, the Mercator atlases, the Paphos icons, the Louis XIV automata, the Simon Bolivar epaulettes, the Maria Theresa samplers, the Cape triangular color varieties, the Rajengari ceremonial kukris, the Tiberius toga, the sixty-three Stradivari, the four Edward VIII proof double sovereigns, the five sections of the Bayeux Tapestry . . . ?

Yes, the Bayeux. Plundered and divided. Divided again and again, as challenges were won and lost by pairs of contestants so that the collection gained was shared between the victors. A Van Gogh for this victor, a Picasso for that. And the tapestry?

Why, divide it!

And, after a later contest, divide it again.

And again.

And what did Xantina's collection contain that would so excite his palate?

As well as the Runnymede Magna Carta, the T'sai Fen silks, the Scottish Stone of Destiny, the Papua Malui black pearls, Saint Cordelia's veil, the Benjamin Franklin onyx snuff-boxes, the Shakespeare folios, the Niger carvings, the Jules Verne headstone, the Wyatt Earp Derringer, the Terengganu ivory . . . Ivory! Shelves and shelves of the most delicate netsuke?

What but another piece of the Bayeux? indeed, perhaps the most prized portion of all, the panel bearing the depiction of Halley's comet.

Yes, a notable and worthy addition to his collection.

Ah, what abundance! When Xantina's collection was absorbed into his own . . .

Already he could envisage the envy and admiration on the faces of Girthald, Thoreaux, M'singa and the others.

Xantina!

What a triumph this would be.

Perhaps he could prolong her dying so that she could appreciate to the full what he was savouring at the moment of victory. Perhaps she'd plead for her life. So many of them had done so, even offering their entire collections in exchange for their paltry lives. As though life without a collection was worth living.

To the victor the spoils. Every time. The very raison d'etre of the Collector Caste, he thought. Let the proles toil, let them expend their worthless energies. We of the Collector Caste, with the expertise of modern transplants and renewals, we are immortal!

As long as we are victorious.

He looked again at the scroll on which the challenge had been delivered.

> *Where Maggie May*
> *Did romp and play*
> *Two birds look down*
> *On port and town*

The script was gothic, the parchment undoubtedly plucked from one of the tombs along the Nile.

No time or date was mentioned. Neither was necessary. A week, one solitary week, to solve the riddle and arrive at the designated location. One day prior to the actual meeting was allowed to prepare the terrain, were it deemed necessary.

Maggie May.? The name meant nothing to him. She was not, he knew, of the Collector Caste. Perhaps an early Collector, one killed in the early days of the Contests. Was her grave marked by a memorial depicting two birds?

Was the Maggie referred to really a Margaret?

Or were the birds, perhaps, symbolic representations gracing some famous work of art?

He turned on the intervid and watched the two proles working in his extensive library, arranging the newly acquired volumes.

He poured himself another glass as he gave his instructions, aware of their pallid prole eyes following his every movement.

Damn proles! It took them almost four hours.

Four long hours to come up with the identity of Maggie May.

Lines from an old sea-song.

> *Oh, Maggie, Maggie May,*
> *They have taken her away.*
> *She'll never walk down*
> *Lime Street any more.*

Almost a further hour to discover that Lime Street was a major thoroughfare in the old English port of Liverpool and that dear Maggie May had been a prostitute who plied her trade for visiting seamen.

The birds themselves meant nothing.

He hauled Leberdik away from his restoration. Minor antiques like Sheraton and Dupadier could wait. The prole did not relish the scouting mission but he had been into the Dead Zones before and, much to his surprise, had survived. Once again he was reminded that there was no danger as long as he did not remain stationary. The proles, even the majors like Leberdik, believe anything.

He returned before nightfall.

He merely confirmed what the others had researched during his absence.

Liverpool stands on the mouth of the wide River Mersey. By the port there are three large office blocks, one being mounted by two massive bronze birds, the mythical liver birds from which the port had, in ancient times, taken its name.

And the birds looked down on a large, open space, a concreted plaza . . .

An ideal place for a contest.

The following day, while his workers prepared and loaded his craft, he attended the usual meeting with his lawyers where the usual formal, perfunctory documents were drawn up and signed. If he lost the contest then his entire collection would become Xantina's property. He was gratified to learn that she had already signed the reciprocal document, as was customary when one issued a challenge.

Thereafter, he wasted no time but took off into the Dead Zones.

He took the direct route over New Arcadia and across Africa's wide veldt which had once teemed with so many now-extinct animals. There was no sign of life until he reached the Mediterranean. On Cyprus a party of perhaps eighty to a hundred proles were busily engaged in removing relics from the ancient site of Salamis.

He smiled. Thoreaux. It had to be Thoreaux. The best relics had long been taken, but a few minor pieces still remained. People like Thoreaux were more scavenger than true collector. Didn't they realize that the acquisition, the ownership, of a truly delectable item was cause for appreciation in its own right?

He skirted Venice and Rome. Fabrizio, he knew, had made a speciality of them. The Venetian bridges had long been dismantled and removed as had the Forum columns and the Trevi Fountain. And the Vatican! Ever a target for those who fed their egos with the acquisition of religious relics.

Over Paris he saw that the Arc de Triomphe had finally collapsed, the result of so many early Collectors removing the occasional stone, each stolen brick making the arch's removal and reassembly an impossible task.

Now any one could take his pick from any one of the thousands scattered across what had been the Etoile. London looked much the same as when he'd last visited the area, though he noted with surprise that there had been further attempts to remove the golden cross which adorned St Paul's Cathedral and that one of the Landseer lions was missing from Trafalgar Square.

Strange! He hadn't heard of anyone having acquired that.

He took his time surveying Liverpool before he landed in a grassed park a kilometer or so from the city centre. There was little evidence of the maelstrom or its resultant decay. Grass had neither withered nor begun to grow, so that the gardens of surrounding houses, as well as park itself with its low shrubbery, were as they had been before that terrible night.

Cars and crude, early versions of the heli-pod parked neatly along the suburban streets were exactly as they had been left, only rust witness to their lengthy neglect, only the leafless trees a testament to what had occurred. He dismantled the heli-pod into its easily managed components, so that each could comfortably be hidden in a half dozen different suburban garages. He inspected the interior of three different houses before he found one which offered a bed to satisfy his standards for comfort and the following day strapped his pack to his back and walked at an easy, steady pace through the dead, litterless streets into the city centre, streets where not even a rat was alive to scavenge.

There was no need for caution. There were still three days before Xantina would arrive to set up whatever little surprise she might have in store for him, four days before he also was expected to arrive.

The fools! Had he built up his collection by playing to their infantile rules!

The surprise would be hers.

Perhaps after all he'd allow her a swift end. They had teamed up on so many occasions. She had meant so much to him.

It was the least he could do.

The three old buildings stood side by side in sombre majesty. He picked out the building on which the large bronze birds were mounted, sentinels looming above the deserted port.

He climbed the marble stairs and made his way through what had been the offices of a successful firm of lawyers and looked out at the plaza between the building and the river.

He would need a high vantage point.

He took the stairs to the roof and stepped out on to the flat concrete. He stood by the chest-high balustrade, scanning the metropolis spread before him, the old commercial heart of the great city, building after building, all silent, all deserted.

The sun drifted out of a cloud and away in the distance to his right its rays reflected from the upper windows of a high office block, mockingly suggesting life where none existed.

He moved through the shadow of one of the great bronze birds to the opposite side of the flat roof.

Before him stretched the wide river, the buildings of another town shadows on its far bank. Immediately beneath him four rusting ships were moored alongside what had been the floating landing stage for the trans-river ferries, a once-sleek nuclear liner and three merchant ships standing by their loading cranes, all dead, all testament to what had been the great port's heart-beat.

Now, all was silent.

There was no horn of approaching ship with wares from distant lands, no churning of ferry boats, not even the cry of a single, surviving sea-bird.

From where he stood he could not even hear the faint lapping of the water urged by an incoming tide against its concrete banking.

Yes, this was an excellent vantage point. He could blast Xantina the moment she arrived.

He began to open his pack.

But wait!

He would be seen. From whichever direction Xantina approached, here he would be easily discernible, the only life in the great port.

He retreated to the floor below. Yes, this was better, far better. He could slide up each of the sash windows and draw down their blinds, leaving a gap wide enough to see through, wide enough to fire through, all excellent vantage points on to the plaza below, each providing a slightly different angle of shot.

All he had to do was wait.

He assembled his laser, adjusting the nozzle so that it would cover as wide an area as possible.

The beam strength would be weakened but it would sufficient to knock her out.

After the hit he'd go down to the plaza and finish her off with the full, concentrated beam.

He spent the remainder of the day amusing himself looking through the various offices in the building, immersing himself in the correspondence of litigation.

Fascinating! He wondered whether it would be admirable to begin a collection of such correspondence. Perhaps it could be suggested to one of the neo-collectors, Perhaps a survey could be carried out on similar correspondence from all corners of the Dead Zones.

He made himself comfortable for the night on a large leather sofa which stood on the landing of the floor below. The food he'd brought with him was tasteless but at least he'd had the good sense to carry a flask of whisky. Not a single malt, for these were not the place in which such could be properly appreciated, but a good enough blend to satisfy the palate in such surroundings.

Only three days to wait.

The following day was warm and sunny. He decided against a pleasant stroll along the waterfront. That could come later, if he so wished, after the triumph of acquisition. It was more likely, he acceded, that he would wish to return to the Antarctic to claim what would rightly be his. Instead, he spent the morning leafing through bills of lading in an adjoining office of a shipping agent.

He broke off when he heard the low hum of a distant craft.

It couldn't be!

Already . . . ?

He ran up the stairs to where he had prepared his lair, carefully looking through the slits left exposed in the shaded windows, mindful not to allow the smallest movement, the slightest reflection reveal his presence.

The heli-pod traversed the river mouth and disappeared from view, the whine of its engines growing louder as it approached, growing almost un-bearable as it reappeared almost close enough for him to touch. It lowered itself on to the edge of the plaza beneath, the sound of its engines dying away to merge into the surrounding silence.

He watched as its door opened.

A man stepped out. He was dressed in silver tunic and pantaloons.

Fordingham!

What was a neo like Fordingham doing here?

He had his answer immediately as Xantina stepped from the craft, the lovely Xantina with her gloss-black hair and her flashing green eyes.

Xantina with a new team-mate.

Xantina with a new lover.

Arriving two days early.

He smiled as he realized that he had been the one to teach her to break the rule. He wondered how she had explained the infraction to Fordingham, how she'd convinced someone so faint-hearted, so conven-tional, to travel with her like this.

He watched as they began to lay the thin, almost invisible, wires to cover the plaza like a grid.

Another trick he'd taught her. Surely she wouldn't think him naive enough to be caught by those?

He checked the laser. There was sufficient charge to take them both. Two short bursts, first Fordingham and then Xantina.

She would still be alive. Stunned, but alive. He would be able to go down to her, show her the wrecked body of her new love and listen dispas-sionately to her pleading.

He adjusted the nozzle and lined up Fordingham in his sights.

He squeezed the trigger.

Fire enveloped the silver tunic and his wearer.

At the same time there was an explosion behind him, the building shaking with the sudden force.

He turned his gaze from the blackened corpse below.

Another explosion shook the interior of the building.

Another and another . . .

A series of explosions.

Smoke billowed in through the open doorway of the office.

He fired quickly and indiscriminately at where Xantina had been a moment earlier.

She was not to be seen.

He ran back into the building. He would have to go down to street level and hunt her.

Those explosions! What had they been?

He knew soon enough.

He made his way cautiously through the thinning smoke, down the staircase, halting abruptly as he realized there was before him a gaping chasm where steps had been. The stairs had been shattered by the explosions, the huge gap too wide to leap.

He made his way to a second staircase.

It, too, had been destroyed by an explosion.

He ran from staircase to staircase, panic rising within him, ice churning around his heart.

All the staircases had been broken in the explosions.

He was marooned on the building's upper floor!

She had outwitted him.

She had been here earlier, probably even before she had issued the challenge. She had rigged the stairs, all of them, the charges set to explode at the triggering of the laser.

Fordingham had been brought along as the decoy. A subtle touch, worthy of his pupil. She'd known he would target Fordingham first.

He forced himself to be calm and examined one by one the shattered staircases. It was impossible to make any descent.

He scoured the corridors and doorways for a staircase, any escape route, that might have been overlooked.

There was none.

At the sound of the whining motors he rushed back to the window, blasting his laser at the rising craft, but already it was out of range.

He ran up the stairs to the flat roof, looking out past the huge bronze birds, watching the heli-pod catch the sun's reflecting rays as it began to spin away along the wide estuary.

She would hole up somewhere, in a hideaway already chosen and prepared, possibly in what remained of a hotel such as the Ritz or Claridge's in London or perhaps the George V in Paris, so that she could return home at the proper time, with the tale of how she'd outwitted him and won the challenge.

His collection, yes, with the four Bayeux panels, would be owned and appreciated by fairer hands than his. Fairer and younger.

He laughed out loud at his appreciation, the appreciation of the irony of the situation in which he now found himself.

He had been out-manoeuvred.

He was lord of a domain which spanned only the roof and top floor of the building. His supplies would last only for another two days.

He could choose to remain and hope that she would return, or that another would come to investigate this region of the Dead Zones.

Was either likely?

He could use the blaster on himself. Or he could jump, first balancing on the roof balustrade, then leaping down to the plaza below, with the great bronze birds behind him, watching his wingless flight with their cold, sightless eyes.

The choice was his.

MOON-PEARLS

David Redd

He had begun as a single cell in a regeneration tank, a cell doubling and redoubling, growing with unnatural swiftness into the shape of a man. Tall and strong he emerged.

His home was a buried city, where apes and distorted humans prowled the sunken levels, where above ground the spreading glaciers, menaced the trees, where in the sky an aviform Senechi soared like a huge purple dragon. He saw these things and learned. Inevitably he, became restless and sought adventure beyond the horizon, as all men, must do to become true men, until suddenly he was recalled to the buried city.

In his present form he was less than four years old.

"You want me to call Ginny?" Corin frowned at the centauroid facing him. "What's wrong?"

"Just call her," said Rol Rauna, red and alien. "I must warn you, do not try to visit her yet. Speak to her first from here."

Around Corin the Holmgard landing pad was bustling with activity. Human or semi-human travellers hurried towards the waiting airship for Lalojiss. During the last month Corin too had been a traveller, piloting his one-man glider across the frozen continent, heading for home and thinking about the one and only Ginny Blanchard.

Corin glared at the grounded airship and its scurrying passengers. "This isn't the best place to talk, Rol Rauna. Can't you explain quickly—is Ginny any worse?"

"Perhaps she may be slightly better. She knows you are coming."

"But what—"

A baggage cart trundled past noisily, interrupting him. The crimson Senechi face of Rol Rauna seemed set in an expressionless mask, and Grin knew that further questions would be useless.

"I'll call Ginny."

Swiftly he found an empty holocom booth, and stepped inside. He spoke the name of Ginny Blanchard.

Corin heard clicking sounds as the scanner checked his identity.

Behind him, a hum of outside noise meant that Rol Rauna had thrust his head into the doorway. "Corin! Be kind to her!" Kind to her? Had he ever been anything else? The holocom bubble glowed.

Waves of blonde hair framed a delicate true-human face: Virginia Blanchard, the heiress of Holmgard. Wealth had not spoiled her.

"Ginny!" Her name burst out of him. She looked well, far better than he had expected, but her worried expression was not normal for Ginny.

"Corin . . . You're back . . . "

He frowned as her words trailed away in hesitation. Behind her image he could see holocom reflections of her apartment—tapestried, golden, sparkling, with a half-glimpsed movement which must be an ape servant waiting discreetly. In that luxurious apartment Ginny had welcomed the alien Rol Rauna, and had helped him educate the newly emerged Corin.

He said gently, "Ginny, I heard from Rol Rauna about your . . . your illness. That's why I came back."

"I know, and I'm grateful, believe me. I'm glad you're back. But there's something I need to tell you first."

He felt himself frowning again. "What's wrong?"

"You've heard of Gilbert Hennequin?"

"No. I don't follow the inner-circle gossip."

"You should." Her face seemed suddenly changed, suddenly older. "Gilbert's a developer from out East. I love him, Corin. We're living together now—officially."

The words echoed in his mind as if he had always known this would happen. An alien whistle of surprise from Rol Rauna pierced his ears. Into the tiny booth came a strange chill, a whisper of the Ice Age waiting outside the city dome.

"Ginny? Living together? You can't mean it!"'

"I'm sorry, Corin. It's true. I haven't known him very long, but—"

"Where is he?' That movement behind her had not been a servant . . .

"Gilbert's here, but we think you'd better not come to our level just yet. You do take bad news badly, Corin, and I know you had other ideas for us even if you didn't like to say so. Please, please take some time to think everything over, work it out for yourself, and then come to see us. Tomorrow?"

He couldn't blame Ginny for snatching at some happiness in the short time left to her. It was himself, the Corin who looked human but was less than human inside, the Corin who had been away exploring the world when he was needed here in Holmgard, that was who he blamed.

"Ginny, why did you do it? He—he's a true-human, I suppose?"

"Yes, he's unaltered, but so are you Corin, whatever you think. You're true-human in law, you're true-human to me. It makes no difference."

But Corin knew that she could not mean what she said. She had watched Rol Rauna create him.

"You know what I am, Ginny. I'm as unnatural as anyone with a Diffusion-altered body, aren't I?"

She whispered "No," unconvincingly.

"I suppose he's rich as well?"

"Oh yes, he gave me these—"

She brushed back her hair momentarily, revealing at each ear a milky jewel shining from her skin.

"Moon-pearls!"

Suddenly he understood. Moon-pearls, the rarest known jewels, were more than mere jewels. Their complex molecules had healing properties. A simple process: implantation, a gradual dissolving into the bloodstream, a halting of malignant growths . . . and a possible cure.

Only fourteen moon-pearls were known to exist, all from a single hoard found a decade or two previously. Despite their fanciful name their origin was unknown. Three were now in museums, three were off-planet, four were believed to be in private collections and the remainder had been used in medical research. Somehow Gilbert Hennequin had brought two of the surviving jewels together and given them to Ginny. A gift of beauty, a gift of life.

"I see," said Corin. "Wealth has its uses. I'm not rich, but I could have given you moon-pearls, not two but a dozen I could tell you how aviforms—" He broke off. The knowledge had been recorded by an earlier Corin Jones, and he wanted no part of it.

"Corin! It wasn't the moon-pearls! I love Gilbert for himself!"

"Because he's human? Because he was *born*?"

"Don't start that again, Corin. You're still a very dear friend and you're as human as I am. These moon-pearls—they're implants, so they'll dissolve away in time. They won't last, Corin. My love for Gilbert will."

He gazed at her image in the bubble, now cruelly unattainable. She would have her Gilbert now for as long as the moon-pearls could keep her alive. But then . . .

Corin said: "Ginny, I hope you're happy with him." He cut the connection.

In silence he turned and stared at the inhuman crimson-and-gold face of Rol Rauna. The glittering eye of the Senechi stared back with alien steadiness.

"My friend, I am most sorry for you. I did not realise the affair had gone so far."

"You could have warned me sooner," said Corin gruffly, but his rebuke was muted. The Senechi, even altered Senechi like Rol Rauna, were not greatly interested in human activities. Rol Rauna's interest in Corin was due to the fact that Rol Rauna had brought him to life, nuturing first his cells, then his body, then his mind . . . but now Rol Rauna could help no more. This was a matter for humans only.

Ginny Blanchard was getting married, tying herself to a man called Hennequin who liked expensive playthings. If Corin met Gilbert Hennequin face to face he would kill the man. The *man*!

"Moon-pearls," said Corin aloud. Hennequin had given her a pair of moon-pearls, both with full authentication documents no doubt. "But I told her, I could have given her a dozen moon-pearls—"

He clamped his jaw shut. Talking was dangerous, his knowledge was dangerous. The origin of moon-pearls was a secret which should have died with the original Corin. He cursed himself for boasting about such things, to Ginny of all people. His temper betrayed him too often.

And yet . . .

Rol Rauna was gazing oddly at him. Rol Rauna was more than a creator; he was mentor and conscience and friend. All of a sudden Corin knew what the Senechi must be thinking, inside that crimson head, and despite his hot anger he was touched by the alien's concern.

"It's not that simple, Rol Rauna. Scattering moon-pearls over her table wouldn't change Ginny's mind—"

"It might. In any event, more moon-pearls would surely aid her."

The red Senechi was very childlike in his simplicity sometimes, having chosen to remain in a body which would never reach full maturity, but the innocence of his logic was arresting. Cory nodded in agreement. What better gift for Ginny than year after year of life? What better revenge on Hennequin than to outshine his two moon-pearls with a dazzling handful?

He needed no time to consider the matter. His mind was made up instantly, even though he knew what lay ahead.

"It'll be dangerous and foul," said Corin. "You can't imagine how desperate winning those moon-pearls will be."

"I will help you," said Rol Rauna, with the easy eagerness of someone who did not understand. "We will get the moon-pearls whereever they come from, because Ginny needs them."

"Because Ginny needs them," Corin repeated. "Follow me!"

The mountain wind was bitterly cold. Dry powdery snow swirled up around Corin as he trudged towards the hut. He regretted leaving his glider behind in the city, but the tasks ahead could only be accomplished on foot. Beside the hut was a sign:

HUNTING STORE

GUNS, FOOD

The airseal door opened automatically for Corin. Rol Rauna followed him inside. In the wide entrance porch they brushed their hunt-suits clean of snow, then went on into the main store area. Bright aisles of merchandise faced Corin, deadly on the left and edible on the right. He went for the guns first.

The storekeeper, a seven-foot ape in semi-military coveralls, eyed Corin watchfully as he and Rol Rauna selected their weapons. The Senechi chose a custom hypodermic rifle, former planetary-occupation police issue, the kind which could knock out even an adult Senechi. Corin scooped up an armful of goods. A machete, a variable-strength heat pistol, an isotope charge gun designed to dissociate watery tissues. The charge gun alarmed Rol Rauna.

"Corin! What do you want that for?" The only purpose of a charge gun was to kill, instantly and messily. "It's deadly!"

"That's right. I'm serious about this."

Rol Rauna hefted the hypodermic rifle uncertainly. "Corin, I don't want anyone to get hurt—"

Corin grinned. He picked up a medikit and a pack of magnasize sealing pads. *"Someone's* going to get hurt."

Rol Rauna looked appalled. The ape storekeeper ambled over and grunted his disapproval. "Seems to me, friends, you should agree your tactics *before* you set out."

Good advice, Corin admitted silently, but that would have meant giving Rol Rauna all the facts, and he didn't want to alarm his friend too soon.

"There's an aviform Senechi in these mountains," said Corin. "If he turns mean, I want something that'll stop him."

Which was as much of the truth as he cared to say just yet.

Swiftly he made the rest of his purchases—food concentrates, carrying harness, inflatable lightweight shelter. Rol Rauna said he could carry more, but Corin wanted both of them to travel as lightly laden as possible.

Under the wary eye of the storekeeper they headed out.

From here on there was no trail, merely the mountain slopes which were frozen all the year round. A winding ridge where the snow was only inches deep made the easiest route. Corin led the way, his backpack heavy across his shoulders.

Before leaving the store Rol Rauna made a call to a Senechi friend, asking for Gilbert Hennequin to be investigated fully and for the police to be informed if anything suspicious was found. Corin insisted on these enquiries, wanting to give Rol Rauna some distraction from other thoughts. But if Hennequin really was the man for Ginny, moon-pearls would never change her mind and this quest was a fool's errand.

If it was madness to seek new life for Ginny—when she had found someone else—then certainly Corin was mad.

The day wore on, grey and dismal as they climbed higher. Once Corin saw an airship gliding overhead along the air path from Lalojiss into Holmgard. Its hull sprouted long struts everywhere – rooting points for the energy analogue envelopes which were its invisible wings.

Corin was still watching the airship, envying its ease of travel, when a police flatwing dropped out of the sky to land beside him.

Corin halted. "They've got no reason to chase me." He watched the ape pilot emerge. "I haven't done anything illegal, yet!'

"Perhaps your intentions are too obvious," said Rol Rauna.

The ape—a sergeant—came straight up to him. "Corin Jones?"

"I'm Corin." He dropped his face mask briefly, as convention demanded. "What's the problem?"

"You've lost some property," the sergeant announced. "A few hours back your place in Holmgard was broken into."

Corin shook his head. "What place?" He had no fixed accommodation in Holmgard. Either he stayed at the main hotel—a toll-free privilege originally given to the first Corin Jones by Ginny's grandfather—or else he found a room with Ginny Blanchard herself. "What place do you mean?"

"That closed-down Diffusion laboratory. It's still in your name according to the city records."

He understood.

"Yes, but—Look, sergeant, the name's the same but that's all. I'm not in the business of changing people. Not me. I haven't been on that level since old Blanchard died two years ago."

"Maybe not, but the place was worked over." The ape shrugged, a gesture which in apes meant annoyance rather than puzzlement or indifference. "It's my duty to inform you and ask your help."

"I'd help if I could, but I don't know what happened. Was anything stolen?"

"That's doubtful. We ran a movement analysis of some debris we found, plus the general disturbance. Somebody got in, searched your files, pulled out some memory boards and melted them. That's all."

It was a puzzle but scarcely relevant to his present life. Or was it?

He said carefully. "I appreciate your trouble in coming out, sergeant, but I don't aim to interrupt my hunting trip here and I can't give you any hints about burglaries in Holmgard. Done by professionals, probably."

"There were metabolic traces of one man only. A human male. The destroyed records were indexed under experiments on Senechi genetic manipulations—especially the aviform conversion. Do you know who might be interested in that stuff?"

"Sorry, nobody. The only human who remembers the laboratory now is Ginny Blanchard—and she wouldn't need to break in."

"We don't consider her a suspect, no." The ape looked disappointed. "Thank you for your help, Dr, Jones. Have a safe trip."

After the sergeant had boarded his flatwing and taken off again into the darkening sky, Rol Rauna looked curiously at Corin.

"I know you, Corin. When you seem most open you are really at your most devious. What fact did you conceal from the sergeant then?"

Corin grinned. "Think back, Rol Rauna. You were listening in the booth when I called Ginny's apartment this morning. Can't you guess who went ransacking the laboratory for facts about the aviform Senechi?"

"Ah!" Rol Rauna grew thoughtful. "The answer to *who* is obvious. The real question is, *why*?"

Corin himself could think of several answers, none of them pleasant.

Towards noon of the next day, after a hard and punishing journey, Corin decided that he and Rol Rauna needed some camouflage.

On a stony windswept ridge he paused. From his pack he got out a light-weight shoulder antenna and set up a polarisation screen in the air above them. Invisible but effective, it would continue the image of the surrounding landscape mirage-like across Rol Rauna and himself, concealing them from any eyes above.

He felt justified in his precautions a mile further on, when the aviform appeared before him.

The thing floated across the narrow valley, a purple hawkshape with arms and long claws under its wings. Corin had never seen that huge shape at such close range before. No natural creature could have been such a size and still flown easily, but the aviform was a product of Diffusion and possessed greater wings than those visible.

Fortunately Corin's polarisation screen was functioning well. The aviform glided away without reacting to the two intruders.

"We're close," said Corin. "From now on we have to track him and find his lair."

"But we do not kill him," said Rol Rauna.

"That's up to him. He's got what Ginny needs. If I see a chance to stop him I'll take it."

"Why will you not tell me where he keeps his moon-pearls? I think it will be better if *I* reach him before you do—" Rol Rauna broke off, and turned his great alien head to one side. "Corin, I can hear engine noise."

Corin listened. He seemed to hear a faint droning far off.

"Sounds like a snowtruck. If it's another ape policeman I don't want to know, not this close to the moon-pearls. Hide!"

Swiftly Corin raced over the ridge and threw himself down on the snowfield beyond the stones. Smooth snow was a better background for his chosen camouflage. He lowered the polarisation screen until the air above himself and Rol Rauna became grey from its nearness.

"I am following your lead in this," said Rol Rauna, "but it disturbs me. A Senechi should not hide."

"You're hiding to help me help Ginny," said Corin, hoping to ease Rol Rauna's doubts. "You want me to get more moon-pearls for her, don't you?"

Rol Rauna said nothing more. Was he wondering where his friendship for humans had taken him? Did the red neotene ever yearn to become adult? Would he one day reverse the alteration he had chosen, and return to a darker full-grown form? Corin himself had no wish to undergo a change of form when his real problem lay deeper.

The noise was louder. He peered through the narrow gap between ground and greyness. Cresting the ridge was a black vehicle on rattling bandwheels, without navigation lights, its front window so dark that only vague shapes could be glimpsed inside. It halted on the stones.

"The snowtruck." Corin drew out the heat pistol from his pack. "They've lost our trail—just! If there's a true-human in that cab, it's got to be Gilbert Hennequin."

But the first person out from the snowtruck was Ginny Blanchard.

Corin knew then that his schemes were over before they had begun, that the moon-pearls would be found by someone else, that his future with Ginny would be decided or ended out here amid the snow and the harsh mountains.

He waited to see the others emerge.

Three of them were humans—of a sort. They were tall and slender, long-limbed, with thin rat-like faces. Corin knew their type. Cowardly and selfish as individuals, yet loyal and aggressive as a group. They were called Ravagers.

The fourth and final man was another true-human, looking young and mild-mannered. He seemed so inoffensive and pleasant that Corin had a distinct shock when Ginny called him by name:

"Gilbert!"

Corin saw him hurry past the Ravagers to reach Ginny. They spoke, but their words were low-pitched and inaudible. Corin whispered to Rol Rauna. "I can't hear them at this distance. Can you understand anything?"

"Yes. The Hennequin is saying that you must be found before you kill someone. He sounds a sensible young man."

Corin took his eyes off Hennequin and Ginny to glare his annoyance at Rol Rauna. That momentary lapse of attention was a mistake.

When he looked back at Ginny purple wings were beating in front of her.

The aviform Senechi had swooped down from above his shield.

It was not attacking. It hovered, huge and powerful, then lowered its wings and alighted on the edge of the snow. Even with folded limbs it was much larger than any of the humans, larger even than the greatest normal Senechi.

Corin gestured for Rol Rauna to hold back. All he could do was watch—and listen. Ginny and the others were facing their challenger.

"We're prospectors," Gilbert was saying, "heading east. I've seen this territory from the airship and it looks promising."

"You are lying. Only hunters come here." The speech of the aviform was deep and resonant, as was to be expected from its purple Senechi-head.

"We're looking for minerals." Ginny took up the explanations.

"Holmgard hasn't had any new developments for years."

"Are the neotene and the man with you?"

"Who?"

So he had been too late in setting up his screen.

Gilbert must have thought fast. "Ah, those two! They're trying to reach our claim first!"

Corin swore angrily and gripped his heat pistol in frustration. It was obvious to anyone that Hennequin was seeking *him* and not any imaginary mineral deposits.

The aviform must have reached the same conclusion. "You are lying," it said again.

Hennequin's face was an image of betrayed innocence. "I'll have to explain this properly. Ginny, stand back." He signalled to the Ravagers. "Boys, please explain to him."

Corin saw the guns come out.

The three Ravagers were fast but the aviform was faster.

Its wings swept open and it lunged forward. Hennequin spun backwards under the blow, either knocked down or falling as he dodged. Before he finished hitting the ground the aviform snatched up Ginny.

She was caught. Corin had the aviform in his sights but dared not fire. Beside him, Rol Rauna had no such qualms. His rifle coughed. The hypodermic dart went through the aviform's wing feathers and took a Ravager in the throat. That one went down but the other two had their guns blazing. Only sheer speed saved the aviform as it surged upwards—still clutching a screaming and struggling Ginny Blanchard.

Corin saw her taken in that horrific moment. The Ravagers went on firing; lightning crackled around the fleeing aviform in dazzling zig-zig waves. The heat beams were cascading against the analogue wings of the aviform—biological energy fields centred around its physical wings, now made visible by Ravager heat pulses pouring even more energy into the sky. The hawk-shape and its captive were black shadows fleeing a sunburst.

"They'll hit Ginny! She'll fall!"

Snapping off the polarisation screen—a necessary precaution before using energy weapons, even though it revealed himself and Rol Rauna to the enemy—Corin fired across the snow at the unprepared Ravagers. Their speed as they saw him, dodged and threw themselves flat under his beam dismayed him. As they swung their guns towards him he realised how very fast the aviform must have been to outmanoeuvre them, and how dreadfully slow his unaltered reactions were by comparison.

Rol Rauna was not unaltered. He used his hypodermic rifle again and again. The Ravagers jerked, ceased to control their guns and simply went limp. Mists boiled up in front of them where the heat guns had vapourised the snow.

"A good idea," said Corin, seizing the opportunity to create some more mist himself. Ravagers, Hennequin and even the bulky snowtruck vanished behind white clouds. He glanced back after the aviform, and saw it dropping out of sight, behind the curve of the mountain. That was the direction to take after Ginny, then. He hoped the Ravager heat beams had been deflected from her by those analogue wings.

His mist screen was clearing already—there had been little depth of snow to vapourise. As the truck became visible he fired into its engine compartment. Hennequin was just rising to his feet, gun in hand, when the explosion blew him over again.

Corin and Rol Rauna departed with extreme haste.

The inevitable happened: they lost track of the aviform.

Hours went by while they searched the valleys and snowfields. Corin grew more and more despairing, wondering why an aviform Senechi should trouble to capture a human girl, hoping that Ginny was still alive and unharmed.

By now Hennequin and his Ravagers would be back on their trail. Ravagers recovered quickly from all things; even the one who had received a dart in his throat would have the wounded tissues regenerated perfectly in a few hours. The anaesthetic from Rol Rauna's rifle would not delay them for long.

The sun was a crimson ball on the horizon by the time his long search was rewarded. An overhanging sweep of ice; a shadow within; clawlike footmarks at the entrance.

Rol Rauna said. "The Ravagers will follow our tracks. One of us should stay outside on guard."

Corin saw the truth of that. "Right. You stay outside, I'll go in after Ginny." He grinned. "It's got to be *me,* Rol Rauna. Only I know where the moon-pearls are."

"You and Gilbert Hennequin, if our guess about that break-in is correct." Rol Rauna held out the hypodermic rifle meaningfully. "Take this, Corin."

Corin looked regretfully at his isotope chargegun, thought of Ginny inside the icy lair and knew that Rol Rauna was right again. They exchanged weapons. "Your way's safer for her."

"Better to lose the moon-pearls and bring out Ginny," said the Senechi. "Bring out yourself too."

He shook his head. "If I get killed you can grow a new Corin any time. Train the next one better."

He turned, and went into the ice and the darkness.

The wall of shadow was not natural. Corin groped his way along in blackness, arms probing the side. Smooth ice first, then something else—metal, or perhaps fused rock?

He felt a sudden burning pain against his chest. Shock gave way to surprise as he realised what had happened: in an inside pocket his neutraliser had heated up. He fished out the little device, but it was cooling into uselessness already and would open no more doors. Unknowingly he must have gone through a high-order barrier in the centre of the shadow. Was the barrier removed now, or would it be there re-formed if he tried to escape? He reached back a little way, felt nothing, and decided to move on. Ginny was somewhere ahead.

Voices. Corin came to the edge of the shadow. As if peering between black curtains he looked into orange brightness. It was a dwelling area. The aviform lived amid scaffolding and storage bins and huge woollen draperies. A strange but comfortable nest for a hermit monster.

With their backs to him, standing before a display tank of live fish, were Ginny and the purple alien. Corin listened.

"I don't know what you mean," Ginny was saying.

"You must see that I am not disturbed," said the aviform, with a trace of impatience. "Use your influence in your city. Why are you so reluctant to use your power? You could be virtually the overlord of Holmgard, should you choose to take up your responsibilities . . . "

If Ginny was being lectured on moral obligations she was in no great danger. That was an immense relief. The aviform must be a regular viewer of Holmgard broadcasts to have recognised her. Corin stared at the creature, at the purple back and the folded wings. The moon-pearls were in there; one shot and they would be his. The machete was in his pack. But could he do what was necessary here where Ginny would see everything?

This was his only chance and he had no time for negotiations. Without moon-pearls Ginny would die. Corin raised his rifle.

The aviform said, "I see you. Put down your weapon."

Above Corin a purple warning light glowed.

From the moment he had seen Ginny step from the snowtruck, back up on the mountain, he had known he would never reach the moonpearls. Corin shrugged with a bravado he did not feel. He lowered his rifle. Then, holding the weapon loosely as though it were a useless toy, he came forward out of the shadow.

"Corin!"

Her voice held shock—and disappointment that he wasn't Gilbert? He made no reply. Corin looked from her to the aviform, then to the aquarium where sinuous forms swam and rippled.

"I knew a *man* who used to collect these once, but I never heard of a *Senechi* keeping fish before."

The aviform showed remarkable restraint. "You have not come here with a rifle merely to discuss my dwarf plectognaths. I do not wish to hear any nonsense about mineral prospecting, either. Why, truthfully, are you here?"

Ginny put in, "It's my fault." Both Corin and the aviform stared at her, and she shrank back. Corin gave her a brief smile which might or might not seem reassuring.

"The facts will be new to both of you," said Corin. This was the time for facts. "The only other person who knows the truth is Gilbert Hennequin—I've no proof of that, but somebody broke into the old Diffusion laboratory yesterday and I'm guessing it was your Gilbert."

Ginny shook her head. "He said it must have been you, faking the traces of a break-in to hide what you were doing. He said you destroyed some very important records."

"How did he know they were important?"

"The police said so when they questioned us—Gilbert couldn't have done it, he was out meeting some Ravagers at the time."

The aviform growled, "Stop interupting, Virginia Blanchard! You, man, tell me why you are here, whatever your name is—"

"Corin Jones."

Despite its impatience the aviform paused. "Corin Jones? The human doctor who helped to perfect body alterations? Yes, there is a resemblance, but you are young and he was old!"

"He died years ago," said Corin. "A friend saved some of his cells and grew a new body from them. My body! I'm not the true-human you think I am—I'm only a clone, not a real person."

Corin discovered that he was trembling. He had not meant to add those last phrases, about not being a real true-human. Discussing it with Rol Rauna was one thing—exposing his inhumanity to this even more inhuman Senechi changeling was another.

"I understand, Cory Jones. I met you in your previous life. Now, without any more delay, *tell me why you are here!*"

Slowly, Corin nodded. In a way this would be easier than explaining who he was. The truth would be good for Ginny, too.

"I came here for moon-pearls," he said. "To give to her."

Ginny gasped, while the aviform gave a harsh cry. "More nonsense! I possess no moon-pearls! Only fourteen exist!"

"You have them inside you," said Corin. "In your second stomach. You don't know about your moon-pearls because they're part of your body."

"Explain fully, Cory Jones. You've no reason to lie now."

"I'm not a Cory and I'm not a liar. Gilbert Hennequin is the liar. He's after your moon-pearls too. He overheard something I said, broke into my laboratory and found the truth about moon-pearls in my records—or rather, in records filed by the real Dr. Corin Jones. It's very simple.

"All Senechi have digestion stones in their inner stomachs little hard pellets which once helped grind up food. Generally these stones aren't affected by body-changing, but with you aviforms it's different. Aviform bodies are expanded and lightened all the way through—and that's how digestion stones become moon-pearls. As old ones wear away new ones develop. I'd guess that you've got dozens of the most valuable jewels in the world inside you!"

He paused. This situation required careful thought. He still had no idea how he was going to get out of here. At least the two of them were quiet while they absorbed the implications of his news.

Ginny said, "I didn't ask for moon-pearls."

"You need them," said Corin.

"They are not for the taking," said the owner of the moonpearls. "So these objects have developed inside me. Why has no-one learned their origin before now?"

"You've been lucky so far," said Corin. "It's about forty years since Diffusion began, and body-changing became common, right? And only about. fifteen since the first aviforms appeared. I suppose that first batch of moon-pearls came from some aviform who died or was sick—maybe you could find out from medical records. It doesn't matter exactly how they were found and taken for jewels, what matters to you now is your personal problem."

"Go on."

"You're a walking, flying, living treasure-house, and when the news goes around you'll get ripped apart for your moon-pearls. I'm sorry, but I had that in mind myself."

"So had I," said a new voice, calm and infinitely confident.

Gilbert Hennequin came through the shadow. Either the barrier had not been restored, or else Hennequin possessed a neutraliser at least as effective as Corin's. Certainly his heat rifle was more deadly than a hypodermic.

Hennequin continued, "I'm glad Corin explained all that to you. It saved me the trouble. Please drop the rifle, Corin."

Corin dropped the rifle. He knew Hennequin would have shot him instantly had he hesitated.

Ginny gazed sadly at Hennequin. "Gilbert, why didn't you tell me the truth about moon-pearls before?"

"I didn't want to worry you. I had hoped to stop your friend here before he went too far, but . . . "

Something else was worrying Corin. "Where's Rol Rauna?"

"Sleeping outside. He got my boys but I knocked him out." Hennequin frowned. "I think, Ginny, it would be a good idea for you to go to Rol Rauna. I know he's a friend of yours—try to wake him up and tell him that everything's under control now, I've found Corin. Go to Rol Rauna."

She looked from Gilbert to Corin and back to Gilbert again. Without a word to either she made her way to the shadow, and disappeared.

Hennequin returned his full attention to Corin and the aviform. He looked very young.

"You two know too much. I won't prolong this—"

The aviform launched itself in a sweep of wings towards Hennequin. Calmly the man whipped up his rifle and fired. A red beam flashed upwards. The analogue wings glowed in sudded brilliance, overloaded, and abruptly the aviform fell back unprotected as the searing heat lanced into it. Hennequin swung his rifle around to Corin.

—Who, without taking his eyes off the combat, had retrieved his weapon and sent a knockout dart thudding satisfyingly into Hennequin's body. He regretted that he had left the chargegun behind with Rol Rauna.

Hennequin and the aviform hit the floor together. Corin was unhurt. He went over to the others and found that both were still alive. Each discovery came as a fresh surprise. He examined the aviform's side, scarred dreadfully by the heat beam.

I could take the moon-pearls now. I could make a small incision . . . seize them . . . no-one would ever know . . .

Instead he took the medikit from his pack, and began covering the wounds. He knew quite clearly that he was a fool. He knew also that Ginny would never accept moon-pearls now that she knew their source. The aviform groaned.

"He shot me . . . but you would have shot me too, Cory Jones?"

Corin rubbed on a sealing pad and did not answer.

"Yes, you would have . . . you cannot remember that I am not a Senechi . . . "

Corin grunted. "Don't try to talk."

"I was never a Senechi I was a man . . . Inside this body my real self is as much a true-human as you are—"

"True-human!" said Corin, and the aviform went quiet.

Footsteps sounded. He looked up, hoping Ginny was back, but instead the ape police sergeant appeared in the entrance.

The sergeant came up to the prone bodies, tut-tutted and spoke swiftly into his pocket communicator. He nodded towards Corin and eyed the makeshift doctoring on the aviform. "Good enough. He'll live. We've got medics flying across. They'll see to him." He moved to Hennequin, gave him an experimental nudge. "I'll keep this one myself. Industrial share rigging, counterfeit moon-pearls, forged certificates—we got him just in time. Another few months and he'd have made everything legitimate."

Counterfeit moon-pearls? Corin understood only too well. "Sergeant, you're welcome to Hennequin. Take him away before I give him what he deserves. And . . . is there a red Senechi outside?"

"Your friend? Yes. He'll be all right when he wakes up, but those three Ravagers around him will take weeks to regenerate." The ape turned to the fish tank, pressed the feed-dispenser button.

"By the way, I contacted the lady's home apartment a while back, after we realised what the Hennequin was up to. There's a crew of apes flying out to take her home."

"Thanks."

There seemed to be nothing more Corin could do. He went back outside, into the soft grey light of evening. Ginny was kneeling on the snow beside the unconscious Rol Rauna.

"Nobody's dead," said Corin. He checked that Rol Rauna was breathing normally, then described the struggle against Hennequin in as few words as possible.

Ginny stood up. Her face was pale. "You didn't get the moon-pearls."

"No."

"I'm glad. It wouldn't have been right."

But what would be right? Finding an aviform who would donate his moon-pearls to her willingly? Trying to produce moon-pearls artificially by Diffusion alteration techniques? A true-human would try everything, and if the aviform was right Corin was true-human inside.

He saw a bright dot appear in the sky, from the direction of Holmgard. Her servants.

Ginny sighed. "Gilbert told me the aviform would help us to find more moon-pearls. I believed him."

She had no reason to have not believed him. Hennequin had given her moon-pearls, or had seemed to.

Counterfeits. She would have died bravely, with Hennequin so loving by her side . . . as he waited for Holmgard to become his . . .

Corin reached out for Ginny. She settled into his arms at last. They stood together while the twilight dimmed and the aircraft from Holmgard drew nearer.

TIME TICKET

B. J. Empson

There was a bronze-colored plate to the stern of the vessel and Ferris leaned forward to make out the printed words: ALBATROSS. **Built by Cobalt and Stone 3006 A.D.**

He nodded to himself, the damn thing was already eighty years old, would it begin to stand up to what they intended to do with it?

Ian Ferris was a tall graying man of fifty with a thin cynical face; years in Undercover had not endeared him to humanity.

"Excuse me," said a voice behind him. "Agent Ferris?"

"Yes—oh, you must be Professor Otto Ludwig." He held out his hand. "Glad to meet you."

Ludwig shook hands with him, smiling. He had a round, rubbery sort of face and wide blue eyes which suggested an innocence he lacked. He had a brilliant scientific mind.

"You can pay the astronomical charges for this experience?" enquired Ferris.

"Candidly no, but the Foundation were prepared to cough it up if I was prepared to investigate."

"They are prepared to take the claims of the consortium seriously then?"

"No, but they are not prepared to take chances—they might have stumbled on something."

"The same view was taken by my department. I take it you are well aware of the dangers if they have succeeded?"

"Too well, Mr. Ferris, I'm wearing a Nullifier. I took the liberty of bringing one for you—just strap it to your wrist above your watch."

"Thank you. What does it do?"

"It dissociates us from repercussions should they occur. If they have stumbled on something, we activate these for our own safety."

"Well, thanks, I appreciate the thought." Ferris changed the subject quickly. "Have you looked round the ship yet?"

"No, I have not even boarded yet or declared myself as a ticket holder."

"Fine, permit me to show you around. There are one or two things on this vessel which I find deeply disturbing."

Ludwig's knowledge of vessels was limited but he had read up on this one first. Clamped close to the quay, she was unmoving in the slightly choppy waters of Great Harbor. She was about ninety meters long and built as if to cut through the waves like a sailboat. This was for artistic effect only, she was flat bottomed and fitted with A/G repellers designed to lift her well above the waves and not through them. Her decks were not clear but covered with a transparent bubble to protect travelers from bad weather. Sections of this could be rolled, back when required.

Ferris led the way forward, stopped after a few paces and pointed. "What do you make of that?"

"Nothing, I know it's ancient, long before my time but, at a guess, it's a weapon."

"You are quite correct. It's a machine gun on a stanchion. Water cooled, fired solid missiles at around ten a second. The thing a couple of meters in front of it works on the same principle but at a much slower rate of fire and was called a Bofors. This fired an explosive missile."

"Is there anyone here who would know how to use a thing like that?"

"Oh, yes, take Delwood Jarvis over there, guy in the red cloak. Collector and specialist in ancient arms. Then Goole, the magnate, multi-billionaire, that's the one with a beard. He owns three Caribbean islands and a slice of the South Americas. He plays around with ancient large arms as a hobby. He boasts of possessing, and using a couple of German 88's from World War Two. Oh, yes, my friend, a fair half these paying guests can use those weapons."

Ludgwig said: "Let's sit down and discuss this. I'm not happy about this business at all."

Before any discussion could begin, however, they were interrupted.

"Excuse me, gentlemen, a word." He was a tall, shaven-headed man in a green shimmering cloak. The smile only showed his teeth.

He bowed a little jerkily. "I represent ship security and I am here to inform you that we have one of the best Type-Recognition Devices on the market. Obviously the device will not tell us who are but it defines, very clearly, *what* you are."

He looked directly at Ferris. "Government agent, top flight, probably A-class."

He turned to Ludwig. "Scientist, also top flight and, if I add my own educated guess, way up on the principles of relativity."

Ferris looked up at him with an expressionless face. "Assuming your conclusions to be correct—so what?"

"Don't get ideas, gentlemen, any attempt to interfere might result in two personal tragedies."

"Well, that makes my premonitions even less happy," said Ludwig when he had gone.

"You have seen something that makes this thing feasible?" Ferris's face seemed suddenly thinner.

"Look," Ludwig was opening and closing his hands nervously. "I once published a paper which gained me a certain reputation, not always favorable but one which other experts admitted contained certain axioms. This paper—bear with me, please, was called, *Relativity in Adjustment to Time/Space.*"

"Can you put that in simple language?"

"Not yet—if ever. Listen, please: walking round this ship, I saw variations. Near the bows are two curiously shaped bulges. The shape betrays them, they're Daimler-Sikert high output variators. There is also a huge bulge near the stern. If I had been adapting this vessel, I would I would have fitted an orbital/spiro-time balance mechanism into that cavity."

"This couldn't be one vast con, could it?"

"It could, of course, but if it is, it's a very elaborate one. More to the point, I'd hate to try and pull it with the type of people we have on board."

Ferris nodded without speaking but his face looked damp. He fumbled in an inner pocket and produced his green plastic ticket.

"This ticket cost exactly one million, world exchange regulation vouchers. Yours cost the same. Can you tell me, in simple language, please, exactly what I have bought?"

Ludwig looked at him bleakly. "In simple language, my friend, *you have bought a ticket to travel in time.*"

Ferris was a trained agent but he could almost feel ice particles forming in his stomach. "What happens? Do we go charging into the future?"

"I do not know where we shall go, I can only tell you that time travel is a possibility."

"Would it strike you as safe?"

"Hazardous is the word I would use. On the other hand, on a rational level, if this is not a con then this cannot be the first trip. Even madmen would not risk their own lives and those of their passengers unless trial runs had not been made first. The danger lies in what happens in transit."

Ferris nodded slowly. "Like you I am very unhappy about this."

"Is it legal?"

"Paradoxically yes until proven that it can be done. The matter transmission of inanimate objects was legal until an Italian cartel proved it possible. World Establishment immediately placed a ban on it until it was proven safe—a ten year test period—by an official body."

Ludwig shrugged. "Nice if you survive."

WILL ALL PASSENGERS PLEASE TAKE TO THEIR SEATS.

Ferris, unashamedly sweating, said: "Where is it?"

"Next to mine, the number is on the back of your ticket."

PLEASE RELAX. THE FIRST STAGE OF OUR JOURNEY WILL BE TAKEN UP IN NORMAL FLIGHT AT FIFTEEN HUNDRED HOURS PRECISELY.

Ludwig glanced at his watch. "I could use a drink."

"No doubt but will your Foundation approve the luxury? Below decks, in the bar, they're asking two thousand a glass."

"Good God!"

STAND BY, VESSEL DETACHING FROM QUAY.

There was a slight bump as the vessel dropped a few centimeters into the water. Almost immediately the Anti-gravitational repellers began to whine.

The ship shuddered slightly, spray rose on either side turning quickly to fountains of water. The whine of the repellers became a howl which seemed quickly to pass beyond hearing.

THE SHIP IS NOW ASCENDING TO THE HEIGHT OF THREE KILOMETERS. UPON REACHING THIS LEVEL, HORIZONTAL FLIGHT WILL BEGIN. PASSENGERS MAY EXPECT A JOURNEY OF NINETY MINUTES BEFORE TIME-TRANSIT BEGINS.

To both men, it was the shortest ninety minutes in their lives. Almost before they had taken it in, the vessel had begun hovering. Far below them, the sea looked corrugated, gray and unreal.

WILL PASSENGERS PLEASE HELP THEMSELVES TO THE BLINDFOLDS NOW AVAILABLE ON THE MAIN DECK. THESE ARE NOT COMPULSORY BUT THEIR USE DOES PREVENT A CERTAIN AMOUNT OF DISORIENTATION.

"Any idea why?" asked Ferris.

"I don't know why but I can make a wild guess. If we travel in time, the days will shorten as we accelerate. Day, night, night day, each growing shorter until they merge and become a blur."

"I wish I hadn't asked," said Ferris.

It seemed a long time to sit in darkness. They could no longer estimate what was happening, as there was no sense of motion. Both realized that they had lost sense of time; five minutes might have passed, or a century.

PASSENGERS MAY REMOVE THEIR MASKS.

They did so and beyond the transparent bubble of the ship was fog, but a boiling fog that rushed desperately round the vessel as if seeking entrance. It was a dull red fog that flickered continually, lessening and increasing in brilliance as they watched.

YOU ARE VIEWING THE BIRTH PANGS OF OUR OWN PLANET EARTH. IT IS NOT FOG WHICH SURROUNDS US BUT STEAM, FIRE AND WATER FIGHTING FOR DOMINANCE; OCEAN AND VOLCANIC ERUPTION.

"All we need is a dramatization," said Ludwig savagely.

"This is genuine?" Ferris sounded as if he didn't believe his own question. "This is not some projected form of virtual reality?"

"No, I took a couple of pictures. It is impossible to photograph an induced illusion."

"Can you explain this simply?"

"I'll try but I won't promise you'll understand it even then. However it goes like this. Everything that has ever happened, from the smallest to the greatest, leaves its impression on time and space like, for example, a footprint in the sand. The highly advanced technology now being used, can tune into the past, find and recreate that footprint. In short, an incident from the past has been attuned to and recreated about us."

"What are we doing—forging ahead into the future?"

"Theoretically travel into the future is an impossibility. One cannot recreate a situation which has not occurred or, put more simply, track footprints which have yet to be left in the sand."

Ferris looked at him with respect. "It may be way out but at least I can follow you."

WILL PASSENGERS PLEASE REPLACE THEIR BLINDFOLDS. YOU WILL BE ADVISED WHEN TO REMOVE THEM. EXPECT AN INTERVAL OF APPROXIMATELY THIRTY MINUTES.

Once more it seemed like a few minutes yet, again, like centuries.

MASKS MAY BE REMOVED WITHIN A SHORT PERIOD BUT FIRST THERE IS A WARNING. YOU WILL BE ENTERING A PERIOD OF EARTH'S EARLY HISTORY. YOU WILL SEE THE WORLD AS IT WAS WHEN THE DINOSAUR WAS KING BUT LET IT BE MADE QUITE CLEAR EVERY LIFE-FORM YOU SEE IS INVIOLATE. SOME OF YOU MAY BE BEARING SECRET AND POWERFUL WEAPONS PERHAPS CHERISHING THE THOUGHT OF A STUFFED PTERODACTYL TO BRAG ABOUT IN YOUR SPORTS ROOM. BE WARNED. FORGET IT. CERTAIN TRAINED MEMBERS OF MY CREW ARE UNDER ORDERS TO SHOOT AT ANY SUCH ATTEMPT. NO CREATURE MAY BE KILLED OR FLY SWATTED. SUCH EVENTS OCCURRING NOW COULD WELL ALTER A GENETIC TREND AND CHANGE THE FUTURE OF EARTH COMPLETELY.

"Well, thank God they've thought that aspect of the bloody thing through," said Ludwig with an audible sigh.

The announcement continued. SOME AMONG YOU ARE NO DOUBT WONDERING WHY WE HAVE ANCIENT WEAPONS ON BOARD AND EXPERIENCING SOME LITTLE DISAPPOINTMENT. DO NOT BE DISCOURAGED, YOUR TURN WILL COME. RECORDS HAVE BEEN EXAMINED AND CONFIRMED. IT WILL BE POSSIBLE TO BLEND IN WITH AND PARTICIPATE IN EVENTS WHICH HAVE ALREADY BEEN RECORDED AS HAVING HAPPENED THUS NOT ALTERING THE FUTURE. PASSENGERS MAY NOW REMOVE THEIR BLINDFOLDS.

Ferris was stopped in the act of reaching for it.

"Switch on your bloody Nullifier for God's sake." Ludwig's voice was urgent. "You will be able to see and speak but you won't be able to move. In brief, you won't be able to *participate*. Blinder off, and switch on—understood? Explain later."

Ferris obeyed but finding his body growing numb and refusing to obey his commands. He could, however, as Ludwig had said, move his eyes and beyond the ship—

Strangely the first thing which impressed him was the heat, it was almost palpable, nearly one could see it. Below and around was a swampy kind of jungle, full of small lakes and stunted pulpy sort of trees. He could tell the whole area was literally sweltering, mist crept up from everywhere.

He did not see as much as he had expected. Below, and close, a head followed by a long green neck rose from the jungle and began to tear at the upper foliage of one of the trees but that was all.

At a distance and in the sky, life abounded. Black things that looked nothing like birds soared and swooped in hundreds.

On the far horizon, a volcano belched smoke and flame angrily at the sky.

PASSENGERS ARE ADVISED TO CLOSE THEIR EYES FOR A BRIEF PERIOD. THEY WILL BE ADVISED WHEN TO OPEN THEM.

BE ADVISED, PLEASE, ALL OF YOU ARE ABOUT TO WITNESS THE MOST SPECTACULAR AND FAR REACHING EVENT IN THE HISTORY OF THE PLANET.

It was night when they opened their eyes, a still sweltering night, mist-wrapped and phosphorescent.

Ferris had a feeling it was close to dawn although there was nothing to confirm it.

It was then that the sky lit, first as a bright white star, turning rapidly to a tiny sun trailing flame.

It passed above ship, lighting it eerily then plunged out of sight below the horizon. The watchers sensed, rather than felt, the enormous impact. They saw an eye-searing brilliance that lit the sky from horizon to horizon. It hung there briefly then dropped away to darkness but a rasping thunder followed by an enormous detonation that shook the ship from bow to stern.

DON YOUR BLINDFOLDS, PLEASE. WE MUST MOVE TO SAFETY.

When they looked again, the jungles had gone and the oceans had arisen.

IT IS NOW MIDDAY WITH THE SUN AT IT'S ZENITH. OBSERVE THAT IT IS TWILIGHT, THE SUN OBSCURED BY THICK CLOUD COMPOSED LARGELY OF ASH AND DUST. THIS IS THE EFFECT OF ALL YOU WITNESSED WHEN A GIANT METEOR STRUCK THE EARTH. WHAT YOU ARE SEEING NOW IS THE BE-GINNING OF THE ICE AGE.

Below, a film of whiteness was gradually covering the ocean. The distant volcano still stabbing crimson in the half-light seemed only to emphasize the spreading cold.

Later they saw the great white cliffs marching across continents already meters deep in snow. Here, winds drove virtual rivers of snow in horizontal streams or spun them around in distorted whirlwinds.

REPLACE YOUR BLINDFOLDS PLEASE.

It seemed a very long wait but it gave the two men time to talk.

"What's all the damn panic?" Ferris wished he could turn his head but even that was denied him. "I suppose you've discovered something?"

"A fallacy in their calculations, I think. They played it by the book in the age of the dinosaur but now they're blundering into the unknown."

"How come?"

"From what they said they have obtained records of actual events. Presumably, therefore, the period of which they speak must be reasonably close to our own age. For example, you and I can access city records and discover details of our grand parents. When they were born, what work they did and when they died etc. The people running this thing have dug up records of past events and, since they have already *happened* they think they can embroil themselves therein without alteration to the time/stream."

"And they can't?"

"Not according to my knowledge and my mathematics, no. They think they can, as it were, slot in on events but it can't be done, not without repercussions."

BLINDFOLDS MAY BE REMOVED NOW. AS WE SHALL BE MOVING RELATIVELY SLOWLY FORWARD. IT WILL BE NECESSARY TO CLOSE THE EYES FOR BRIEF PERIODS ONLY. AT THIS PERIOD IN EARTH'S HISTORY, THE ICE AGE IS FAR PAST AND THE RACE OF MAN HAS BEGUN TO EXPAND AND CONQUER.

THE PERIOD IN WHICH WE NOW FIND OURSELVES IS AT THE BIRTH OF THE ROME EMPIRE.

The world was smiling again, there was green and warmth and blue seas.

Ferris thought they were over the Mediterranean but was never sure. No Roman Galleys were seen but two dhows were spotted near a rocky coast.

It was clear to the two men that the vessel was shifting quickly from decade to decade. Clearly there was some end in view and intervals of eye-closure became shorter but more frequent.

PASSENGERS MAY NOW OPEN THEIR EYES AGAIN. PLEASE NOTE, OUR POSITION BOTH IN TIME AND SPACE IS PRECISE. THE YEAR IS NINETEEN SIXTEEN AND BELOW US ARE THE BATTLEFIELDS OF WORLD WAR TWO.

Both men were as shocked as those on board. There was an immediate rush to the rails to see and record. Interest was far greater than that aroused by the Jurassic period or even the impact of the giant meteor.

From their fixed seated position neither man could see too much but they saw enough to make them close their eyes. They saw running men in a mass attack mown down in hundreds by concentrated machine gun fire. A surviving group, sheltering in a crater, literally blown to nothing by a heavy shell.

Nothing was missed, all the agonies of mud and trench warfare were selected and almost served up as a contrived drama.

"I could kill them," said Ferris in a strained voice. "The shows put on by the Roman Emperors were mild sports compared to this. The human race is supposed to have advanced since those days of barbarism."

It was some seconds before Ludwig spoke and, when he did, his voice sounded quavery. "There's nothing we can do, nothing to alter things but this, I fear, is but the beginning."

"I don't follow you."

"You will. Dear God in Heaven, I think I know what those ancient guns on board are for. Worse still, if correct, it will confirm the fallacy I mentioned earlier."

Ferris was still stressed. "How can they act like this? We're educated, psychiatry and genetic manipulation are supposed to have improved the race."

"Not for the very rich—every advance is slanted to increase their dominance with each succeeding generation."

Ferris became suddenly aware of the other's previous words. "You can work out future events?"

"Not really but I can work out quite a lot with observation, some background knowledge and one or two wild guesses. Those guns are not their for show, they're there to be used."

"But if they do, won't they interfere with the future? I mean, they stressed that time and time again, even an insect must not be harmed."

"They think they've found a way of getting around the problem, and therein lies the fallacy."

Ludwig paused and drew a deep shuddering breath. "I think it goes something like this. Unless I am very much mistaken, our next time stop will be in the middle of World War Two. The British, the Germans and the Americans kept meticulous records of events, many of which are open to interested research people such as historians. It is on record what ships or aircraft were lost, and in many cases how. 'Sunk by air attack', 'shot down by Spitfire,' etc, etc."

Ludwig paused again then continued. "The people running this show think they have found the answer—since these events have actually *happened*, their influence on the future has already *taken place*. It is, therefore, according to their theory, quite in order to move in and participate without endangering the present or the future."

"And the fallacy?"

"The fallacy is that whatever decisive action might be taken in the past, it *must* effect the future."

"Then we could return to a changed world—an alien world?"

"I wouldn't discount that possibility, no. Although there are so many variations in the study of time and space that I wouldn't care to be dogmatic."

PASSENGERS MAY NOW OPEN THEIR EYES. HERE IS AN ANNOUNCEMENT OF PARTICULAR IMPORTANCE. THE PERIOD IN WHICH YOU NOW FIND YOUR-SELVES IS THE EARLY AUTUMN OF 1942. IN THIS PERIOD WE SHALL BE COVERING A LARGE AREA OF THE ATLANTIC AT NORMAL SPEED IN ORDER TO BRING ABOUT CONJUNCTIONS WITH EVENTS WHICH HAVE ALREADY OCCURRED. THE USE OF THIS VESSEL'S WEAPONS IS THEREFORE IMMINENT.

PASSENGERS WISHING TO PARTICIPATE SHOULD MAKE THEMSELVES AVAILABLE TO THE PURSER IN CHARGE.

PARTICIPANTS WILL BE TAKEN IN STRICT ALPHABETICAL ORDER WITH THE FIRING TIME OF ANY WEAPON LIMITED TO FIVE MINUTES.

THESE MINUTES HIRED WILL COST, AT STANDARD EXCHANGE RATES, FIFTY THOUSAND PER MINUTE. SEVENTY FIVE THOUSAND WILL BE CHARGED FOR EVERY SHELL FIRED FROM THE BOFORS GUN. SOLID MIS-SILES USED BY THE MACHINE GUN WILL BRING A CHARGE OF TEN THOU-SAND FOR EACH MISSILE FIRED.

Ludwig shook his head. "Why? What's the point?"

Ferris's mouth twisted slightly. "Well, in the first place, these people can afford it. They're rich enough to buy complete cities without a second thought. Again this is a one-off for the promoters so they have to make a killing for the profit. At a guess this vessel cost twenty five million to buy and equip, the sponsors want to do a damn sight more than break even."

Ferris stopped abruptly then continued: "This whole bloody conversation is a pointless exercise, isn't it? We don't care about profit or loss, we're talking to stop ourselves thinking."

ATTENTION! YOUR FIRST TARGET IS A FAST, HEAVILY ARMED MOTOR

VESSEL WHICH CARRIED QUICK-FIRING GUNS AND TORPEDOES. IT WAS GENERALLY KNOWN AS AN E—BOAT.

GERMAN RECORDS SHOW THAT IT WAS DESTROYED BY ENEMY ACTION, PROBABLY A COMBINED AIR ATTACK. CONFIRMATION WAS LATER PROVIDED BY A BODY WASHED UP ON THE FRENCH COAST TOGETHER WITH SOME OF THE SHIP'S PAPERS.

This E-Boat might just have made base, the starboard engine was still running erratically but the port engine had seized up.

Ludwig who enjoyed sailing himself, estimated her speed at six knots with her bows just clear the water.

She had taken a beating, there were splintered holes in her upper surface and one of her smaller guns had been blown off its stanchion.

Ferris thought he saw two dead bodies but was not quite sure, his attention was taken up by the man at the wheel. If he had had a uniform, what was left of it was gone above the waist. He was obviously steering the vessel yet holding himself upright at the same time. It was obviously an application of sheer will power—he was doing it with his right arm only. The left arm, a bloody mess of bone and tendon, hung limply at his side.

As the vessel passed from his line of vision, there were three ear-splitting reports.

The Bofors Gun! Ferris was a appalled yet at the same time filled with fury. In his job he had seen and reported upon many dreadful things, but somehow this act of slaughter surpassed everything.

He knew, of course, even if the man had survived at the time, he would have died of natural cause over a thousand years ago but, even so, he was in emotional revolt against the whole business. To him, to use an ancient word, there was something *evil* about it.

SUNDERLAND FLYING BOAT, RETURNING FROM ROUTINE SUBMARINE PATROL. BRITISH REPORT STATES THAT THE AIRCRAFT FAILED TO RETURN FROM MISSION.

Both men saw the aircraft approach, both heard the chatter of machine guns. They saw the aircraft veer suddenly sideways and one of its four engines begin to smoke—

"They can't fit that in," said Ludwig in a choked voice. "The plane was undamaged, there was no evidence whatever of enemy action. *We* brought it down, no one else."

It was but a beginning. The A/G vessel with her immense air speed ranged the Atlantic and the Western Approaches for several hours, knowing just where to find victims. One of which included a torpedoed tanker with survivors. One boat had been launched and was half full. Others struggled desperately in the water.

The worst part to the two men was the conversations they heard afterward.

"What the hell, as far as we are concerned the whole bloody lot have been dead over a thousand years."

"Actually we did the poor bastards a favor, they died quickly—"

Ferris for his part was reviewing his own life. He'd always thought he had a tough job. He had convinced himself he was a hard man but not anymore. Pray to God he never sank as low as these. Their main concern, their primary aim had not been the wonders of the past, they were just frills. Their real aim had been an unlicensed slaughter for which they could never be accused for the proof was too far in the past.

Ludwig, equally distressed, was more concerned with the effects of their actions. When they got back to their own age—if they got back—would the world have changed through their actions? Would some dreadful plague or volcanic upheaval bring distress to thousands of innocent people?

There was a further problem, quite personal, which also refused to leave him in peace. It had come to him in a very short time that he, the alleged expert on time, space and relativity, knew absolutely nothing about the subject. In truth he was like some idiot student who, having learned to add and subtract, considered himself an expert in mathematics. Worse, like Albert Einstein before him, he was beginning to sense that there was something beyond science. There were vast unchangeable laws one could not move. Certain actions brought about certain results even in simple terms. You could, if you were smart and cultish, call it Karma or if old fashioned, what you sow, you will damn well reap. Ludwig knew in that brief moment that somewhere was absolute truth.

Ferris broke his train of thought. "We stuck here, I see your reasons for being unable to move but how the hell do we turn these damn wrist things off if we're part paralyzed?"

"We can't, not physically—but both will respond to a vocal command, a key word."

"And when are you going to use that?"

"I don't honestly know. You'll have to trust me, when I feel the time is right."

Ferris made no comment. He had grown to like his companion and, in any cases, the man was the only hope he had.

PASSENGERS MAY DON THEIR BLINDFOLDS OR CLOSE THEIR EYES ACCORDING TO PREFERENCE. WAITING PERIOD WILL BE APPROXIMATELY THIRTY MINUTES. AT THE END OF THAT PERIOD OUR JOURNEY WILL BE OVER, WE SHALL HAVE RETURNED TO OUR OWN AGE ON THE SAME DAY WE DEPARTED. IN RELATIVE TIME WE HAVE BEEN AWAY FROM GREAT HARBOR FOR SEVEN HOURS AND NINE MINUTES. AN AVERAGE CRUISE ON AN AVERAGE DAY, GENTLEMEN. THANK YOU.

The Earth looked the same, there was Grand Harbor below seeming to rise up and meet them as they descended. Along the coast, on either side of the harbor, the sea was dotted with swimmers and the usual pleasure craft normal for a Summer day. It looked the same, felt the same, but Ludwig could not convince himself that it was.

They had, almost reached their mooring place beside the quay when alarm bells seemed to awake inside him.

He heard himself shout the command word releasing them from their enforced stasis.

He turned to Ferris. "*Jump!*" he shouted desperately. "Jump now!"

They were still some three meters above the quay but both sensed that escape was urgent.

Both landed awkwardly, sprawling as they landed, but before they could draw breath there was an immense rush of wind.

Ferris had a brief impression of the vessel rocketing upwards again but was too absorbed after that to look further. He was being swept across the quay and he clutched desperately at one of the old-fashioned mooring rings that no one had bothered to remove. Somehow he caught it with one hand and, mainly from reflex, caught Ludwig's ankle as he slid past.

For some seconds the two men lay on their backs, shaken, trying to regain their breath.

The wind had stopped and finally Ludwig sat up. "You saved my life—you know that? I owe you."

"I've got a feeling you saved mine more than once." Ferris sat up himself and sucked at the edge of his hand that was bleeding from a lot of small scratches. "That blasted mooring ring is jagged in parts."

Ludwig said: "What's happened to the bloody ship?"

"God knows, the last glimpse I got of it, she was sort of shooting upwards."

"No sign now, not a single one, and it's a clear sky."

Ferris struggled shakily to his feet and extended his hand to the other. "Take a hold, you're shakier than I am."

"Can you wonder, look over the edge—it's nearly a twenty meter drop to the water. You saved me from that."

"Where's the bloody ship?" said Ferris. Suddenly the answer to that question was all-important to him. On that answer alone, he thought, his whole future, possibly his entire life depended.

"I don't know." Ludwig had a handkerchief pressed to his forehead, he was sweating profusely. "No, I don't know but I have an idea, no, a theory, as to what might have happened."

He paused and drew a deep but uneven breath. "As I said a few hours ago, any decisive action taken in the past *must* affect the future. Where I went wrong, I think, were my conclusions as to *how* it would influence the future. It didn't affect the environment, the climate or the comings and goings of men, it was a limited reaction."

"I don't quite follow."

"Put it this way then: I think this is personal. I think that these men, by their actions in the past, *have altered their own future*. They fulfilled a cycle by returning but, at that point, their future *here* has ended."

"I follow you." Ferris, sweating himself now, was dabbing at his face pith a shaking hand. "Whatever happened it did us no good; I feel downright ill."

"There's a bench about every thirty meters up from the land. I suggest we make the nearest and sit for a while. I'm not feeling too good myself." Ludwig was aware that his legs were shaking. He had the alarming feeling that they might buckle at the knees without warning.

By the time they reached the nearest bench, they were compelled to hold each other up.

We must look like a couple of drunks thought Ferris, sourly. Surely they were not going through this because of one rather high jump, and even shock would not account for a reaction like this.

They dropped heavily on the soft pseudowood with almost a whimper of sheer relief—a relief which was not to last.

What happened to them both could not be called a vision. They could see the rest of Grand Harbor clearly. They could see down the quay to the wide road and the thriving city beyond. Whet was happening was occurring in their minds.

In a way it was like memory, only they knew it wasn't memory, although it was the closest they could get to it. The events that they were seeing was not happening to them yet they were somehow living it in their minds. They were like accident victims rescued from some major tragedy like a multiple pile-up or horrendous earthquake. They were not involved in it but they were reliving every detail again vividly. The experience was just like that, they were not *there* but the whole scene was vivid in their minds.

There was a long rocky coast of low black cliffs. In front of the cliffs was a wide gray beach that stretched away as far as the eye could see. Huge gray boulders were strewn over the beach and all were draped with green seaweed as if to prove that somewhere beyond the horizon was an ocean.

There was light, oddly bluish, but the sun from which it came was concealed behind thick cloud.

About eight meters out, however, was the Albatross, the A/G vessel which they had left a bare twenty minutes earlier.

She lay half on and half off a huge black rock but it was clear that her back was broken. Something had gone wrong close to landing.

Rescue tunnels had been extended to the beach and emergency ladders been lowered down the sides of the vessel.

A large angry crowd had collected in front of the vessel and, although the two men could not actually hear the words, they knew what was being said.

"I thought that bloody pilot was supposed to be experienced."

"You'll pay for this, Boyce, you owe me well over a hundred million."

"Where the hell are we anyway, I don't recognize this coast at all?"

"Can't get a bloody thing on either of my callers."

"We'd better get beyond those cliffs, must be a road or some sort of civilization there."

Ludwig was almost shocked with disbelief. Couldn't they *see*, couldn't they *feel* that this was no beach on the planet Earth? He realized slowly that so far they couldn't. They were too taken up with their personal problems to really open their eyes and look.

Ferris, on the other hand, was thinking more of their situation. It made a certain sense really. Even in the normal world, decisions made in the past affected the future. How many millions of people must have looked back and regretted, or applauded, a past decision—

His thoughts came to an abrupt stop—Why, in the name of God, hadn't he noticed it before? He hadn't realized that he'd been so intent on the crowd on the beach. Hell! The damn thing was relatively—at least in this mind picture—-right beside him.

He sensed Ludwig's tension suddenly increase beside him so he must have seen it too: a prehensile claw on a rising black rock beside him. Yet it was not quite a claw, it was more of a normal hand, four fingers and an opposing thumb but large, more supple and faintly green. He followed upwards, thought 'lizard' and dismissed the word instantly. At a glance, yes, but closely, it resembled nothing he had ever seen. Four legs terminating in human hands, yes, but after that—

It was about four meters long and, in its own way, beautiful, both in a serpentine sort of grace and in its color. It was a soft cream from the top of its head to the curve of its tail. Cream yet subtly iridescent, a shifting of colors like petrol spilled on a wet road.

As the crowds came shouting and arguing up the beach, it lifted its long head slightly and watched them approach with bright green, slightly protuberant eyes.

It was at that moment that both men realized that here was a creature so utterly alien that it was beyond their comprehension. Here was no cold-blooded reptile, here was—They knew that here was an intelligence probably ten times greater than that of man but that, too, was wholly alien. It thought from different reference points and from racial knowledge.

The creature lifted its head a little higher and, as if in response other heads lifted around the bay. Then, in one curved line, they began to slide softly forward.

They were still shouting angrily at one another on the beach.

"I'll take you for everything you've bloody got, you can depend on that. I'll stamp you into the ground!"

They stumbled on, shouting, swearing, often exchanging blows. Unaware, as yet, that their past actions had destroyed their original future and redirected them unto another. Ignorant, of course, that an alien reception committee was coming down to meet them . . .

The vivid reality in the two men's minds seemed slowly to fade. They would always remember it, of course, but the life had gone from the picture. From hereon they would have to recall it, all else would not be pushed from their minds by it.

Ludwig rose first. "I'm feeling a damn sight better . . . God, I could use a drink."

Ferris rose also, drawing deep breaths. "Couldn't agree more—" He broke off, frowning. "What are you trying to do?"

The other made an irritable gesture. "Bloody thing won't tear." He leaned forward and pushed something into a refuse disposal slot by the bench. "That's my time ticket—not something I want to keep as a souvenir."

www.ingramcontent.com/pod-product-compliance
Ingram Content Group UK Ltd.
Pitfield, Milton Keynes, MK11 3LW, UK
UKHW031433191224
3776UKWH00039B/277

9 781587 155154